Ladies Night Out

Ladies Night Out

Mary Rea

Enjoy!
Mary Rea

This book is a work of fiction. Names, characters, places and incidents either are products of the imagination or used fictiously. All resemblance to actual events or locales or persons, living or dead, is entirely coincidental.

Copyright © 2010 by Mary Rea

All rights reserved.

www.maryreabooks.com

ISBN: 1449986145
EAN-13 9781449986148

Printed in USA

Cover by Mary Sharman
Yatta Yatta Yatta Design

For Marc, who kept after me to tell this story.

1

Rita Lee Taylor felt like she had a wad of sandpaper stuck in her throat. There was a gritty scratch when she swallowed, and an alarming catch made breathing difficult. She tried to take a deep breath, but stale air in the overheated meeting room only made things worse.

Stop it! Rita sternly ordered herself. *There is no reason to get this stressed. You've known everybody up there for years. You're not going to die. You will not even faint.*

Speaking before a crowd, even a small one, wasn't easy. One at a time in the Beauty Mark Rita Lee did just fine. But she totally understood why public speaking was the number one fear people reported, way ahead of death and injury.

You're on a mission, Rita reminded herself. *It's okay to sound stupid, as long as the community center board gives its approval. Just think of them as heads of hair.*

She visualized chairman Ray Caru's unmanageable cowlick, and the bald spot hidden under Gene Closser's baseball cap. Gracie Melmont always complained about the shampoo so she didn't have to leave a tip. Louise Peterson secretly permed the curls she claimed were natural.

Thinking of them in that way helped Rita relax a little, but the palms of her hands remained clammy.

"That's it for old business, is there any new business?" chairman Ray Caru asked, gazing around the almost empty room at the Hobart Junction Community Center.

Just four of seven board members were on hand for the monthly meeting, and Gene Closser, sitting down at the end of the table, looked like he might be asleep. The only other person in attendance, Irene Slump, was sitting in her usual seat in the last row, furiously taking notes and muttering to herself.

"Ray, I have some new business." Rita Lee croaked, slowly rising from a metal folding chair that made an embarrassing thunk as she got to her feet. Despite the gravel in her throat, Rita Lee did her best to sound confident and in control.

"I'm here representing the volunteer fire department." She took a second to clear her throat.

"We've been trying for years to get enough money together to buy a decent camcorder and a DVD player, so we can watch training films and video ourselves during practice drills. But every time we think we've got it covered, something else breaks down.

"Tax funds barely cover the cost of maintaining the vehicles. There's never enough money to buy anything extra. We've tried bake sales and raffles. What the department really needs is a blockbuster fundraiser. And I think we've found it."

Rita Lee paused to be sure she had the board's full attention.

Louise Peterson, sitting next to Gene Closser, gave him a poke with her elbow.

"I'm listening," Gene protested, eyes snapping open. "The fire department is tired of holding bake sales. Rita Lee wants to do something different. Tell us about it, honey."

Bald spot, Rita Lee reminded herself as she tried again to clear her throat. "We want to put on a show, and I'm here to ask the board for your okay to use the community center stage."

"Sounds fine to me," said Ray Caru. "What are you planning to do? Put on a talent contest or something?"

"Not exactly," Rita Lee replied. "We've contacted a group in Chicago that puts on a male dance review. These guys have played Las Vegas and are really well known. They're called the Top Cats. There's a master of ceremonies and six dancers. They're like the Chippendales, if you've ever heard of them."

"Did I hear right?" gasped Gracie Melmont. "You want to have men taking off their clothes in our community center?"

"I'm not sure I'd put it exactly that way, but, yes, that's what we want to do. I've been talking this over with my customers at the Beauty Mark, and every woman I've spoken to says she'll buy a ticket. If we charge ten dollars apiece and three hundred people show up, that's three thousand dollars. Subtract the Top Cats' fee, and the volunteer fire department makes at least twenty-one hundred dollars just on ticket sales."

"That certainly sounds good to me, dear," Louise Peterson said. "I move we let the volunteer fire department use the community center for the show. Where do I buy a ticket, Rita Lee?"

"Over my dead body," roared Gracie Melmont. A flush moved up her neck and throbbed in her plump jowls. "What are you people thinking? Kids roller skate in the gym on Friday nights. Do you want children roller skating in the same room where men take off their clothes in front of nasty-minded women?"

"Now wait a minute," Rita Lee objected, all her fear of public speaking buried by indignation. "I resent you calling us nasty-minded. This is a legitimate fundraiser. It's a show for adults who can make up their own minds whether they want to come. All the kids have to do is turn on their TV sets to see worst shows than this."

At the back of the room Irene Slump flipped a page in her spiral notebook and shook out her cramped writing hand. "Lord help us," she snorted.

"We have family values in Hobart Junction," Gracie declared. "The reputation of the town and the community center is at stake. Think what people will say. They'll cancel their memberships. They'll stop supporting us with donations. The community center can't be part of anything like this."

Rita Lee watched Ray Caru eyes wander first toward her and then to Gracie. She could almost see the wheels turning in his brain.

Both women had valid points. He was sure the ladies would enjoy the show, and the fire department certainly needed the money. On the other hand, he didn't want to jeopardize the center's reputation, and he definitely didn't want to cross Gracie Melmont. That woman could be hell on wheels when she got her back up.

Rita Lee took a step forward. "May I say one more thing? When I came up with the idea, I didn't think anyone would object to a group of grown women having a little innocent fun. The last thing I want to do is hurt the reputation of the fire department or the community center. If you think this is not a good idea, I'll call the Top Cats and cancel the show."

"The sooner, the better!" Gracie shot back.

Ray glared darkly in Gracie's direction. "One point, which I was going to make before Gracie interrupted, is that three board members aren't here tonight. This is a complicated issue, and everybody on the board should be part of the decision."

"Exactly!" Gracie's voice rolled out over the meeting room like Reverend Goss on Sunday morning. "We'll just see how people feel about nudity and perversion in our community center."

"Let's put off the vote until next month's meeting," Gene suggested. "At that time all board members have got to show up, no excuses accepted."

After a unanimous vote to delay the decision, Rita Lee thanked the board members for their time and turned to leave. As she passed Irene Slump, she heard a low, nasty hiss.

Oh my, what have I gotten myself into now? Rita Lee wondered with growing dismay as the meeting room door banged closed behind her.

When Ray Caru arrived at his home on Lincoln Street not long afterwards, his wife Betty was waiting at the door, a cocktail in hand. "Here," she said, taking his jacket and handing him the drink. "I think you're going to need this."

"Not a good sign," Ray groaned. "Did the dog dig up Mrs. Ostell's daffodils again?"

"Worse than that. I just got a phone call from Marge Overstreet. She said she heard you voted to allow perversion at the community center."

"Where did she hear that? We just got out of the meeting five minutes ago."

"Marge heard it from Estelle Conroy. Estelle heard it from Gloria Spilling. Gloria heard it from Joe Junior. Marge's story is that Joe Junior was walking by the meeting room after his violin lesson and heard Gracie Melmont shout something about a pervert vote."

Betty hung Ray's jacket in the closet and turned back to her husband with a questioning look. "What kind of perversion did you vote for, dear?"

The next morning Rita Lee had barely turned on the lights at the Beauty Mark when she heard an insistent rap on the front window. Teenie Williams waved through the glass and pushed at the locked door. Rita Lee and Teenie were best friends from forever. They knew each other's deepest secrets and wildest dreams. Newcomers to town assumed they were sisters. Those who had been around them awhile thought of them as partners in crime.

"Well girl, you really did it this time," Teenie declared as Rita Lee unlocked the door and let her in.

"Me?" Rita Lee protested. "It was your idea as much as mine."

Teenie plopped into the black and chrome chair at Rita Lee's haircutting station. The aroma of strong coffee wafted from a plastic travel mug she slid onto a shelf, pushing aside two silver cans of hair spray and a collection of styling brushes. Teenie, like Rita Lee, recently celebrated her thirty-fourth birthday. She was dressed in jeans and an oversized sweater that concealed her curvy figure. "I dropped the kids off at school and came straight here," Teenie said. "Tell me everything that happened. I heard Gracie Melmont about had a heart attack."

"She was pretty upset," Rita Lee admitted, removing combs from a tall jar of disinfectant solution. The astringent fumes made the inside of her nose tingle. "I told the board how we want to put on the Top Cats show. They talked about it for a few minutes, and the next thing Gracie was raving. She said we're dirty minded!"

"Dirty-minded?" Wendy Johnson asked as she came in through the back entrance of the Beauty Mark. "Not any of us!"

Wendy had worked in Rita Lee's salon off and on for six years. Every so often she got sick of doing the same heads of hair over and over and moved to Foxville or Belfort--and once even to Denver--to work in bigger salons. But she always came back, lonesome for her regulars and the small town where she grew up.

As usual, Wendy's hair was flying in all directions. A miracle worker with other people's hair, Wendy never seemed to have time for her own. When her appearance got downright embarrassing, Rita Lee made Wendy sit still for a cut.

"You're a professional stylist and a walking advertisement for this salon. Do me a favor and at least look human," Rita Lee implored.

Today Wendy was dressed in a black leather mini skirt, black boatneck T-shirt, and dark green tights. Dangling beaded earrings completed the outfit. She talked occasionally about getting her nose pierced, but so far Rita Lee and Teenie had been able to talk her out of it by telling her that it wouldn't look good, what with her nose being so big and all.

Wendy dropped into one of the shampoo chairs and blew her shaggy bangs out of the way. "Okay, Ree, tell all. What happened last night? From beginning to end."

Rita Lee recounted the story, starting with Ray Caru asking for new business and ending with Irene Slump hissing at her.

"It can't be true," Wendy shrieked. "Do you think

they'll actually tell us we can't have the Top Cats?"

"Somebody should just shoot Gracie and put her out of her misery," Teenie said glumly. "You notice the woman knows all about the Chippendales. If she's so pure, how come she even knows who they are? I'll bet she secretly watches those triple-x cable channels."

"I really didn't see this coming," Rita Lee told her friends "Especially since we asked around and everyone seemed so up for the show."

Teenie gave her a skeptical look.

"Well, maybe not all the guys in the fire department were that enthusiastic," Rita conceded.

Truth was, only the promise of finally being able to buy the camera and DVD player overcame their objections. This was the first fundraiser with prospects since Gloria Spilling got the idea to collect a quarter every time a person used a swear word in the fire hall. Every Saturday afternoon Gloria went to the Quickie Stop and bought lottery tickets with whatever was collected at the previous week's meeting. So far the effort hadn't produced a winning number, but cussing was down some.

"Don't worry about it, Rita Lee," Teenie advised. "Gracie is just one person. She's not the whole town."

"I hope not," Rita Lee said, trying to ignore the knot of muscles tightening between her shoulder blades.

Wendy stirred herself out of the salon chair, headed over to the make-up display and carefully applied a bit of the First Rose blush tester to her cheeks. When the phone rang, she reached for it.

The shrill voice was so loud Teenie could hear it from across the room, though she couldn't make out all the words. Wendy's face began to turn a splotchy red, the way it always did when she was upset.

Suddenly the one-sided conversation was over and Wendy stood there, staring at the phone, a puzzled look on her face.

"What was that all about?"

"It was Rita Lee's 11 o'clock appointment, calling to cancel. I'm not exactly sure why. But it has something to do with the Top Cats."

"Rita Lee's not going to be happy," her friend predicted.

Outsiders might be surprised that word about the Top Cats got around Hobart Junction so quickly. But those who lived in town were used to it. It was sort of like that game kids play--you whisper something in the ear of the person next to you, and that person whispers what she heard to the next person, until it goes around the circle. And by the time the words get to the last person, they are not at all like what the first person said. In the game, there are always one or two people who don't hear the words right, and a few others who make changes on purpose. That's pretty much the way gossip worked in Hobart Junction, too.

When the town first got telephones, everyone was on a party line and eavesdropping provided a lot of local entertainment. After the last party line was eliminated in the late Seventies, everyone gave a sigh of relief--privacy at last.

Fat chance!

Gossip still continued to fly around town faster than the speed of sound.

Hobart Junction was established by Ezra Hobart in 1859. He recognized the site, a long day's wagon ride from Foxville to the east and Belfort to the west, was an excellent location for travelers to spend the night. He opened a rustic inn and saloon, with a special room for ladies to rest on their journey. It quickly it became news central as women passed gossip from one town to the next.

From its earliest days, Hobart Junction thrived. In just a few years, Ezra's wife no longer had to serve as hotel cleaning maid and desk clerk, and she opened a one-room school for the increasing number of children in the village. It was her idea to lay out a plan for the settlement. On the Fourth of July, she was inspired to name the streets of the budding village after presidents of the United States.

The need for a strong fire department was proven in 1927 when a blaze started in the kitchen of the Hobart Hotel. Before local volunteers could get the town's aging fire fighting equipment on the scene and operating, a third of downtown Hobart Junction was in flames. Men, women and children worked for hours hauling water in buckets to augment a broken-down water wagon and leaking hoses.

"Never again," they vowed when the destructive fire was finally reduced to smoking ashes.

The fire department was re-organized and a fund-raising effort got underway which continued until the day Rita Lee Taylor appeared before the community center board to talk about the Top Cats show.

The first to get a chance to chew on the Top Cats gossip bone were members of the Hobart Junction Sewing and Knitting Guild--better known as Stitch and Bitch.

The commotion started in the parking lot. "Did you hear the Chippendales are on their way to Hobart Junction?" Billie Jo Baxter called as she exited her dusty van.

"No way!" shouted Ronda Porter out the window of the blue Ford Tempo she'd been driving since high school.

"It's true." Billie Jo insisted. "I just heard it from Joe Spilling at the gas station."

"The Chippendales, the real Chippendales? Can't be."

"That's what I heard."

Stitch and Bitch met the first Tuesday of the month in the community center meeting room. Members and invited guests brought needlework and mending to occupy their hands while they traded opinion and gossip. There was one strict rule: whatever was said at Stitch and Bitch never left the room. This allowed the women to complain about their husbands, and talk about friends and relatives who weren't at the meeting. They mulled over divorces, grudges and methods of revenge. They passed on juicy scandal and flimsy rumor.

One time, a member told her husband about a rumor she'd heard at Stitch and Bitch concerning an especially shocking affair. Since men never can remember which gossip is supposed to be kept strictly secret, he brought up the affair at a neighborhood potluck. Word got back to Stitch and Bitch that the sacred silence had been broken. The woman was immediately ostracized by everybody in the club. Not long after, she and her family moved away. She couldn't take the evil looks she got when she went downtown.

"You have to be tough to belong to Stitch and Bitch," Edna Olson, a thirty-six year veteran of the club, often said. Not only did the group talk about people who weren't there, they freely critiqued each other. One time a member started a hooked rug in shades of blue and yellow to match her bathroom colors. Other members hated both the pattern and the colors and told her so in strong terms. She left in tears, but immediately stopped work on the rug and was back the next month with a cross-stitch pillow cover she was sure would pass public review.

That's the way it was at Stitch and Bitch. As Edna also often said, "If you can't stand the heat, stay out of the kitchen."

Sex was definitely a subject for discussion at Stitch and Bitch. Members freely talked about performances of their husbands and boyfriends. They speculated about the love lives of movie stars and television personalities. They told dirty jokes, warning straight-laced members to cover their ears. No one did.

Inside the community center meeting room, talk was heating up. Since the Top Cats rumor was only eleven hours old, a few lurid details were still missing, but the scuttlebutt was rapidly gaining momentum. Some were already calling the proposed performance disgusting. Others were cheering the arrival of city-style entertainment to town. A few women were disappointed to learn it was the Top Cats who were coming, not the Chippendales. But most didn't care. Male strippers of any kind were going to be a hoot.

"Exactly what is it these guys do?" Edna asked, as she stitched on a pink and white quilt for her niece, who was expecting in June.

"They do a striptease, just like women, only they're men taking off their clothes," Billie Jo explained.

"Do they actually get naked? Edna was aghast.

"Pretty close. They get down to a sort of G-string that covers just enough to make it legal."

"I'm in heat already," Ronda moaned.

"I can't imagine why the volunteer fire department approved such a thing," Gloria Spilling said. She'd been knitting on the same navy blue cable sweater for over two years.

"Well, I've been to every fire meeting for months, and I can tell you for sure the topic never, ever came up until it was a done deal," another woman reported. "This is all Rita Lee Taylor's idea. Don't blame the fire department."

"I'm not blaming anyone," Gloria said in a conciliatory tone. "We have freedom of expression in this country. If Rita Lee wants to put on a strip show, and is willing to do all the work, I say let her go for it."

"Freedom of expression is one thing," the other woman answered, "but an X-rated show is no way to raise money for the fire department. Sex always leads to trouble."

"And it only took you three kids to figure that out," Ronda said dryly.

Stitch and Bitch was off and running.

2

While Stitch and Bitch buzzed around the Top Cats show, it was nearing deadline at the Hobart Junction Independent. Editor and publisher Walt Billings was feeling unusually pressured. His mind was blank. His computer screen was blank. The space on the page where his editorial was supposed to go was blank.

Walt always planned to get his editorial written early in the week, but it did not happen very often. Walt and his office assistant Ellie Foster ran the paper together. "Walt's in charge of words, I'm in charge of money," Ellie told people. Ellie manned the front desk, took care of the books, and occasionally sold advertising. Walt wrote up the news, took photos and supervised the work of his one reporter, Tommy Gates, a recent journalism grad.

It had been a busy news week and Walt didn't get around to writing the editorial until Tuesday morning, the day the newspaper went to press. He was still struggling to find a topic. The one good idea he'd had in the shower that morning had somehow escaped into the steam.

Walt had been writing an editorial every issue for nearly eight years. Sometimes the editorials were brilliant, usually they were pretty good, and once in a while they didn't make sense to anybody but him.

Walt first learned about the Independent though the classified section of a professional journal. At the time, he was a burned-out mid-level editor on a big-city paper. He was divorced, cynical and sick at heart from the violence and corruption that are a reporter's stock in trade. Taking over the newspaper turned out to be the perfect antidote. Residents of the small Nebraska farm community wanted to read about high school sports and doings around town, not muggings and murders. Most of the paper's readers began with the letters to the editor and then turned to the classified section. After that they caught up on the news.

That suited Walt just fine.

He often got bored attending town council meetings, and after eight years it was hard to come up with something new to say about the annual Strawberry Festival, but in general Walt Billings was a happy man. He was thirty-six, lived a simple life and felt he had found his place in the universe.

Now, if he could just find an idea for an editorial.

Walt leaned back in his squeaky wooden desk chair and let his mind wander. Unfocused, his eyes ranged around the room, not seeing the thick layer of dust settled on neglected files, yellowed clippings and a stack of worn reference books scattered across the top of an oversized roll top desk that took up a good quarter of the room. A dog-eared copy of Roget's Thesaurus, a 30-year old world atlas, and several histories of the state of Nebraska partially hid cigarette burns scarred into the surface by a previous editor.

When Ellie walked in his office, Walt wasn't sure if the front desk manager was an annoying interruption or a welcome relief. "There's a call on line one that maybe you should take. It's Ray Caru. He says there was some kind of blow-up at the community center board meeting last night. It may be front page."

It wasn't often the Independent got a late breaking story. Most of the news was all over town by the time the paper came out. The best Walt usually could do was set the record straight, sorting facts from the misinformation spread among local residents.

It wasn't uncommon for readers to claim he had the story all wrong. "I was misquoted," claimed the mayor, even though Walt had him on tape. "I never said that," someone else objected, though a third of the town heard her say those very words at a crowded meeting.

Despite the occasional criticism, Walt relished small town journalism and openly enjoyed stirring things up.

"Walt here," he said into the receiver, searching for a pen on his cluttered desk. "What's up, Ray? Ellie says you may have a story for us."

Ray was calling from his office in the back of the pharmacy. His voice sounded weary and a little worried. "Well, I'm not sure it's a news story, but I thought I better call you before you heard it from Gracie Melmont or somebody else.

"We had a meeting of the community center board of directors last night. Rita Lee Taylor was there representing the volunteer fire department. She asked the board for permission to put on a show."

Ray hesitated.

"And...?" Walt prompted, glancing out the window

at cars parked across the street at Gretta's Good Food Café. After he finished this call, maybe he would slip over for a cinnamon roll and coffee. He missed breakfast and was feeling a bit undernourished.

"And the show she wants to put on is a bunch of male strippers called the Top Cats." Ray said.

Walt forgot all about the cinnamon roll.

"Okay, start at the beginning. What happened?"

Walt quickly scribbled notes, filling one page and going on to a second. "Where did you say these guys are from?"

"Can't recall. You'll have to get ahold of Rita Lee over at the Beauty Mark to get those details."

Walt had barely put the phone down when Sylvia Crocker sailed into his office. Ellie was right behind, rolling her eyes and silently mouthing, "I tried to stop her."

"What are you going to do about it?" Sylvia indignantly demanded. She was dressed in twill pants and a yellow fleece jacket. She stood five-foot-two in her crepe-soled oxfords. But what she lacked in stature, she made up for in pure officiousness.

Sylvia was almost a fixture in the news office. People always said if anything happened in town Sylvia was the first to know. She kept a scanner on her kitchen counter, set on the frequency used by the police and fire departments. When the dispatcher called out personnel, Sylvia jumped in her rusty Pinto and drove to the scene. Top speed for the ancient vehicle was around 45 miles an hour.

She staked out the post office every morning, peering over people's shoulders as they removed mail from their boxes. She stood close and gave advice while the guys from public works fixed leaky water mains. Sylvia knew more about construction than the contractors, more about medicine than the town doc, and more about raising kids than their parents. And she never missed an opportunity to tell each and every one of them about it.

Sylvia had a husband at one time, but hardly anyone could remember him. Edna Olson thought his name was William.

"Sylvia talked him to death," Edna observed one morning at Stitch and Bitch.

Walt usually didn't mind Sylvia's stopping by his office. Except for the fact it was so hard to shut her up, Sylvia was a great source for news.

"What am I going to do about what?" Walt asked innocently, knowing full well he was about to get an earful about the fire department fundraiser.

"Strippers, that's what I'm talking about. Strippers! Bare naked men running around Hobart Junction with no clothes on."

Walt worked hard not to chuckle.

"I'll tell you why Rita Lee Taylor is doing this," Sylvia went on, shaking her finger in Walt's face. "She hasn't been out on a date since that no-good husband of hers left town. This is just a sick way of getting her kicks."

"I heard it's a fundraiser for the volunteer fire department," Walt said mildly, his gaze straying to his empty computer screen.

"She doesn't care about the fire department." Sylvia was incensed. "She just wants to get more business down there at the Beauty Mark. She knows every woman in town is going to come in and get her hair done before she goes to that thing."

Every second it got more difficult to hold back the laughter roiling inside. Walt knew he must get Sylvia out of his office or insult her by guffawing right in her face.

He stood, gently took Sylvia's elbow and began steering her toward the exit. "The center board will make the right decision," he assured her

"Don't count on it," Sylvia shrilly retorted as Walt propelled her through the front door.

"If they let those strippers get up and dance, the people of this town are going to see something they've never seen before!" Sylvia yelled through the crack in the closing door.

Walt couldn't hold back any longer. He turned away and rocked with laugher.

Still dabbing at his eyes, Walt sat back down in front of his computer. It was now or never.

The phone rang again.

"Walt here," impatience clearly in his voice.

"Hey Walt!" a familiar voice came back. "People are sure stirred up about those Top Cats. My wife's telling me this is pure and simple a matter of women's rights. What the heck's going on?"

Instantly, Walt recognized the voice of Joe Spilling, owner of the Chevron station. "Joe, I'd really like to talk to you, but my editorial was due an hour ago and right now my mind's a blank. The phone's been ringing off the hook, and Sylvia Crocker just finished bending my ear. If I don't get this editorial written in the next half hour, we're not going to get the paste-up to the printer in time and my goose is cooked."

"I understand," Joe reassured him. "If you want something to write about, how about those morons at the state wildlife department deciding to close down fishing at Fish Lake? Somebody needs to tell them a thing or two."

"Excellent idea!"

"After you get the paper done, give me a call. We'll go to the Pub & Grub for a beer. And you'd better call

Rita Lee."

Walt heard a click and then the dial tone. He turned to his computer and began banging out the editorial.

Rita Lee felt as though she was riding along on the leading edge of a hurricane, with dangerous winds getting stronger by the minute. What seemed a tiny breeze when she came into the salon that morning had all the prospects of turning into a gale. She nervously glanced out the front window, expecting to see angry black clouds gathering in the west. She saw no signs of a storm, but a sense of dread kept her nervous and out of sorts.

There was only that one cancellation so far, but Rita Lee suspected it was only a matter of time before there would be more.

She used the time opened up by the cancellation to dial Walt Billings. The editor listened without interruption while she explained the volunteer fire department's need and how they hoped to clear several thousand dollars from the show. She told him she thoroughly checked out the Top Cats and the performance they put on was in good taste and wasn't anything smutty. She said she was already getting calls for tickets and Teenie was taking down names. She didn't mention the customer who cancelled her hair appointment.

Rita Lee hoped she was making a good impression on Walt. A positive story in the newspaper would go a long ways toward convincing the board of directors to let them use the community center.

As she answered his questions, she made wavy doodles through the lines of the open appointment book. Flowers flowed from curlicues around 9 o'clock, stars dripped from 9:45. By the time the phone interview was nearly over, most of the morning was filled in with swooping curves.

"Thanks for calling," Walt said. "It sounds like you ladies are planning a real night out."

"LADIES NIGHT OUT" spilled from Rita Lee's pen across the bottom of the appointment book.

Perfect. She had a name for the event.

Maybe the hurricane was going to miss her.

After a final few words, Walt hung up and took a slow draw from his coffee mug. He had known Rita Lee Taylor in an off-handed way for as long as he had lived in Hobart Junction. They were introduced at the first chamber of commerce meeting he attended. A few weeks later, he stopped by the Beauty Mark to talk to Rita Lee about advertising, and they got well enough acquainted to feel comfortable chatting whenever they saw each other around town. Walt sometimes thought about asking Rita Lee out, but so far hadn't gotten around to actually doing it. He wasn't sure what was holding him back other than it had been years since he had been on a date, and he wasn't sure he could pull it off. Women always wanted to know about his past, which inevitably led to his failed marriage, which he really didn't like to talk about.

Walt gazed at his computer screen, intent on finishing his story on the community center controversy, but to his surprise he couldn't get his mind off Rita Lee. He recalled the sound of her voice, the funny little twang that made her sound both tough and sweet at the same time. He thought of her wide generous smile and the soft green sparkle of her eyes. Grabbing a pad, he wrote himself a reminder to call her in a day or two. Maybe they could get together for another interview about the show.

That evening Rita Lee sorted through the notes she

was starting to accumulate on Ladies Night Out. She wasn't quite sure how she was going to manage to get everything done. Along with owning the salon, Rita Lee volunteered at the grade school on Mondays reading to third graders. It started when her niece Jennifer invited her to a first grade Reading In The Family program. Rita Lee had so much fun she asked Jenny's teacher if she could come back and read with the kids again. The teacher was delighted. It wasn't often that adults came into the classroom to spend time with children. Rita Lee followed her niece to the second grade, and now they were both in the third grade. Rita Lee read stories to small groups and listened to kids read to her. She wondered why more grown-ups didn't volunteer in schools.

Her other labor of love was the fire department. Rita Lee joined shortly after her ex-husband Jason left town. They had been married almost three years and though Rita Lee knew the relationship wasn't perfect, she was stunned when she came home from work one day and found his truck and all his belongings gone. She waited a couple of years to see if he would call and explain. Then she filed for divorce. During the wait, she joined the fire department. The weekly meetings gave her a chance to get out, and it was a nice change from doing hair.

One of the things Rita Lee discovered when she went out on her first fire call was that if she wasn't in good shape, fighting fires was way too much work. That put her on an exercise program. She tried to jog three times a week. She also worked out with a rowing machine to build upper body strength. The exercise helped in another way--it burned calories. Rita Lee needed that because she loved to eat.

She could never understand how her friends existed on one meal a day or got by on salads and coffee. Rita

Lee liked all kinds of food--except maybe liver--and enjoyed cooking, even for herself. Her specialty was Asian food, with its exotic tastes and ingredients. She collected cookbooks featuring recipes of the Far East, and had fun ordering strange sounding products to experiment with. So far though, the dried shark fins were still in a package on a kitchen shelf, waiting for the day she got up nerve to turn them into soup.

When Rita Lee first started thinking about a blockbuster fundraiser for the fire department, she considered putting on a Chinese dinner. But it took a lot of effort and food costs would be huge. The Top Cats show sounded so easy: sell tickets and watch the money roll in.

The idea to do something different to raise money started the morning after the annual firefighters Valentine dance. Rita Lee counted the proceeds and was depressed to find that expenses had nearly eaten up all the profit. It was Teenie, high on ladder pulling down red and white crepe-paper streamers, who said out loud what Rita Lee was thinking. "This dance is too damn much work. There's got to be a better way to get more money for the fire department."

That afternoon Teenie received a package from her Aunt Carol in Omaha. Packed around family keepsakes was an old issue of the Omaha World Herald. On the front page of the entertainment section was a picture and story about the Top Cats.

Teenie showed Rita Lee the photograph--six guys dressed in top hats, bow ties and nothing else from the waist up. Rita Lee had a flash of inspiration. She called the newspaper, talked to the entertainment editor and got the name and number of the Top Cat's manager. Turned out the group had engagements in the region on consecutive weekends in May. If the fire department could work with a mid-week date, the Top Cats were available to perform. In fact, they would be very happy to come to Hobart Junction.

Rita Lee seldom acted on impulse, but without talking it over with the fire department she made a provisional commitment. Then she asked around to see if the women she knew would come to the show. All her friends were excited; they thought bringing male strippers to town was an excellent idea. Several volunteered to buy tickets on the spot. So Rita Lee mailed off a $500 booking deposit.

Now all she had to do was convince the community center board of directors to allow the show to go on.

3

On the second Wednesday of the month, the Hobart Junction Chamber of Commerce met for breakfast in the community center. Breakfast was catered by the women's guild of the First Baptist Church. This morning the ladies were serving up oatmeal with brown sugar and raisins, blueberry muffins and link sausage.

Walt Billings could smell the cooking sausage as he walked across the parking lot. It reminded him of farm breakfasts when he was a kid. Thankfully, when this was over he would be going back to the newspaper office and not out for a long hot day throwing hundred-pound bales onto his dad's old flatbed hay trailer.

Walt's story on the fire department fundraiser had been on the street for a week. He was looking forward to hearing what folks had to say this morning.

He didn't have long to wait.

"It sounds like a great business opportunity to me,"

declared Trixie Smith, owner of Smitty's Food City. She inherited the grocery store when her father passed on and now operated it with her husband George. Trixie was one of the chamber's staunchest supporters. Being a keen reader of "Woman Business Owner" magazine, she knew the organization was an important place to network.

"There'll be women coming from Foxville and Belfort to see the show," Trixie continued, speaking to fellow members sitting along both sides of a long table. "They're going to have to eat, some are going to want to stay overnight, and they'll probably buy gas and other things. As a business owner I intend to make them feel welcome."

"But what about Hobart Junction's reputation?" Roy Overstreet asked as he helped himself to a couple more sausages and another blueberry muffin. Roy liked coming to chamber meetings because he could eat whatever he wanted without his wife nagging him about high cholesterol.

"What reputation is that?" Joe Spilling asked skeptically. Joe was wearing a freshly pressed shirt bearing the Chevron logo. The front stretched across his hefty frame and its blue buttons strained in their holes.

"I don't see how this can hurt the town's reputation," chimed in Twila Switzer, owner of the Cozy Corner Bookstore. "The Top Cats appear all over the United States. If their appearance ruins reputations, there are lots of ruined towns around."

"But those other towns aren't like us," Doyle Baxter objected from across the table. "We're different. We have higher moral standards here."

"That's debatable," Twila argued. "Ask Frank Beemer how many morals he thinks this town has."

All eyes turned to the police chief, who was busy

stirring brown sugar and raisins deep into his oatmeal. His wife and kids hated the stuff, which happened to be one of his personal breakfast favorites. He hoped it wasn't going to get cold while he answered questions.

"We do have our share of domestic violence," Frank said, quickly lifting a steaming spoonful of oatmeal to his lips.

"But not sex crimes, right Frank?" This from Roy Overstreet.

"Right." Frank shoved more oatmeal into his mouth and dipped his spoon again, hoping to get another spoonful in before he was expected to say more.

"I sincerely doubt that a group of women having fun watching men strip dance is going to lead to sex crimes," Twila said. "What do you think is going to happen? Wild-eyed females running through town attacking everything in sight?"

"Could happen," Trixie said. "You never can tell what stirred up hot-blooded women might do."

Laughter erupted around the table.

"Especially those crazies from Foxville and Belfort," Twila put in.

More laughter.

Chamber president Arland Bryson clinked a silver spoon against his coffee cup in a mock call to order.

When the laughter subsided, he spoke. "I have to agree with Trixie that the Top Cats show presents a unique opportunity for the town's business community. It has potential to bring in considerable outside dollars. Besides, if I don't support it, my wife and daughters will never speak to me again."

"Don't let 'em henpeck you, Arland," a voice called from the far end of the table. It was Clint Small, the town's mayor and owner of the local Ford dealership. Clint had been selling cars in town for close to thirty years. He was serving his third term as mayor.

"What do you think, Clint?" Twila asked, a sharp look on her face. It was a well known fact that Clint Small spent most of his time refereeing battles between his wife Judy and his mother, who lived with them. Rumor was the mayor's mother was demanding he shut down the show. His wife was among the first to put her name in for a ticket. Judy dared Clint to stand in the way of the fire department fundraiser. "I'll picket town hall," she threatened. "You'll never get re-elected again."

The mayor blew air out his lips. "Personally, I don't really care one way or the other. I do know the fire department needs money, and there's nothing for them in the town budget. The most important thing right now is getting those leaks in the water main fixed. A new video camera for the fire department is pretty low priority."

Talk about the Top Cats show continued through breakfast. The general consensus seemed to favor the dance troupe because it would be good for business. Ray Overstreet and Doyle Baxter weren't convinced, but almost everybody else agreed with Trixie when she suggested that a petition in support of the show was in order.

She volunteered to write up the petition and get copies to other business people as soon as possible. With the next center board vote less than a month away, time was running short.

"My goal is at least 300 signatures," she told those around the table. "That should shut up Gracie Melmont."

Arland signaled for one of the church ladies to bring the pot of coffee around again.

"One more thing we need to talk about. It's the Citizen of the Year award. Some of you may have noticed that Hazel Bell isn't here this morning. That's because we're putting off presenting the award till next meeting.

"We had a little trouble with her plaque," Arland explained. "That place over in Foxville got the orders mixed up and put Hazel's name on a bowling trophy. So they're redoing it."

Walt said silent a thank you to the news gods. He'd forgotten about the Citizen of the Year presentation and left his camera back at the office.

He thought Hazel Bell was an excellent choice for the "Citizen" award. She was a long-time 4-H leader, Sunday school teacher, and the person the kids always called when they needed a chaperone for a high school dance. She was fondly known as Ma Bell by almost everybody in town. There was no question, Hazel deserved the award.

It was getting close to 8 o'clock, when most businesses in Hobart Junction opened for the day. Arland looked around the table. "If there's nothing else to talk about, let's call it good for this morning. See you all next week."

Chairs scraped along the wood floor as everyone got up to leave. Several took a moment to thank the church ladies for breakfast. Joe Spilling asked one woman if she would give him the blueberry muffin recipe to take home to Gloria.

Out in the parking lot, Twila and Trixie made plans to meet for lunch to figure out the exact wording for the petition. Trixie would then go back and print out copies on the store's copy machine.

"I'll help you pass them out around town," Twila promised.

The chamber of commerce meeting got over at 7:48. By 8:01 Sylvia Crocker heard the news about the petition and was on the phone. By 8:20 a hasty meeting had been called of a select group of citizens strongly opposed to the Top Cats show. They met in the private dining room at the rear of the Pub & Grub.

Sylvia and Marge Overstreet were there, along with two deacons from the Lutheran church, Irene Slump, and a stray from the bar who thought he was going to get a free breakfast out of the deal. When he realized his mistake, he wandered away, uncomfortable with the gathering's angry mood.

Sure they were small in number, but what else could you expect on such short notice? They considered themselves the vanguard of a group that would soon grow into the hundreds--people who thought the community center shouldn't be turned into a strip joint.

Later in the morning Sylvia filled in Berlene Goss, the pastor's wife, about what had been accomplished during the meeting at the Pub & Grub. It was Sylvia's seventeenth phone call of the day.

She told Berlene the group agreed it was unlikely the board members on record would change their votes. Gracie was a sure no, Louise was a yes, and Gene Closser was claiming he couldn't vote because of conflict of interest--he was a volunteer fireman. But there were three others, who hadn't been at the board meeting, who could still be influenced. The strategy was to concentrate energy on convincing those folks to vote against the Top Cats show when the final ballot came.

"Excellent idea," Berlene agreed. She had the phone receiver perched on her shoulder, leaving both hands free to load breakfast dishes into the dishwasher. She was already dressed in a comfortable powder blue sport knit set and had her make-up on. She was due at the church in fifteen minutes to sort rummage for the upcoming sale.

"I'll see Ellen Green this morning and make our

feelings known to her. And at least three people are going to talk to Audrey Willis and Phil Miller. That should cover it," Sylvia said with satisfaction. "We'll stop this thing in its tracks."

Just as Sylvia hoped, by the time Ellen Green heard about all the opposition she decided to vote against the Top Cats show.

Then her phone started ringing. The first call was from Teenie Williams, giving her five good reasons to vote yes. Then Janice Bryson called, followed by Wendy Johnson. They all reminded her of the fire department's needs and how much money the show was going to make. Next came a call from Pastor Goss inviting her to church on Sunday. He also happened to mention he hoped she wasn't planning a yes vote on that terrible strip show.

After that she let her answering machine take messages.

The calls seemed to be running mostly against the show, but Ellen knew there was a petition going around and thought maybe she was only hearing one side.

Phil Miller had a similar problem. When he took early retirement from the auto parts factory in Belfort, he looked forward to having more time for his two hobbies, gardening and golf. It worked out just as he planned. Phil and his wife Linda had two wonderful years together before she was diagnosed with terminal lung cancer. After the funeral he felt lost, and had only accepted the community board center job because it gave him something to do. But half the time he felt so low he couldn't get up the energy to go to the meetings.

Now there was this Top Cats thing, and he barely had time to think about Linda.

The third targeted board member, Audrey Willis, was also feeling the pressure. At Smitty's Food City,

Audrey didn't get all the way down the first aisle before someone stopped her to talk about the show. In the meat section, a member of her church thanked her in advance for voting no. Audrey was on a diet and didn't need many groceries. She got out of the store as fast as she could.

The worst came on Saturday night when she was invited to dinner with her late husband's cousins. They all opposed the Top Cats performance and spent the whole evening insisting she had to vote against the show. She was getting more and more confused. Most of her close women friends were urging her to vote yes. Audrey certainly didn't want to be disloyal to those who'd supported her through her grief and continued to ask her to dinner and include her in outings.

It was tough to know how to vote.

Finally, in desperation, she called Phil Miller and asked if he would mind discussing the matter with her.

"I'm sick of this whole business," Phil admitted to Audrey in a low, weary voice. They were sitting at an out-of-the way table at the Pub & Grub. The place was nearly empty. The late lunch crowd was back at work and the early-bird senior citizens wouldn't show up to dinner for another hour or two.

The pair had been acquainted for a number of years, going back to the days when they both had spouses. But other than serving on the community center board, now neither got out much. Phil was still laid low from his beloved's death. Audrey was long over the worst of her loss but still stayed pretty close to home. She went to church and did grocery shopping, but mostly she worked in her flower garden, which was the town's showstopper.

Phil was wearing a blue polo shirt with "Willow Springs Golf Resort" discreetly embroidered on the pocket. Audrey couldn't help but notice the shade of his shirt closely matched the blue of his eyes. She worried when she put on her new denim jumper that she might be overdressing, but now she was certain she'd made the right decision.

It wasn't long before they were swapping stories about annoying phone calls and comparing notes on the mafia-style tactics various supposedly upstanding members of the community were using to influence their votes.

"Joe Spilling gave me a free lube and oil change."

"Trixie Smith threatened to cut off my charge account."

"Doyle Baxter offered to drive me to church. And he's hasn't been inside a church since his mother died in 1986."

"Irene Slump was out in my backyard yesterday. Lord knows what she was doing."

Phil signaled for the waitress. "I'm ordering a glass of white wine. You want one?"

Audrey looked down at her empty coffee cup. What the heck, it was a little early in the day to be drinking, but who cared? She could use a glass of wine to steady her nerves.

After considering a moment, Phil decided to go ahead and order a bottle. What they didn't drink he'd send home with Audrey.

An hour later, the wine bottle was three-quarters empty and they were chuckling over the whole Top Cats controversy. In the course of the discussion they learned they had a mutual enthusiasm for growing roses, and that Audrey had been thinking for years she ought to take golf lessons.

Phil knew a golf pro who was especially good with beginners and offered to introduce her.

She promised to bring the latest Jackson and Perkins rose catalog to the next board meeting. There was new hybrid floribunda she wanted him to see.

The mention of the board meeting brought them full circle. How, they asked each other, were they going to vote?

"I want to say yes for my friends," Audrey confessed, "but I think I'll probably vote no. My late husband's relations are really opposed to the show, and it's them I'm going to have to face at every family get-together from now on. My friends will eventually forgive me, my relatives never will."

Phil nodded with understanding. "I should vote yes because the fire department needs the money. But somehow, and I hope I don't sound too old fashioned, the idea of women sitting around watching men take off their clothes just doesn't seem right to me. Women are supposed to be better than that."

Without realizing what she was doing, Audrey reached across the table to take his hand. At the last second she pulled back, a pale pink blush flooding her face.

"Well," Phil said, pouring the last of the wine into their glasses, "the worst of this is facing the people on the side I don't vote for. Wish there was a way to get out of the whole meeting."

Audrey swirled the white wine in her glass. She was feeling a little giddy and reckless. "What if we don't go?" she asked. "What if we leave town and send in proxies? We could say we've been asked to be judges at that big rose show that's going on in Foxville. Nobody would ever know the difference."

Phil thought it over. If he stayed in town and voted no, Trixie Smith was going to cut off his Food City charge account. Maybe if he left for a couple of days, the whole thing would work itself out and life would get back to normal.

"How about if we make this into an expedition?" he suggested. "We go to the rose show one day, and I'll play that new course over there the next. You can ride along in the cart and I'll explain the rules of golf as we go."

Audrey looked doubtful.

Phil began to speak faster as his vision of the expedition expanded. He saw them lingering over an especially spectacular Princess Diana rose, examining its perfect color. Afterwards they'd go out to dinner at the place that served that great pot roast.

Audrey couldn't help herself. She wanted to go to the rose show and learn about golf, and eat pot roast.

"Best of all, when they take that vote, we'll be far, far away."

That did it! Audrey raised her glass. "Here's to the expedition."

That left Ellen Green as the only undecided board member.

A week before the meeting Ellen finally had to admit she'd backed herself into a corner. She accepted the free lube and oil change from Joe Spilling. She let Wendy Johnson cut her hair at no charge. When Gretta of Gretta's Good Food Café told her their anniversary dinner was taken care of, Ellen knew without a doubt Gretta was expecting a yes vote in return.

But she smiled and agreed with Pastor Goss every time he talked about the wicked show. She told Sylvia Crocker she was absolutely right when Sylvia dropped by with a batch of her famous lemon squares and a lecture on the deviltry that was about to be set loose in town. And worst of all, she'd all but promised a delegation from the Christian Women's Society that she'd vote no.

What was she to do? Wendy and Gretta said the show was all harmless good fun. The Christian Women called it the work of Satan.

Who was right?

Ellen changed her mind one way, then the other, twenty times a day for the rest of the week.

However, by Sunday morning she had definitely decided to vote no.

That afternoon Twila and Teenie knocked on her door. They brought her a petition signed by 338 people who asked for a yes vote.

When they left, Ellen went straight to the bathroom and threw up.

Then she went to bed.

4

"Go get more folding chairs out of the closet," Ray Caru instructed those clustered at the rear of the community center meeting room. "No reason you all should have to stand through this."

Ray was aware a number of people planned to show up for the showdown vote, but this crowd was way more than he expected.

Only a few empty chairs remained. And there were still people out in the hall.

Gracie settled down to the right of Gene Closser. Of all the center board members, Gracie had experienced the least turmoil during the past month. Her views on the Top Cats were widely known. After the first two or three people tried to change her vote and failed, word went out she was a hopeless case and everybody else left her alone.

Since Gene was claiming conflict of interest, he was

off the hook.

Louise Peterson enjoyed the attention she received from opponents of the show, but told each and every one of them she wasn't changing her yes vote, no matter how many pans of lemon squares they brought her.

"I'm sending around a list for people to sign, so we'll have a record of who's here," Ray announced to the assembled crowd. "If you want to stand up and say something, put a check after your name."

When the clipboard got to Trixie, she saw there were already nine names with checks. Hers made ten. She was glad she'd gotten there early and found a good place to sit. It promised to be a long evening, and she wanted to be able to see and hear everything. The petition was in her lap, ready to present when her name was called.

Walt Billings leaned against one wall. As usual, a camera dangled from a strap around his neck. He caught Rita Lee's eye and gave her an encouraging smile.

Rita Lee responded with a little wave. Tonight she was wearing a navy dress with a prim white collar. The dress was selected by the Beauty Mark regulars after going through Rita Lee's closet. With all the rumors circulating around town, they felt she should appear as demure as possible. "No point in giving those crackpots something else to talk about," Wendy advised.

At first Rita Lee resisted. Let them talk, she didn't care.

But Teenie reminded her if they didn't put on the Top Cats show they'd be right back planning another Valentine dance. So she agreed to wear the navy dress she usually reserved for funerals.

Rita Lee glanced around the room to see who was there. A large contingent from the volunteer fire department filled up one row of chairs and part of another.

Fire Chief Arvid Smiley was sitting on the aisle next to his wife Ruth. On the other side of Ruth were the deputy chief, Dick Tanner, and his wife. It was great to know she had so much support from the fire hall. Not everyone in the department agreed the Top Cats show was a good idea, but they were standing by her. It was either the Top Cats or more bake sales.

The smell of flowery perfume and odors from recently cooked dinners mingled in the close quarters. Chairs squeaked as folks scooted over to make room for their neighbors. The swelling crowd generated its own heat. Soon people were taking off coats and draping them over the backs of their chairs.

Rita Lee's nerves were on red alert. If talking in front of four people was a trial, speaking before a whole roomful was going to be trial by fire. She clutched one hand tightly with the other to keep them from shaking and prayed the meeting would start soon, so she could get it over with. Then she prayed it would never start and everyone would go home.

At the front of the room, Ray Caru glanced at his fellow board members. Gene, Louise and Gracie were ensconced in their usual spots. The three other seats were vacant.

He knew about Ellen. She was home, sick in bed. The whereabouts of Phil and Audrey was a mystery.

A glance at the clock on the far wall told him he had waited about as long as he could for the missing pair. Reluctantly, Ray called the board meeting to order. After the Pledge of Allegiance and reading of the minutes, he moved right to the main business of the evening.

Rita Lee spoke first. She again explained the needs of the fire department and her idea about the Top Cats show, which she was now calling "Ladies Night Out."

As Rita Lee made her case, she could hear angry

whispers around her. She did her best to ignore them.

Then Ray began calling off the names with checks after them. He told the speakers they could each take three minutes to have their say. "Otherwise we're going to be here all night."

Members of the volunteer fire department got up to support the show. Ladies from the Christian Women's Society, using words like "lewd" and "offensive," went on record as opposing use of the community center. Trixie dramatically handed each board member a copy of the signed petition. She started to read all 338 names out loud, but Ray cut her off after the first page, saying her three minutes were up.

As the evening went on, tempers began to fray and harsh words were tossed back and forth between proponents and opponents sitting too close together in the crowded meeting room. Walt snapped several photographs of an excited Reverend Goss shaking his fist angrily at Teenie. In between taking photos the editor scribbled quotes into his notebook.

Rita Lee gazed up at the three empty seats at the front table. The whole reason for delaying the decision for a month was to allow the entire board to be there. So where were they?

Ray Caru was wondering the same thing.

Finally everybody had been heard from, and it was time for the vote.

Ray turned to his fellow board members. "I got a call from Ellen right before the meeting. She says she's sick as a dog and can't get out of bed. I asked her how she wanted to vote, but couldn't get a straight answer. So I guess she's out. I haven't heard a single word from Phil and Audrey."

"Excuse me Ray," came a low voice from the back of the room. Everyone turned to look in the direction of

Darrell Miller, who advanced toward the chairman, an envelope in his hand. "My brother asked me to give this to you."

Ray accepted the sealed envelope, looking confused. "Am I supposed to open it now?"

"That's what Phil said."

Ray broke the seal and slipped out two pages of letter-sized paper. He quickly read the top page to himself: "Sorry I can't make the meeting. I'm sending my brother Darrell to act as my proxy. He'll tell you my vote." It was signed by Phil Miller

With a deepening frown, Ray turned to the other sheet. It read, "I'm sorry to report that urgent business has taken me out of town. I hereby appoint Darrell Miller to vote in my stead." Audrey's flowery signature followed.

Ray was stunned, not exactly sure what to do next. He looked with distress at his wife Betty, sitting in the third row, with a faint hope that somehow she'd use mental telepathy to tell him how to get out of this mess.

Betty gave him an encouraging smile, having no clue what his problem was.

After considering for a moment, Ray decided there was nothing to do but plunge ahead. He addressed the board. "Rita Lee Taylor has asked the board of directors to let the volunteer fire department use the community center stage for a benefit show with male strippers. How do you vote?"

Rita Lee held her breath. Teenie said a little prayer.

The three at the front table quickly responded with a firm yes, a thunderous no, and a weak mumble about conflict of interest.

Ray looked in the direction of Darrell Miller. "What about Phil and Audrey?"

"They vote no."

The room was quiet for a long moment and then erupted. Rita Lee sagged in her chair, not entirely comprehending what had just happened. The only thing she knew for sure was that Ladies Night Out was over.

Across the room, Walt watched a flood of emotion cross Rita Lee's face. First agitation, followed by hurt, anger and, more slowly, resignation. He came to the meeting with a secret hope the board would approve the show for no other reason than it would make her happy.

However, at the moment Rita Lee looked anything but happy.

Walt waited till she was through talking to her supporters and started putting on her coat to leave.

"Got time for a short interview?" he asked, knowing full well he already had enough notes to write three stories. "I thought we might get a cup of coffee, if you like. We could talk then."

Rita Lee gave him an odd look. "I'm not sure there's much to say at this point. But if you want to go for coffee, I guess we can. Only could we go to Gretta's? Everybody said they were going to the Pub after the meeting, and I just can't face that right now."

"Fine. How about we just leave the cars here and walk over?"

The night air was unusually warm for early April, and the walk felt good, especially after sitting so long in the stuffy meeting room. Neither said much on the way to the café. Rita Lee was still in shock. She thought she came to the meeting prepared for any outcome, but obviously that wasn't true.

Don't take it personally, she silently instructed herself. *They weren't voting against you, they were voting against the Top Cats.*

Walt glanced sideways at the serious look on Rita Lee's face. "Don't take it personally," he said in a soft voice. "They weren't voting against you, they just didn't like the idea of strippers at the community center."

Rita Lee's heart skipped a long beat, then took up again. She was startled to hear Walt's words echoing her own thoughts so closely. Were her emotions so obvious?

"I know you're right, but..." Rita Lee's words trailed off and she walked on in silence.

It was near closing time at Gretta's and only a few customers remained. Walt led Rita Lee to a booth in the back, and got out his reporter's notebook.

"Actually," he confessed, shoving the notebook back into his jacket pocket, "I've got more than enough notes for a story. Why don't I call you tomorrow morning for an official quote? And tonight, how about we go off the record and just enjoy our coffee?"

"Fine with me," Rita Lee said, relieved. She was suddenly aware of how prim she looked in the dark blue funeral dress and wished she was wearing something a little less grim. The dress hadn't made any difference in the way the vote turned out, and now she was sorry she let her friends talk her into wearing it.

"Walt...Rita Lee," Gretta greeted them as she came toward the booth carrying two mugs in one hand and a pot of hot coffee in the other. "Hope you like decaf, because that's all that's fresh."

"That'll be fine," they said, almost in unison. Their eyes met and Rita Lee was struck with what a soft brown Walt's eyes were--almost like velvet. She'd talked to him hundreds of times and never noticed before. As his smile came, she watched nice little crinkles appear at the outer corners of his lips. Next thing she knew she was smiling back, and with the smile the tension began to flood out of her. Rita Lee slumped back in the booth, sagging into the worn cushions.

"Whew, am I glad that's over," she sighed.

Neither of them was really aware of Gretta pouring coffee until she spoke. "How did the vote go at the board meeting?" she asked, setting down the pot on the edge of the table. "Are we going to get to see those gorgeous hunks?"

"Doesn't look that way," Walt responded, as Rita Lee vainly tried to frame an answer.

"Darn. I was saving up my dollar tips to stick in their G-strings." Gretta gave a hearty laugh. "Oh well, I should have known it was too good to be true."

Without waiting for an invitation, Gretta shoved her ample body into the booth beside Rita Lee. "Wow! Surely feels good to get off my feet. So what happened? Did Gracie and her crowd totally take over the meeting?"

"Not exactly," Walt said quickly." "The vote was three against and one in favor."

Movement at the front of the café caught Gretta's attention. "More customers," she groaned. "Sorry, feet, you still have work to do."

She turned to Rita Lee as she picked up the coffee pot. "Don't worry, hon, something will work out."

"I sure hope so," Rita Lee said, more to herself than Gretta. Then, straightening up in the booth, she focused her attention on Walt. "Enough of this. Let's talk about something interesting. How are things at the paper?"

Before long the Top Cats and Ladies Night Out slipped to the outer edge of Rita Lee's mind. As they conversed, she discovered the same people who tickled her funnybone when they came into the Beauty Mark made Walt chuckle when they stopped by the news office. Rita Lee was amused to find out Sylvia Crocker was one of Walt's regular news sources.

"Half of what she tells you, she hears in my shop. Not that she ever gets her hair done. She just stops by to give us free advice and pick up whatever gossip she can."

"How did you end up in the beauty business?" Walt asked. Like all reporters, he had built-in curiosity.

Rita Lee explained how she'd started out to get a fine arts degree, but one summer as an intern cataloging acquisitions in a musty museum basement convinced her to try something different.

"I know you're going to think I'm crazy," she told him, shifting with embarrassment, "but I see the styles I create sort of like works of art--not all of them, you understand--but sometimes. I've been working with some heads of hair for over 10 years It's a creative challenge to come up with a style that looks good on a person and isn't always the same.

"Of course," she went on, "some women don't want to change. They prefer to go on looking the same forever because it's comfortable for them. Hair is such a personal thing--it's a way of telling the world who we are and how we want to be viewed. Some people wear their hair a certain way because it functions well for them. Others choose a hairstyle because they think it will make them attractive to the opposite sex--not that it always does, but they think it will. Other people chose a style because some movie star or famous person has their hair a certain way. My job is to come up with a style that fulfills their needs and also looks great."

"Are men the same about their hair?"

"Pretty much. Especially since men started wearing their hair longer. You'd be surprised how many come in for a perm or color."

Walt self-consciously touched his own brown wavy hair, wondering what he looked like. It had been years since he'd been to visit a real stylist. Instead, he dropped in to see Boyd-The-Barber-No-Waiting whenever his hair got so long his hat didn't fit any more. Walt was in and out in ten minutes, and that included time spent listening to Boyd's endless supply of knock-knock jokes.

Otherwise he didn't pay much attention to his hair. *What does that say about me?* Walt asked himself. Maybe it was time to make an appointment with Rita Lee for a real haircut.

"Sorry to kick you kids out," Gretta called from behind the counter. "But my tired feet tell me it's time to call it a day. I'll give you more coffee to go if you like, but I gotta close this joint down and get on home and soak my tootsies."

Rita Lee glanced at her watch. It was nearly 10:15. Gretta usually closed at about 9. She'd been keeping the café open so they could talk. "Sorry, Gretta," she apologized. "I guess we lost track of time."

Gretta hung up her apron and started shutting off lights.

The couple strolled slowly through pale pools of street light, past tidy brick storefronts, pausing occasionally to inspect window displays. Anyone who saw them would assume they were trying hard not to get back to the community center parking lot any sooner than they had to.

"I'll call you tomorrow," Walt promised when they finally parted.

Teenie was outside in her mini van waiting when Rita Lee arrived at the shop the next morning. "Timmy had to be at school early for band practice," she explained "I'm dying to talk to you about last night. Where did you disappear to? You weren't at the Pub, and when I called your house your machine answered."

"I had coffee with Walt Billings. He wanted to interview me for the paper."

For some reason Rita Lee was reluctant to tell her closest friend about her long conversation with the editor. She couldn't deny a spark of excitement at the prospect of a new man in her life, but it was important to remain level-headed. After all, you couldn't exactly call last evening's chat at Gretta's a date.

Teenie didn't seem to notice Rita Lee's reluctance to talk about Walt. She followed close behind into the Beauty Mark, chattering about the vote and how extremely bummed she was that the Top Cats weren't coming. "I can't believe it! After all we've gone through. It's just not fair."

She helped stash fresh towels at each hair cutting station and at the shampoo sink. "No Top Cats, no Ladies Night Out, no fun. Dang, this is a boring place to live. Booorring! How do I stand it?

Teenie grabbed a brush from the counter and glumly started messing with her hair. "I had a whole new look I was going to do for the show. Now look at me, stuck with the same old boring Teenie."

Rita Lee smiled at her friend. "One thing you'll never be is boring, Teen. Don't worry."

Wendy flew in the back just as Ronda Porter, her first client of the day, came in through the front.

"Rita Lee, I heard," Ronda said, stricken. "What's wrong with people around here?"

"Mud wrestling is okay for the guys," Teenie grumbled. "But the girls can't have male strippers. If that's not a double standard, I don't know what is."

"Mud wrestling?" Ronda was puzzled.

"About five years ago, the guys got the idea to hire female mud wrestlers as a fundraiser. They got one of those big plastic swimming pools, set it up in the community center, and filled it with mud. The women, in these skimpy little bathing suits, got in and wrestled around. I guess they sold a lot of beer and made a bunch of money for some group--I forget which one."

"So how come they let the men put on women's mud wrestling, but the women can't have the Top Cats?" Ronda wanted to know. "How about this? We hire the Top Cats to wrestle in a big vat of Jell-O. Fair's fair, after all."

"You've got a point, but I don't think Gracie's going to go for that either," Rita Lee said, looking in the appointment book. Berlene Goss was due in at 11:30. Then the mayor's mother was getting a cut and color at 2. Rita Lee was certain both women would carry on about Ladies Night Out. She was sick of the whole topic and wished it would just go away.

Unfortunately, it didn't.

By 11:30 Rita Lee had a splitting headache and was rummaging around in her purse for aspirin when Berlene Goss arrived. Accompanying the pastor's wife was her daughter Charity, who had recently celebrated her twenty-third birthday with a big surprise party at the Pub & Grub. Charity had three earrings in one ear and two in the other. A small butterfly tattoo peaked out from between her purple capri pants and black leather boots.

"Hi Ree," Charity said. "I'm here to help my mother with her big make-over. Her hair needs a total overhaul. She looks twenty years older than she should." Charity began digging through a stack of hair style magazines.

She turned to Berlene waving a copy with a glamorous over-fifties model on the cover. "This would look great on you," she declared.

While neither would admit it publicly, both Reverend and Berlene Goss were a bit in shock about the way Charity turned out. They'd always imagined their only daughter marrying a fine young man she met at Bible College. Instead, she insisted on going to State, and look at the results. A tattoo, for heavens sake! And no good husband prospect in sight.

Berlene was more than a little dubious as Charity continued to flip magazine pages, flashing a variety of hair styles before her. "I'm not sure what your father is going to think about this."

"Forget Dad," Charity advised. "Think for yourself. It's your life and your hair we're talking about here."

An unconvinced Berlene was soon draped in a mauve plastic cape, nervously watching in the wide mirror as Rita Lee pensively shifted her hair this way and that.

"You'll want to keep some length," Rita Lee mused, pushing Berlene's bangs to one side. "Your hair's in pretty good condition, especially considering you've been wearing it pulled back in a bun for so many years. Usually, when people do that they end up with a lot of split ends, and there's nothing to do but cut it quite a bit shorter. But in your case I think something just below your ears should work well."

"Nothing too far out," Berlene cautioned.

"Bring her up to date," Charity demanded.

"Keep it simple," pleaded Berlene. "I'm all thumbs with a brush and comb. If it's not simple, I won't be able to keep it looking right."

"Ahh, Mom, you're too hard on yourself. Look at all that stuff you make for the church bazaar. If you can do that, you can handle a hair brush."

"Please just don't get too fancy," Berlene beseeched, shoulders hunched beneath the cape.

"I'll do my best," Rita Lee promised as she led the pastor's wife to the sink. "You just relax and enjoy the shampoo. I'm going to give you a little scalp and neck massage. You seem awfully tense to me."

By the time Berlene's shampoo was complete and she was back in front of the mirror with her damp hair wrapped in a towel, more customers had entered the salon.

In the next chair Wendy was starting a perm on Hazel Bell, due to receive her Citizen of the Year award the next morning at the chamber of commerce meeting. The strong chemical odor of permanent wave solution spread throughout the salon. "Hit the switch on the fan," Wendy directed Ruth Smiley.

Across a little table from the manicurist, Billie Jo Baxter had her fingers spread out, getting maintenance done on her acrylic nails.

"What do you think? Should I stick with the red or switch over to a pink since it's spring?" Billie Jo asked everyone.

Personally, Berlene couldn't understand how women got anything done with those long nails, but they did seem to be popular. In fact, she'd seen a checker at Smitty's with rhinestones embedded in her nails. She prayed Charity wasn't getting any wild ideas about doing her fingernails that way.

"What's this?" asked Wendy, sorting through the mail on the front counter. She held up a manila envelope. "The return address says "Midnight Productions."

"It's from the Top Cats," shrieked Ronda. "Open it up."

"Oh my," Wendy sighed as a half dozen large glossy photographs fell into her hands. "Look at these."

There were the Top Cats--six sexy guys in their twenties who obviously spent a lot of time working out.

"Hot. These guys are definitely hot!" Ronda said in a breathless voice, fanning herself with one of the photos.

"Hey ladies!" Hazel protested. "Don't be hogs. Send those pictures this way." She extended a hand from beneath her cape and snapped her fingers impatiently.

"Would you look at that," Hazel said, swiveling in her chair to show one of the photos to Berlene. "Isn't that blond a cutie?"

Not knowing what to say, but realizing that some response was expected, Berlene blurted, "I like the Italian looking one."

Charity stared at her mother. The Italian one? Who would have guessed!

"Well yes," Hazel agreed, "a lot of women go for those passionate Latin types. But I've always had a soft spot for Swedes myself."

"You know what they say: cold country, hot heart," Rita Lee teased.

"It's not his heart I'm looking at," Hazel shot back.

The salon exploded in laughter. "Don't let the chamber hear that. They'll take away your Citizen of the Year award."

"You can bet Arland Bryson and the rest of those chamber guys take a peek at Playboy once in a while," said Wendy, as she unhooked the clip on a roller to check the effect of the perm solution. "Just a few more minutes," she predicted as she rolled the curl back up.

"It's just too bad we can't see the Top Cats in person," Billie Jo said. "Not to mention the fire department could use the money."

"There's got to be another place to hold it," Charity declared. "Think everybody. Think."

"There's the grange hall," Wendy suggested, as she removed the latex gloves protecting her hands from the perm solution.

"Same crowd that controls the community center controls the grange hall," Charity pointed out. "How about the fire hall?"

"Too cold, no stage, not enough room."

"I don't suppose the high school gym is a possibility," mused Ruth.

The others looked at her in disbelief.

"How about the American Legion hall?" asked Hazel. "Harry's a member there. He might be able to help us talk them into it."

"Do you mean you actually approve of this show?" Berlene asked in amazement.

"Well why not? Nothing wrong with it as far as I can see. Of course I wouldn't want my Sunday school students to be there. But we're all grown women, we've all seen naked men before. It sounds like fun to me."

"Maybe it's okay for younger women..." Berlene ventured.

"Pooh! I'm seventy-three years old, but that doesn't mean the fire's gone out. I still like the sight of a well-built man just as much as I did when I was twenty. You never get too old to enjoy looking."

"Right on, Hazel!" chirped Ruth.

"Take the men around here. Most of them have bellies that sag so low a belt can hardly get under it to hold up their pants. It's a shame how they're letting themselves go. Makes you want to cry. I don't see anything wrong with sneaking a peek at a guy with a well built body. It does a woman good."

"Do you think so?" Berlene asked hesitantly, tightening her grip on the arms of the chair. "Actually, I've never seen a man nude except for my husband. Oh, and statues of course."

"Time you did, girl," Hazel roared. "Then again, I don't think these guys are going to be totally naked, that might be a little much. But those G-strings will cover up the private parts and we can enjoy all the rest.

"Give me a hard body anytime," declared Charity.

"Hard body," Berlene repeated faintly.

"But back to the problem at hand," Rita Lee interjected briskly, before Berlene bolted. "Do you think there's a chance at the Legion hall?"

"Don't see why not. But we've got to have a plan-- give the Legion boys a good reason to let a bunch of screaming females take over their building."

"We could split the profits from the liquor sales with them," suggested Ruth. "I know their treasury is low after donating to the high school scholarship fund and the town improvement committee."

"Excellent idea," said Billie Jo, holding her fingers perfectly still as the second coat of Tulip Pink polish dried. "My dad's always complaining about that old pool table down at the Legion hall. Says the surface is totally worn out. Maybe we should put a bug in their ear about buying a new one."

While Hazel's perm solution performed its magic and hair cascaded to the floor around Berlene, the regulars tossed around options, trying to come up with the best way to approach the American Legion.

The final strategy had two parts. First they would contact sympathetic members of the Legion's women's auxiliary to ask them to use their influence with their husbands to get the guys to go along with the idea. Then after the auxiliary did its work, a committee from the volunteer fire department would go to the Legionnaires, armed with projected figures on how much the Legion stood to make on liquor sales.

As an added incentive, Hazel volunteered to see if she could pick up some pool table brochures to leave around the Legion hall, just to give the members something to think about.

"This haircut turned out way better than I expected," Berelene told her daughter as they left the salon. "And perhaps Hazel's right about Ladies Night Out. Maybe I was too quick to condemn it. The more I hear about it, the more fun it sounds. But your father probably wouldn't understand, so let's not say anything to him just yet."

"My lips are sealed," Charity assured her mother.

5

A week and a half later it was set--Ladies Night Out had changed venues. Instead of the community center, the show was scheduled for May 7 at the American Legion Post.

The Ladies Night Out committee came to the American Legion armed with homemade coconut oatmeal cookies, an apple pie, and an impressive spreadsheet Teenie created on a computer at the insurance office. It showed the Legion had the potential to make over nine hundred dollars on the event.

Rita Lee once again explained what the fire department hoped to do with the money they raised. She pointed out that the Legion hall was a prime candidate for a fire. The old wooden building was constructed nearly fifty years ago, shortly after World War II. Surely the Legion wanted department volunteers to be as highly trained as possible--just in case.

Legion officials ate cookies and apple pie while they

listened with interest to Trixie Smith, who came representing the business community in support of the show. She passed around copies of the petition, in case the Legionnaires hadn't already seen it. Twila backed her up, pointing out how many Legion members and their wives signed the petition.

The mention of wives reminded several of the decision-makers of strict instructions they had received from their better halves before leaving home.

All in all, a yes vote appeared to be in order.

Walking out of the Legion hall, Rita Lee was filled with relief. She was glad to have the show back on track. Now she could concentrate on advertising and ticket sales. The first thing she needed to do was get her lists out from under the bed. Frustrated and depressed after the no vote at the community center, she dumped her lists into a manila envelop and stuffed the whole works behind the dust ruffle. When she got home, she'd retrieve the envelope and get started compiling a new master "to-do" list.

On impulse, Rita Lee walked down Main to the newspaper office.

"Late breaking news!" she announced as Walt came forward to greet her.

"From the smile on your face, I'd say the Legion must have given you the go-ahead. Congratulations. I'll bet that's a load off your mind." Walt gave Rita Lee a quick hug.

"Oh Walt, you have no idea." A glow spread through Rita Lee. His hug was having a remarkable effect, and she had to force herself concentrate on his next question.

"Did they give you any trouble?

"That's the funny part. There was nothing to it. We all made our presentations, they asked a few easy questions, and then told us we could have the hall."

"So what's next?"

Rita Lee's smile got even brighter, if that was possible. "Sell as many tickets as we can. Want to buy one? Oh, I forgot. You don't need one. You'll get a press pass."

Walt was slightly startled. He hadn't really thought about covering the male strip show. It was hard to imagine sitting among hundreds of women watching men undress. "Thanks for the offer," he told Rita Lee, "but I'm not sure that's a place I want to be."

"You don't need to be self conscious," Rita Lee teased. "No one expects a mere newspaper editor to look as good as a Top Cat. Those guys are professional dancers."

"It's not my body I'm worried about," he told her. "I remember when I was a kid and my mom used to have her club over to play cards. I can still hear those screechy voices getting louder and louder as the night went on. I imagine this show is going to be something like that, only a lot worse."

"You're right," Rita Lee nodded, a wicked glint in her green eyes. "It could get wild."

"On the other hand, there just might be some great photo ops--like the mayor's wife taking off her bra and throwing it at one of the dancers."

"It's probably not going to get quite that wild."

"Don't think I'm going to make it then.

Out of the blue Walt changed the subject. "What are you doing on Sunday? Want to take a drive up to Fish Lake with me?"

"Didn't you write an editorial about fishing there a couple of weeks ago?"

"I did indeed," Walt said, pleased she remembered. "I've been thinking about maybe interviewing a few fishermen to get their opinions on closing the lake for a follow-up story. We could take a picnic."

"Have you ever eaten a Chinese picnic?" Rita Lee inquired, remembering an intriguing set of recipes she'd once seen in Gourmet magazine.

"Can't say as I have. What's to eat at a Chinese picnic? Fortune cookies dipped in soy sauce?"

"You just wait. This is going to knock your socks off."

"Okay," Walt agreed, somewhat dubiously. "I'll be by your house about 11 on Sunday morning. If you've got fishing gear, bring it along."

After a few more minutes of talking about the Top Cats show, Rita Lee left the newspaper office. As she strolled down the street toward the Beauty Mark, she kept coming back to Walt's hug, recalling the faint, spicy tang of his aftershave, the nubby texture of his sweater as he drew her close. She found herself wondering what it would be like to kiss him and was shocked by the need she felt.

"Get a grip, girl. It's just a picnic. Nothing else!" Rita Lee said out loud. Hearing the sound of her own voice, she quickly glanced around, embarrassed, to see if anyone had heard. But the only person on the street was Sylvia Crocker driving her old Pinto to the post office.

Talking to yourself, not a good sign, Rita Lee's inner voice cautioned. *People in town already think you're not quite right.*

"Who cares!" Rita Lee shouted with glee to an empty street. Then, instead of going back to the salon to make out a bank deposit as she'd planned, she walked home.

The little bungalow she and Jason bought with her savings soon after they married was the only remainder of that devastating relationship. On the day their divorce became final she held a giant yard sale and got rid of everything that belonged to him. Clean Sweep Sale was what she called it in her classified ad. She sold whatever he left behind and everything else that reminded her of him, including clothes she'd worn on dates and gifts he'd given her. What didn't sell, she donated to the Salvation Army.

Then she repainted the house inside and out, bought as much new furniture as she could afford, and swore she was never going to let a man into her life again.

However, her vow seemed forgotten as Rita Lee searched for recipes suitable for a Chinese picnic. Her mind bounced from five spice and ginger to wondering whether Walt would like preserved tea eggs. Maybe she shouldn't get too exotic at this point. She didn't want Walt to think she was totally loopy. Going fishing with a Chinese picnic was strange enough.

We have to have chopsticks, her mind raced on. *Chinese food always tastes better with chopsticks.*

But maybe he'd never used chopsticks, maybe he'd be more comfortable with a regular spoon and fork. Rita Lee was on her feet and pacing around the kitchen, absently opening drawers and peering inside. She needed more soy sauce. She needed a grocery list. But first she needed to find recipes. She sat back down and tried her best to concentrate, but the memory of Walt's hug kept interrupting.

It took Rita Lee nearly two hours to decide on a menu and make up a grocery list. Of course, some of the time was spent on sidetracks reading other interesting recipes that wouldn't do now, but might later. Without being aware of it, she was planning future meals with Walt; dinners of Pho from Viet Nam and curry from Bali. She was startled when the phone rang. Cradling the headset on her shoulder, she began to gather recipes and put them back in their file folders.

"Just calling to remind you about the bank deposit," Wendy said breezily. Then the tone of her voice changed. "Trixie stopped by to talk to you about the Top Cats. She said the Legion guys said it was okay to have it there. I'm surprised you didn't tell us. What's going on?"

"Oh my gosh!" Rita Lee gasped. "I forgot all about the deposit. I'll be right there." She quickly tucked the recipe folders back on the shelf among her large cookbook collection. The grocery list went into her purse. Gathering up her jacket, Rita Lee checked to be sure the coffee pot was off and walked swiftly out the back door. But the spot where her faithful blue Subaru was supposed to be was empty. She felt the first stabs of panic--had someone stolen her car?

Then it came to her: the Subaru was still parked out in front of the Legion hall--right where she left it when she had that sudden urge to share her good news with Walt.

"Good grief...get a grip, girl" she told herself for the second time that day, taking off at a brisk pace toward the Legion Hall and her car. The exercise suddenly felt wonderful. She wondered if it was possible to lose a few pounds before Sunday if she really watched her diet and jogged an hour or two every day.

Back at the Beauty Mark, Rita Lee was greeted with cheers.

"Good going, Ree," Wendy said proudly, giving her boss a hug. "I'm not sure what I'm happiest about--knowing I'm going to get to see the Top Cats or knowing we managed to beat out Gracie Melmont and her crowd."

"Excellent!" exclaimed Billie Jo, who was in for highlighting. The silver tinfoil squares covering the top of her head shimmered as she turned to grin at Rita Lee. "When are you going to start selling tickets?"

"As soon as Teenie gets them printed. She's got the

tickets designed and ready to go on her computer."

As if she heard her name called, Teenie came through the front door, an oversized white envelope clutched in her hand.

"Tickets, get your Top Cat tickets right here," she whooped, pulling out a handful of shocking pink tickets. "Who wants to be the first to buy a ticket to paradise?"

"Me!" shouted Billie Jo, grabbing for her purse. "Do you take checks?"

"Make it out to Hobart Junction Volunteer Fire Department," Teenie instructed.

Again the front door swung open with a rush. "Heard the tickets are on sale. I want to get twelve of them to sell at book club tonight," a fire department volunteer announced.

"You've come to the right place," Teenie said, as she counted out a dozen tickets. "Tell everybody the show's back on. The Top Cats are on their way."

"Fantastic. I'll pay for the tickets now and collect from everyone tonight. That will keep your bookkeeping down," the woman said as she handed Rita Lee a check for $120. "I hope the fire department makes a bundle."

"So do we," Rita Lee agreed, gratefully accepting the money.

Word that the show was a go quickly spread around town. Sylvia Crocker did more than her share to get the word out. She posted herself at the front door of the post office and complained to everyone who came by.

"It's shameful," she huffed. "The devil's at work in our town."

Some people agreed with Sylvia. "Something should be done," they muttered, though no one had a clear idea of what. There was talk of picketing a fire department meeting or sending off a strongly worded letter to the county fire commissioners, but no one actually volunteered to do the work.

"We need to get better organized," Pansy Hatfield advised Sylvia. She moved closer to her friend and spoke in a low urgent voice.

"I'll get in touch with the other members of the Library Watch Committee. I know they'll want to help. We're not officially connected with the library you understand, but the committee does quietly monitor books the library buys, just to be sure they're proper literature for this town. I serve by staying alert for questionable books and advising everyone to be careful about what they check out. I'm just sorry the librarian pays so little attention to my opinions."

"There are many of us who appreciate what you do, dear," Sylvia assured Pansy. "Gracie was telling me just the other day how you warned her about that southern writer, what's-his-name. The standards of literature have dropped so low it's hard to find anything fit to read."

Sylvia crossed her arms and glared at Twila Switzer, who was getting out of her car with an armload of outgoing letters and packages. "The trash that woman sells in her bookstore would turn your hair gray,"

"I know exactly what you mean," Pansy concurred. "I stopped buying anything from her years ago."

"It's all the newcomers," Sylvia said. They've completely ruined this town."

The definition of "newcomer" changed, depending on who you talked to. The folks born and raised in Hobart Junction thought a newcomer was anybody who moved in, no matter how many years ago. According to some, to be "local" meant both you and your parents were born in Hobart Junction. A couple of generous souls were willing to give local status to anyone residing in town for more than 50 years.

Of course, the so-called newcomers didn't agree. Residents who moved in at least twenty years ago considered twenty as the break-off point between local and newcomer. Five-year residents thought of themselves as local, and they claimed a newcomer was anybody who had taken up residence since.

Whatever their definition, few people in Hobart Junction had a good word to say about newcomers--who tended to get blamed for everything from lines in the supermarket to racy novels at the bookstore.

"There's Frank Beemer," Sylvia indicated with a little wave, as the police chief rolled by in his cruiser. She gave him a friendly smile.

"I'm surprised there's not a town ordinance against strip tease dancing," Pansy said, watching the back of the cruiser slowly round the corner.

"Who would have thought we would ever need one?" Sylvia sighed.

"Good afternoon, ladies," Twila greeted the pair.

Twila could tell that both Pansy and Sylvia would love to ignore her, but she wasn't going to give them the satisfaction. "Would you mind opening the door for me? My hands are quite full, as you can see."

Sylvia pushed open the heavy post office door, saying not one word.

"Thanks, Sylvia," said Twila sweetly as she moved past the scowling woman.

"You're not welcome," Sylvia snorted once Twila was inside.

"As I was saying," Pansy went on. "The Library Watch Committee can be a great help in putting a halt to this show."

She glanced in both directions up and down Main. "We do have influence in high quarters," she cryptically added.

"Well, I guess I could call Irene Slump and the deacons into action again," Sylvia said, remembering the success her committee had in influencing the community center vote. "I assumed all was lost. But you may be right. If we pull together on this, we can run those boys out of town before they even get here."

"Now you're talking," Pansy said, rubbing her hands together in anticipation of the battle ahead. "I'll alert the Library Watch Committee. You call your group. We'll get together for a meeting after church on Sunday."

A missionary zeal blazed in Sylvia's heart. "A crusade to begin on the holy day," she noted with approval. "Those heathens will be sent packing."

The post office door opened and Twila stepped back out into the sunlight. She knew she shouldn't, but the temptation was just too great. Stopping in front of Sylvia and Pansy, she began a pretend search through her purse. "Would you be interested in buying a ticket for the Top Cats show?" she asked most innocently. "It's a benefit for the volunteer fire department." She dug around in her purse some more. "I know I have those tickets in here somewhere."

"No thank you," said Sylvia, giving her a look that would turn butter rancid. "We certainly will not be going."

Twila looked up. "No? Well, let me know if you change your mind." She closed her handbag and started back to her car. "Ciao," she called over her shoulder to the two prim women pretending not to hear.

6

Sunday was one of those spring days that came as a lovely surprise, even to those who had watched the season arrive in Hobart Junction for more years than they cared to count. A tender breeze gently tickled new green leaves. There was a fragrance in the air that couldn't be tracked to a certain source, but seemed to come from just around the corner or up the hill. It was the kind of morning that put residents in mind of gardening and washing the car. Around Hobart Junction, husbands offered to take care of outdoor chores they'd put off for months and kids actually volunteered to mow the lawn.

Rita Lee was up and out in the kitchen early. It wasn't that she had so much cooking to do, it was a picnic after all. But she didn't want to miss a moment of this gorgeous day. After brewing up a pot of fragrant jasmine tea, she wandered into her back yard, cup in hand.

"Morning, Bill," she called to her neighbor, who was already out pruning fruit trees that lined the back of his property. "Looks like you've got your work cut out for you."

"Morning, Rita Lee," he called back. "Been meaning to get to this for weeks. The wife wanted me to go to church and then to some meeting over at Pansy's, but I told her no way. Just too nice to be inside. Told her I'd be attending the Church of Mother Nature today."

He hung his pruners over a tree branch and slipped out of his garden-stained jacket. "Getting warm already."

"Nice day for a picnic," Rita Lee observed.

"Yes, indeed," Bill agreed, snipping a wayward branch. "Was thinking of going out to the lake later to see if the fish are biting. The kids gave me a jar of garlic-flavored fish eggs for my birthday. Can't imagine the darn things are going to work, but who knows, maybe I'll get lucky."

A pile of pale green twigs began to grow on the ground beneath the thick limbs of the cherry tree.

Rita Lee turned her face a little to catch the warm rays of the morning sun. She thought she could actually feel the earth heating up through the thin soles of her bedroom slippers.

The mention of fishing brought her mind back to the picnic. Doubt hit her like a brick tossed from the top of a nearby peach tree. *Whatever was I thinking?* she thought with rising panic. *Whoever heard of a Chinese picnic? The man is going to think I'm an idiot. I should just fix fried chicken and potato salad. That's what normal people eat at a picnic.*

Abruptly she poured the jasmine tea onto the ground.

Please let there be a chicken in the freezer, Rita Lee

begged as she trotted back to her kitchen. She yanked open the freezer door and pushed aside a jar of soup broth and two cartons of ice cream.

Nothing came into view that resembled a chicken.

"But things do get buried in this mess."

Not this time.

Rita Lee stared forlornly at the Chinese recipes spread out on the counter and the hardboiled eggs soaking in a gallon of oolong tea. She could make a run to Smitty's Food City, but it would take at least an hour after she got home to get the chicken fried properly. She glanced at the clock on the stove. There wasn't time. A Chinese picnic was it. She'd just have to look like a crazy.

But wearing the silk blouse with the Mandarin collar was definitely out. That was a really goofy idea.

Rita Lee removed a package of raw shrimp from the refrigerator. A quick stir-fry and they would be ready to go with the Asian dipping sauce she made last night.

"Oh god, what if he's allergic to shrimp? This is awful. Why didn't I stick to potato salad?" she wailed.

Rita Lee stopped and took a deep breath. Time was short. She'd have to get hysterical later.

Walt was out in his yard, too, lured by the fine morning and spring promises. As he stared intently at the long lump under a tarp next to the fence, he thought about the upcoming picnic.

Over the years, he'd been on lots of picnics with lots of women, and they usually seemed to bring fried chicken and potato salad. Not that there was anything wrong with a good potato salad, but the idea of a Chinese picnic had him speculating about Rita Lee and anticipating an unusual day.

Walt walked over and pulled the tarp away from the lump. Beneath was a red canoe resting upside down on small wooden blocks. He'd been thinking about the canoe ever since he asked Rita Lee to come with him to the lake. He ran his fingers lightly over the hull. It still seemed sea-worthy, though he hadn't had it on water for months.

He wondered if Rita Lee would enjoy exploring the lake in the canoe. *Might be fun*, he told himself. *I'll load the boat on the top of the car. If she's not interested, no big deal. I won't even have to unload it.*

He looked at his watch. Still plenty of time to gather up the paddles and another life vest.

As Rita Lee fussed over her Chinese picnic and Walt searched for a life vest, Reverend Gilford Goss was putting the finishing touches on his Sunday sermon. He usually tried to get started some time during the day on Thursday. A rough draft was done by Friday. Saturday the sermon sat in a desk drawer. Early Sunday it came out for last minute changes or, very occasionally, a total rewrite.

This was one of those awful total rewrite Sundays. The pages of Gilford's sermon were spread in disarray across his desk. Several sheets were scrunched into balls and scattered on the floor around his waste basket. What on Thursday seemed so easy--warning his flock against sinful temptations like the Top Cats--went sour on Friday.

It all started when someone asked if he planned to attend the meeting Pansy Hatfield was organizing after church on Sunday. Even though the reverend definitely didn't approve of the Top Cats show, he couldn't support the way certain church members were handling the situation. It seemed to him that the show was stirring up a lot of animosity that had little to do with its production values. Instead of opposing the event, his parishioners were getting personal. People were saying malicious things about each other rather than concentrating on the negative aspects of the show.

He overheard one woman at Bible Study call Trixie Smith a bitch--hardly a Christian term by any measure. Worst of all, he suspected the pejorative was primarily based on an incident several months before when Trixie called in a complaint to the health department about the many cats the woman kept in her house.

That Beauty Mark crowd had really stirred up a hornet's nest. This morning he'd even overheard Berlene and Charity discussing something to do with the Top Cats, but they stopped talking when he came into the room.

Things hadn't been the same since Berlene got her hair done.

Reverent Goss tried to focus his mind on the sermon, but soon found himself off track again thinking about Berlene's new hair style. Berlene had her long brown hair pulled back and tucked into a bun when he met her twenty-five years ago. He thought the style becoming for a minister's wife, and he was accustomed to her looking that way. Now all of a sudden, her hair was shorter and wavy. His daughter Charity insisted it was a long-overdue change. He wasn't so sure.

Reverend Goss usually didn't pay much attention to the way women's hair looked. Once in a while, gazing out over the congregation, an especially fancy hat would catch his attention, but since women didn't wear hats to church much any more, that didn't happen often.

The men all pretty much blended together. There were the usual Sunday suits and ties, though like ladies hats he saw fewer of those these days. A couple of young guys had long hair, but generally the men looked pretty much the same, hair-wise. Charity said she could tell which guys got their hair cut at Boyd-The-Barber-No-Waiting and refused to date them on principle. He tried to imagine what kind of hair the Top Cats had. One of the Bible Study ladies told him about a photo of six near naked men that was posted in the window of the Beauty Mark with a notice that said, "Get your tickets here!" But she hadn't said anything about their hair.

There was a soft knock at his study door. Berlene poked her head in.

"Breakfast will be ready in about ten minutes," she said quietly. "How's the sermon coming?"

"I'm not sure," Gilford confessed. "I feel it's my duty to preach on the lowering of morals in our community that led to this strip show, but to tell you the truth I'm more concerned about some of the other effects it's having. I don't know if you heard or not, but someone called Trixie Smith a bitch at Wednesday Bible Study."

"Oh dear," Berlene sighed. "It wasn't that woman with all the cats, was it?"

"Afraid so."

"Well, that explains it."

"My point exactly!" said Gilford, pounding the edge of his desk and pointing an accusing finger at his wife.

Berlene nervously wondered just how much her husband had overheard when she and Charity were gossiping about the Top Cats.

"We're told to love one another and practice compassion. And here they are, Christian women, calling each other names and holding secret meetings." He swirled back to his bookcase. "I need a scripture. Where's my compendium of scriptural quotes?"

Gilford began jerking volumes off the shelf.

"Oh dear," Berlene thought as she softly closed the study door. The Sunday sermon was obviously in deep trouble.

Pansy Hatfield would have been shocked to know her decency committee meeting was causing Reverend Goss such distress. She saw herself as an evangelist, doing her best to protect the community from evil that lurked ever nearer at hand. You only had to turn on the TV or go to a movie to know how bad things were getting.

Pansy lived with her husband Lester in a doublewide on a large lot at the end of Adams Street. The interior was decorated all in lavender--her favorite color. An overstuffed lavender sofa, matched by a pair of identical lavender chairs, set off a plush dark lavender rug. Lavender roses on the drapes added to the look. Several pillows in an eggplant shade sat on the sofa. On top of the TV rested a pale gray vase filled with silk flowers--lilacs, of course.

At the moment, Pansy was in the bathroom making sure everything was tidy in case a guest decided to visit the powder room. She made a small adjustment to the fuzzy purple bathmat hanging over the edge of the tub and closed down the lid of the toilet, revealing its fuzzy cover. Both items were an exact color match to the purple bath towels and shower curtain. Flowered hand towels hung graciously above a glass bowl filled to the brim with individual soaps giving off a faint hint of grape.

Pansy stepped back to make one final inspection. Her reflection in the mirror revealed a thin woman with the look of someone perpetually sucking on lemons. She had spent so many years frowning about selections made by library patrons, the lines in her face were permanently etched downward. But beauty is only skin deep, as Pansy was fond of telling people. It's what's in the heart that counts.

She primly moved several soaps in the dish closer together to make the grouping more uniform. Then satisfied at last, she headed for the kitchen.

Knowing everyone would be hungry by the time church services were over, Pansy began arranging Velveeta cheese, Ritz crackers and rolled baloney slices on a plate. She felt a bit guilty about not attending church this morning. But there was that last speck of dust to eliminate. She had her reputation as a spotless housekeeper to think of. It would be horrible if they started talking about her dirty cupboards at Stitch and Bitch.

It was embarrassing enough that Lester absolutely refused to come to the meeting. "I'm sick and tired of looking at all that purple," he declared as he loaded fishing gear into the back of his pickup. "I'm going to go out to the lake and gaze at some green and blue for a while."

Even without Lester, Pansy was expecting a large crowd. She knew she wasn't alone in her disgust at the depravity about to descend upon Hobart Junction. Among those attending were almost all of the members of her Library Watch Committee, along with a contingent of concerned Lutherans and Presbyterians. And that wasn't counting all the other folks outraged by the filthy fundraiser.

Pansy added another dozen crackers to the plate.

7

Rita Lee was tucking the last little container of soy-cilantro dipping sauce into a corner of a large wicker picnic basket when Walt drove up. She sure hoped he wasn't allergic to shrimp.

"Gung hoy fat choy!" he called through the open door.

"What?" She turned in confusion.

"That's the only thing I know how to say in Chinese. It think it means Happy New Year. But don't quote me. I might be saying my cat has fleas."

Walt was dressed in a blue chambray shirt and tan chinos. Over the shirt was a well-worn fishing vest. He seemed to be taking the prospect of a Chinese picnic with such good humor that for an instant Rita Lee thought maybe she should have worn the mandarin blouse after all.

Then again, maybe not.

"That basket looks heavy. How about I carry it out to the car?"

"A canoe!" Rita Lee exclaimed as they headed down the walk. "Haven't been in one of those since I went to Camp Zecki Wecki back in fifth grade. Are we going canoeing?"

"If you'd like."

"Give me a sec to get my water shoes."

Rita Lee dashed back up to the porch, grabbed an old pair of tennies, and returned before Walt had time to shift the basket from one arm to the other.

"Ready when you are, sir," she said, delight in her voice.

The ride to the lake went quickly. Walt got Rita Lee telling stories about her adventures at Camp Zecki Wecki. He followed up with the tale of a dreadful week spent at music camp the summer his mother decided he should master the violin.

"The maestro cringed every time I came through the door. Mom paid him extra for me to take private lessons. While the rest of the kids were around a campfire cooking lunch in tinfoil, I was sawing away in the music room."

Walt took his eyes off the road for a moment to look across at Rita Lee. "Actually, I tried to play bad. Figured if I was rotten enough, he'd give up on me. He never did though. If my mom was paying, he was determined to teach me something. It was the longest week of my life!"

As they rounded the last curve, the lake spread out before them, a dark blue mirror. Budding trees along the edge, reflected in the still water, gave the impression of a second watery glade spreading out into the lake. There was little sound except the occasional call of a distant bird or the low murmur of a fisherman.

"Half the town's here!" Rita Lee exclaimed, surprised at the number of cars parked near the public boat launch.

"Must be the weather," Walt said. "Nothing like a warm spring day to get a guy thinking about fishing. Especially if his wife's got a long list of jobs for him to do around the house."

"Wait a minute there," Rita Lee protested. "Women like to fish, too."

"Point well taken," Walt said, releasing the first of the tie-down straps holding the canoe securely to the car-top rack. "My sister can out-fish me any day of the week."

It didn't take long to get the canoe off the car and into shallow water. Walt handed Rita Lee a yellow life vest. "Hope this fits," he said. "Last person to use it was my ex-wife."

Rita Lee's heart did a little flip. She'd heard Walt's former wife was a high-powered advertising executive in Chicago. How was she supposed to look good next to someone like that?

Forget it, she quickly told herself. *The guy asked you to go out to the lake with him, that's all.*

Paddles, picnic, and seat cushions were loaded. Then Rita Lee waded out several feet and carefully stepped into the craft. Reaching back to pick up a paddle, she gave Walt a happy smile. "Ready for launch, captain."

Walt shoved the red canoe forward until there was enough draft to accommodate his weight and gingerly climbed in. "Gung Hoy!" he proclaimed. And they were off.

For nearly 15 minutes hardly a word was spoken. Once they got their paddle strokes synchronized, the pair skimmed smoothly along, hugging the shoreline. Ahead was the reflected forest; behind, fractured ripples of brown, gray and pale green.

When her right arm began to tire, Rita Lee rested her paddle on one knee and watched reflected sun sparkle like diamonds on the surface, the points of light caught in the gentle wake of fishing boats moving slowly down the center of the lake. A pair of mallards paddled out of the reeds, quacking softly as they made their way past the couple in the canoe.

"Walt," she whispered, "Do you suppose they have a nest back in there?"

"Hard to tell. It seems a little early. Most ducks don't start laying eggs until it warms up a bit more."

Walt watched as Rita Lee smoothly powered the boat forward. He imagined her as an Indian princess, proud and bold. He found himself strongly aware of her feminine curves, the grace of her movements, her strength and confidence.

"By the shores of Gicheegoomee, by the shining deep sea waters," Rita Lee loudly intoned.

"What?" Walt's mental picture of a beautiful Indian maiden was brought up short.

"Didn't your teacher ever read that poem to you?" Rita Lee asked. "It's by Longfellow. "We had to learn the first part of it by heart when we studied Indians in sixth grade. You just heard all I remember."

"Can't say I know that one. Where did you go to school, anyway?"

"Right here in Hobart Junction."

"That explains it." Walt chuckled as he began steering for a sandy point sticking out into the lake. "Tell me more. What other poems do you know?"

"I can say all of 'The Midnight Ride of Paul Revere,'" she bragged.

"Maybe some other time," Walt suggested. "I think I'm sorry I asked."

"Listen my children and you will hear of the midnight ride of Paul Revere." she began.

"Please, no!" Walt begged, poking her in the back with his paddle.

His sudden movement and Rita Lee's quick reaction when she felt the paddle bounce off her life vest, set the canoe rocking violently. For a few seconds both feared the craft might capsize and send them overboard into the chilly water of Fish Lake. But a coordinated effort soon had them righted and back on an even keel.

When Walt started to apologize, Rita Lee interrupted. "That was certainly exciting. I had visions of our lunch going to the bottom off the lake. And after all my work."

"I suggest we eat that lunch before we drown it," He pointed to the sandy beach ahead. "Let's stop there."

On shore, Walt hauled out a waterproof bag he had stored in the back of the boat. With a flourish he shook out a blanket and then produced two green bottles with long necks.

"Chinese," Rita Lee marveled, examining the label. "Where did you find these?"

"In the imported beer section of that big new super market in Belfort."

Rita Lee spread lunch out on the blanket: cold shrimp with dipping sauces, spring rolls, pickled asparagus, and finally, hesitantly, the tea soaked eggs.

"Interesting taste," Walt said, biting into one. "Quite strange. But good strange."

Finally assured Walt didn't think her a total weirdo, the last bit of Rita Lee's nervousness evaporated. "Hope you aren't allergic to shrimp, because if you are I'm going to have to eat this whole thing," she joked, as she uncovered the container.

"Just so happens I love shrimp. You may not get

any at all."

Walt hoisted his bottle in a toast. "To the Indian princess and Chinese cook."

"To the red canoe," Rita Lee responded.

They clinked bottles and began lunch.

As Walt finished off the last hard boiled tea egg, he asked Rita Lee how ticket sales were going for Ladies Night Out.

"Just great. We got off to a pretty terrible start, but things are going super now. I was so depressed after the vote at the community center. I thought everybody in town hated me. When I was little, Hobart Junction was really a hick town. But with all the new people and the changing times, it's hard to understand why this has caused such a flap. You see male strippers on TV, for heavens sake."

"But not too often right in Hobart Junction," Walt reminded her.

"Still..." Rita Lee's voice faded.

But her eyes brightened, as she shook off the gloomy thoughts. "That's all in the past now. The show's going on. We've already sold over a hundred tickets. No more bake sales this year," she gloated.

But in less than three hours, Rita Lee was to wonder if her boast had been premature.

After repacking remnants of the picnic, which Walt declared the best he'd ever eaten, the pair continued their exploration of Fish Lake's many small bays. Several hours later, when the wind started to come up, they agreed it was probably time to head back to the car. Their leisurely pace was replaced by concentrated paddling, both putting maximum effort into moving rapidly, before small swells turned into menacing whitecaps.

"Well, captain," Rita Lee groaned, as they drifted the last few feet into the public boat launch, "that was a workout."

"Yep," Walt agreed. "You're pretty strong for a girl."

Rita Lee felt a flush of pleasure. Not the usual compliment she got from a guy, that's for sure, but coming from Walt, they seemed fine words indeed.

Lifting the canoe back onto the car's rack went smoothly, and they were just about to leave when Joe Spilling and Arvid Smiley walked by, carrying the last of their fishing gear to the parking lot.

They didn't see Walt and Rita Lee, out of sight on the other side of the car and canoe.

Spotting a brown jacket hanging from a post, Joe exclaimed, "Looks like Lester Hatfield forgot his coat. I better grab it and drop it by his house."

"I don't know if he's there or not," Arvid replied. "Pansy's holding that big meeting about the strippers today. She and her friends are still trying to put a stop to the show. Formed some kind of decency committee. Lester says he's sick of the whole thing."

"Can't say as I blame him," Joe responded. "It's got the whole town in an uproar. My wife won't stop talking about it."

"Well, if Pansy and her gang get their way, the volunteer fire department is going to be out of luck, that's for sure."

The two fishermen walked out of earshot, leaving Rita Lee feeling ill.

"Oh Walt," she cried, tears welling up. "Everything was going so well. What are we going to do now?" She laid her forehead against the damp hull of the red canoe.

"Daaaamn," Rita Lee wailed.

Monday was Rita Lee's day to read with the third graders. She thought about calling Jennifer's teacher to cancel, but didn't want to disappoint the kids. As usual on Monday, the salon was closed, which gave her a day to recover from the damaging news she'd overhead at the lake.

She sat at her kitchen table, still in flannel pajamas and blue fleece robe, even though it was close to noon and she needed to be at school soon. The phone rang several times, but she let the machine take the calls. Rita Lee didn't want to talk to anyone right now. Depressed? She couldn't even describe how depressed she was.

Rita Lee tried to remember the good parts of yesterday--Walt and the canoe and how much fun they'd been having--right up till the moment Joe and Arvid walked by. The worst was not knowing exactly what was going to happen next. She could imagine all sorts of things--each more disastrous than the last. But until the gossip got back to her, there was no way to tell for sure what Pansy and her decency committee had planned. All she could do was wait.

Morosely cradling her teacup, Rita Lee listened as another phone call came in.

It was Teenie. "Hi Ree, I heard you were out at the lake with Walt yesterday. What gives? Keeping secrets from us? Also, we just sold ticket number 150. That means we're halfway there. Give me a call, okay?"

Oh great. I hope we don't have to give all that money back.

Dejected, she slumped even further down in her chair, tea going cold. She picked up another chocolate chip cookie, seeking comfort in its sweet flavor.

But eventually curiosity overrode desperation. Exactly what had Teenie heard about her and Walt out at the lake?

Rita Lee cleared the table and put away the cookies. It was time to face the world. When the bad news came, she'd take care of it just like she always did. She was tough. Jason had made her that way, dang his hide.

Teenie, Dale and their kids lived in a two-story Victorian on Adams Street. It was built by one of the early Hobarts and retained much of its old fashioned charm. The cozy kitchen was her favorite spot in the house and it was there Teenie led Rita Lee later that afternoon.

Rita Lee sniffed the air like a dog. "I smell chocolate. Does this mean you've been playing PTA mom again?"

"Cupcakes for Tina's Campfire group. There are a few extras, if you want one."

"Actually, I ate at least fourteen chocolate chip cookies this morning. Think I've probably had my carbohydrate allotment for the day."

"Not me," Teen said, picking up one of the pink frosted cupcakes. "As far as I'm concerned, a girl can't get too much chocolate.

"Tell all," she coaxed. "What's this about you and Walt out at the lake?"

"None of your business. And where did you hear we were out at the lake?"

"None of your business."

"Okay, okay. I'll tell you, if you'll tell me."

"You first."

"No, you first."

"No, you first," It was a game they'd played since childhood.

Rita Lee filled a glass from the automatic ice maker in the refrigerator door and poured a diet drink. Posted on the door were the kids' school pictures, a photo of Larry and the rest of the guys on the Pub & Grub slow-pitch softball team, Libby's straight-A report card, and at least a half-dozen sheets of kiddie art held on with teddy bear magnets. She secretly wondered if she would ever have a refrigerator door that showcased so many emblems of love.

Sitting down at the round oak table, she described her day with Walt.

"Oh, Ree, that's great. It sounds wonderful. Did he ask you out again?"

"No." Rita Lee hesitated. "But there's something that happened right at the end I haven't told you about yet."

"Oh, no," Teenie groaned. "What?"

"It has to do with Ladies Night Out. Have you heard anything?"

Teenie stared at her friend, mystified. "Heard anything? Just that tickets are selling like hotcakes."

"Well something's going on that might change that."

"What are you talking about? Something to do with Walt?"

"No it's not Walt, but I don't know what it is."

"Rita Lee, you're not making much sense."

"I know that," Rita Lee moaned.

She absently picked one of the chocolate cupcakes off the plate. Between bites she described the conversation she and Walt overheard. "So what's going on? What have you heard?"

"Not a word, I swear. I didn't even know Pansy was holding a meeting, or I would have warned you."

"What should we do?"

"Send out the spies. It's impossible to keep a secret in this town. Somebody will tell us."

Rita Lee waited impatiently for word on what the decency committee was up to. Every time the phone rang she stopped short, thinking it might be bad news. She asked each of her customers if they knew anything, but they were just as much in the dark as she. No one had even heard there was a meeting--which seemed particularly strange.

Finally, Rita Lee could stand it no longer and called Walt, though she knew it was Tuesday and he was swamped getting the paper ready for the printer.

"Hobart Independent, Thomas G. Gates speaking," said an official-sounding male voice Rita Lee recognized as the young reporter.

"Hi Tommy, this is Rita Lee over at the Beauty Mark. Is Walt available?"

"Got a hot story for us?" he eagerly asked.

"Afraid not."

"Too bad. I'd like a chance to write about something besides the Strawberry parade."

Rita Lee took a few extra deep breaths to calm herself while she waited for Walt.

"I know you're busy and I won't keep you," Rita Lee said quickly when Walt picked up the phone. "You remember that conversation we overheard out at the lake about a meeting at Pansy Hatfield's house? Have you heard any more?"

"No, and that's got me puzzled. Maybe the meeting got postponed. Sylvia Crocker cruised through here this morning, but she never mentioned it. And you know Sylvia, she prides herself on being the first to give me the word on the street."

"Do you suppose we misunderstood?" Rita Lee asked, faint hope in her voice.

"Seemed pretty plain to me."

Rita Lee leaned against the front counter and watched absently as Irene Slump parked her car, got out and started down the sidewalk. When she came to the Beauty Mark, Irene stopped short and stared for a long moment at the publicity photo of the Top Cats in the window. Her lips begin to curl upward into an odd sort of smile--a look that Rita Lee immediately recognized.

"Walt," Rita gasped into the phone. "Irene just walked by here and she stopped and looked at the Top Cats poster in the window. I swear, Walt, she started to smirk. She smirked!"

"What is going on?" she shouted.

But before Walt could answer, Rita Lee abruptly cut him off. "Sorry to bother you. Let me know if you hear anything, okay?" She slammed down the receiver.

Totally undone, Rita Lee grabbed a hair brush and pounded it frantically on the counter.

"Ree, it can't be that bad," Wendy told her, once the racket subsided. "What can they do? This is an official volunteer fire department event, co-sponsored by the American Legion. If certain people don't like it, that's just tough. It's a free country."

The next morning, long before business opened, Walt Billings was in Gretta's, his visit timed to catch the early breakfast crowd. On each table, a fresh carnation and a few sprigs of baby's breath stood in a small vase between the cut glass salt and pepper shakers. Gretta's German plate collection was displayed on a high shelf, but it had been there for so long nobody but the occasional tourist noticed it any more. The odor of frying bacon filled the air.

As Walt's gaze passed around the restaurant he recognized the usual suspects. Contractors sat at their regular table closest to the coffee pot. Phil Miller and the other retirees bunched together at a table to the rear. Police Chief Frank Beemer, Clint Small, several delivery truck drivers, and one or two people Walt didn't recognize filled out the room.

"Better watch what you say, the press has arrived," boomed Chief Beemer, shoving aside his newspaper to make room for Walt. "Mornin', Editor."

"Mornin', Chief. What's up? Any new crime in town?"

"Nothing to speak of. Just the usual complaints about barking dogs. There was a one-car rollover down on the state highway last night. Some guy from Kansas fell asleep at the wheel. Banged up his car pretty bad, but he wasn't hurt."

Walt smiled at Gretta as she plunked down a mug and filled it with steaming coffee. "Looks like they're keeping you busy this morning. What's the special?"

"Same as every Wednesday. French toast, two eggs and bacon."

"Sounds good to me--when you get time. I see Burley Spilling's shaking his cup at you like he's out of coffee. Don't those old timers give you any respect at all?"

"Ol' Burley's a case," Gretta said fondly. "He's been coming in here every morning for forty years and thinks that makes him eligible for special service."

"He may be right," Walt acknowledged.

Frank Beemer's eyes narrowed as he pulled at a sleeve of his uniform. "I see you've got my nephew Jerry back there in the kitchen cooking for you again. That mean he's out of the county jail for good this time?"

"Now Frank, take it easy." Gretta said, patting his shoulder with a plump hand. "The kid deserves another chance. Besides, Jerry's one of the best breakfast cooks I've ever had...as long as I can keep him sober."

After topping off the police chief's coffee, Gretta hastened to pour Burley's refill.

"Heard anything new about that show the fire department is putting on?" Walt cautiously asked.

"Nothing since..." Frank' sentence was interrupted by Steve Bryson, over at the contractors' table.

"If you ask me, it's a violation of my civil rights. The

women are putting on a show and men aren't allowed in. It's time men got treated equal with women."

"Right on, brother," exclaimed the fellow next to him.

"Don't have any desire to go, even if men were allowed," chimed in the Frito-Lay driver.

"Why not, man? Someone needs to be there to protect the women in case one of those dancer guys tries to get too friendly."

"It's my impression it's usually the other way around--the dancers need to be protected from the women," Walt said.

"No way," the first man objected. "Why do you think those guys do it? It's for the good lookin' chicks they can pick up."

"More likely it's for the fat tips," said the Frito-Lay driver. "I saw some of those Chippendale guys dancing on TV one time and the women were just stuffing money into their shorts."

"No kidding?" said a retiree. "What a way to make a living."

"I'm definitely in the wrong business," declared a plumbing contractor.

"Not with your body," chided the fellow across the table. "Besides you can't dance worth beans."

"Like you're such a hotshot dancer," retorted the plumber. "I've seen you down at the Pub & Grub. You look like an elephant on roller skates."

"Still better than you are," the other man shot back, as laughter filled the room.

Steve Bryson smile faded. He thoughtfully pushed the last of his French toast through the egg yoke oozing along the edge of his plate. "I want to go see those guys."

"That sounds pretty strange to me," a retiree noted. "If I didn't know you from high school sports and on the job for so many years, I'd wonder if you were a little girlie."

"I'm talking equal rights here," Steve explained earnestly. "Women are always saying that men don't treat them fairly, but here's a case where the shoe's on the other foot and look at the treatment us men are getting."

"Do you really want to go see those guys? Seriously?" asked an electrician at the end of the table.

"Not really," Steve admitted. "It's a men's rights matter. That's all."

"Not me," said Jim Porter from the counter. "I want to go because it sounds like fun. Ronda told me all about it. The Top Cats put on a great show. Lots of jokes and stuff. There's a female impersonator who looks and sounds just like Joan Rivers. A buddy and I went to one of those impersonator shows in San Francisco and it was wild and crazy."

"That's what I'm telling you, man. We should all buy tickets."

"Count me out," declared the electrician.

"How much are the tickets, anyway?"

"Ah, you're too chicken to show up," said the plumber. "Five bucks says you don't have the nerve to go."

"You're on, man. Let's see your money.

"Hey Gretta," Andy called out. "Will you hold the money for us? I don't trust this guy to pay up when he loses."

Gretta slipped the soiled dishes she had collected from around the restaurant into a gray plastic bin behind the counter, wiped her hands on a nearby towel, and walked over the contractors' table. At least a couple of times a week she held money on a bet. Two days ago the wager was who was going to get the first strike when the guys played in the weekly bowling league. Before that it had to do with rushing statistics.

Experience taught her to require bettors to put all wagers in writing. She'd spent way too many mornings listening to the crowd argue over who won a bet. Usually the arguments started because her customers disagreed about the exact wording of the wager. Sometimes that argument lasted longer than the original discussion that led to the bet.

"Here you go fellas," Gretta said, handing the plumber a blank page out of her order book. "You know the rules. Write down the bet and give me the money."

The plumber pulled a fat pencil out of the chest pocket of his coveralls. "The bet is that Jim Porter is too chicken to actually go to the Top Cats show. Right?"

"Not me," Jim protested. "I said I thought it was going to be a good show and I'd like to go. I didn't say I was really going to buy a ticket."

"You're betting with Andy," corrected Phil Miller.

"Oh yeah. Anybody else want to join in?"

"We're going to buy tickets, just to support the fire department. But my wife and I don't plan to go," noted a retiree.

"Last call before I write down the bet. Any other takers?"

The room was silent.

"Okay, the bet is that Andy is too chicken to show up."

"Say so long to your five dollars," Andy told the plumber, handing the envelope to Gretta.

The restaurant's owner folded the receipt over the two bills and went back to the counter to add them to the clutter in the drawer under the cash register. Several other long-term wagers were in there already. One fat envelope contained money on the outcome of the World Series. Another was a pool on how many piglets Doyle

Baxter's sow would produce that year.

Chewing on a piece of toast, Jim Porter looked over at Walt. "You haven't had much to say. What do you think about all this Top Cat business? You going to go?"

"Rita Lee offered me a press pass, but I'm not so sure I want to put up with a bunch of howling women. Going to Little League games is bad enough"

Walt turned to the police chief. "I suppose you're going to have to be there."

Frank Beemer suddenly shoved himself out of the booth and hurried over to pay his bill without saying so much as a word. Walt thought Frank had a distinctly uncomfortable look on his face.

"Gotta run, Gretta," the chief called, as he dropped money next to the cash register. He grabbed a toothpick from the holder, pushed open the door and was gone.

"That's odd," Walt remarked. "Wonder what got into Frank."

Walt and Phil Miller stood up to leave at the same time. Walt headed to the cash register to pay his bill. He didn't see Phil, a few steps behind, give a slight nod toward the pass-through into the kitchen. Jerry, flipping a flapjack, saw the signal and acknowledged it with a nod of his own.

8

Phil Miller thought he might be in love. At his age! Not that he was that old. He saw on television just the other day that some 89-year-old millionaire was marrying his 31-year-old secretary. The old boy told reporters he was happy to have a love life again. Phil wondered if it was the millionaire or his millions that attracted the young secretary.

In the weeks since they first got together at the Pub to talk about the community center vote, Phil and Audrey had seen a lot of each other. The weekend over at Foxville was a huge success. The rose show was excellent and they had a lot of fun at the golf course, where Phil showed Audrey how to putt on the practice green. A few days later Audrey had him over for dinner. Then they went to Belfort to a movie. Soon they were seeing each other every day.

Stitch and Bitch declared them an item.

Audrey had a birthday coming up the first week in May, and Phil wanted to do something really nice for her. His gift idea was so good he could barely keep it secret. During dinner one evening Audrey mentioned how much she liked the fountain in the town park. The fountain was modeled after one in Saint Louis, the original home of the Hobart family. The Saint Louis fountain, in turn, was a copy of a famous fountain in the courtyard of a castle in France. In the middle of a round pool, standing outward in a circle, stood three seahorses. On their heads balanced a scalloped shell. Rising above the shell was a fanciful mermaid. From stars she held in each hand, water spouted.

Audrey wished she had a fountain like that in the middle of her rose garden. And Phil was going to give it to her.

At first it was just a fuzzy notion, but on a trip to Foxville a solid plan began to develop. Phil missed the turn to the golf course and had to drive a few blocks out of his way. On a side street he passed a sales yard filled with concrete animals, benches and other backyard ornaments. Birdbaths were on prominent display. He didn't see many fountains, but that didn't mean they couldn't make him one. He stopped long enough to jot down the phone number displayed on a sign attached to a cement deer.

The next day Phil dialed the number for Creative Concrete. He described what he wanted to the company's owner, Don Johnson. Don was used to filling peculiar custom orders, but usually the finished product ended up in a cemetery. Angels were common, a lot of people asked for those. Once he made a replica of a family's cocker spaniel to stand next to the angel.

Another time a customer wanted a whole set of concrete lawn furniture. The guy said he was tired of repairing broken chaise lounges.

But this fountain sounded like a real challenge. It wasn't going to be cheap, he cautioned Phil.

"That's fine," Phil said, "as long as it's done right. This is a birthday present."

"I'm going to need photographs of the park fountain to get started," the owner said. "I think I have forms for seahorses in the warehouse somewhere. And the scallop shell won't be a problem. But I'm not sure about the mermaid. I need to see what she looks like."

First thing the next morning Phil shot up a 24 exposure roll of film, taking pictures of the fountain from every angle and distance. Then he drove to Foxville to the one-hour photo place to get them developed. "Hope this does it for you," he said, handing the envelope to the concrete man.

"Wow," Don Johnson said, sorting through the stack of photos. "This is going to be tougher than I thought. The mermaid will be real tricky, I can tell you that. And the whole thing is much taller than I had in my mind when you described it to me."

"So, you think you can do it?"

"Can't promise one hundred percent. But we're going to give it a big try. Should be fun. Never did anything this tall before."

On Wednesday evenings the calm of Hobart Junction was shattered by the wail of the siren at the fire hall. It was the weekly test of the fire alarm system and a reminder to the volunteers that the fire department meeting was about to begin. The first thought of most residents when they heard the alarm go off was "Oh no, not a fire." The next was "What day is this?" If it was Wednesday, they relaxed and went on eating dinner or watching TV.

There was a core group of volunteers who always showed up, including fire chief Arvid Smiley, the Kanute brothers and Gene Closser. Others members came when they remembered or didn't have anything else to do.

The fire hall sat at the corner of Lincoln and Jefferson. The red wooden building housed the fire engine and tanker truck. Pegs on the wall held a motley collection of uniforms. Battered boots stood in a row below silver flame-proof jackets and pants. That night, both garage doors were thrown open and light spilled into the street.

Rita Lee was surprised to see so many vehicles parked around the fire station. There hadn't been such a big crowd since the vote to serve snacks and beer. The concept was to increase attendance, but after a couple of weeks some of the wives started to complain, and then the Baptists threatened to boycott the fire department. So the scheme was dropped.

Rita Lee pulled her Subaru in beside Will Kanute's battered pickup. Next to it was his twin brother Bill's shiny new Camry. Wilma Kanute, their mother, named the identical twins William and Willard, after two favorite uncles. For years she kept them dressed in identical outfits, which made it even more difficult to tell one from the other. Most people in town called both little boys BillWill, since they couldn't tell them apart. When the boys were about fourteen, the Kanute twins decided they didn't want to be BillWill anymore. Will took to wearing Hawaiian shirts and sandals. Bill came to school in preppy attire he purchased at Simon's Men's Store in Foxville. From then on people could always tell who was who.

After high school both went to college. Will attended for a year, dropped out and moved to Australia. While Bill worked on a degree in finance, Will was down under drinking beer and riding the surf. To almost everyone's surprise, both boys ended up back in town. When their father decided to retire, they agreed to take over the family business. Bill was the manager, Will spent most of his time on the road calling on customers.

They shared a duplex on Lincoln Street. Bill's side was neat and tidy. Will had a rusty VW bus on blocks among the weeds on his side.

Bill was pulling the tanker truck out of the fire hall when Rita Lee arrived. The smell of diesel exhaust hung in the air where the volunteers congregated. She had mixed feelings about coming to the meeting. She was excited because 178 tickets were already sold. But she knew not everyone in the department approved of the fundraiser, and some were upset she'd gone ahead and set up the whole thing without asking anybody.

Most of the female volunteers were talking together in front of the fire engine. The men, led by Arvid, were dragging a hose off of a reel at the back of the truck.

"Hey, ladies," Arvid called. "Give us a hand back here."

Rita Lee smiled. Unwinding the hose wasn't that big a deal. Arvid just liked giving orders.

"Rita Lee, glad you're here," the fire chief said. "How are ticket sales going?"

"Very well. We've sold 178, which is more than half way to our goal of 300. And there's three weeks to go."

Arvid did some quick math in his head. "So, at $10 a ticket, that means we've got $1,780 in the bank already."

"That's right. Can you believe it?"

"Earning interest all the while," Bill Kanute noted.

Will, who liked to spend money as much as his twin brother liked saving it, had a flash. "Sounds to me like there's enough money to buy that camera and player right now. I'm going to Foxville tomorrow. How about I go ahead and buy what we need?"

"There are still expenses we've got to cover," Bill cautioned.

"Can't be too much," Will returned.

The twins glared at each other with identically stubborn looks.

"What do you think, Rita Lee?" the chief asked. "How many more bills are there going to be?"

"Well, it depends. The Top Cats say we have to provide a sound system. There's one at the Legion Post, so I think that's covered. I'm still working on the lights. Teenie and Dale donated the tickets and posters. We've decided to pay the high school pep club to clean up afterwards. So I'm going to take a wild guess and say, maybe, a hundred dollars more in expenses. We have to pay the Top Cats a thousand dollars. After that, it's all profit."

"Plenty of money for a camcorder," Will said.

"I'd wait if I were you," Bill cautioned again.

"While we're at it, why don't we go ahead and order a couple more air packs?"

"Better hold off on air packs until the show is over," Arvid said. "Once we know exactly how much we have to work with, we'll come up with a list of priorities. Just stick with the player and camcorder for right now."

"Right," Will said.

The fire chief turned to Rita Lee. "Anything else you need help with?"

"Just keep selling tickets."

She thought about bringing up the mysterious decency committee, but it was all so vague. It was probably better not to worry about it. Maybe the committee didn't even exist.

Rita Lee decided to walk to the salon on Friday. It was a warm morning and she needed the exercise. Her rowing machine was collecting dust while she organized Ladies Night Out, and she hadn't been out for a run in three weeks.

After folding and stacking towels, Rita Lee sat down in Wendy's styling chair to take a quick look at last week's Independent. There was a prominent advertisement for the show on page three. She was listed at as the contact person to call for more information. Seeing her name in print always made her want to march right down to the judge and ask for a name change. Rita Lee was the name of a big-haired country singer or some airhead who took orders at the drive-in, not a thirty-four year old woman who owned her own business.

But what name should she change to? She'd always liked Victoria, and Anne wasn't too bad. She could be seventy-five and those names would still sound good.

Rita Lee regarded herself in the mirror. *What kind of person do I look like? Do I look like a Victoria? Do I feel like a Victoria?*

She was still staring pensively at her reflection when Wendy came in a few minutes later.

"Wake up," Wendy said, snapping her fingers. "Looks like you need a lot more coffee this morning...or maybe a transfusion."

"I'm thinking about changing my name."

"To what?"

"Victoria, actually."

"Victoria's an option, I guess. What's wrong with Rita Lee?"

"I'm sick of being a country singer."

"How about you go out and buy some new clothes? That's what most women do when they feel restless and ready for a change. A whole different name seems a bit radical."

Rita Lee was about to reply when she heard a sharp

rap on the front door. Teenie was standing outside, both hands full. She kicked at the door with the toe of one shoe.

"Good news," Teenie said a moment later, setting a cardboard box, coffee mug, and two large manila envelopes down on the counter. "Couldn't wait to come and tell you. As soon as the bank opens I'm going to make a deposit. We've now sold 189 tickets. And I haven't even told you the best part. I got a call last night from my cousin Susan in Foxville. She's sold 30 tickets. They're renting a school bus to come over for the show."

"And Victoria was afraid we wouldn't be able to sell enough tickets," Wendy said.

"Who's Victoria?

"The former Rita Lee, who's changing her name."

"Why? What's wrong with Rita Lee?"

"That's what I asked. Not sure if I can get used to calling her Victoria. Don't you think Stephanie fits her better?"

"Get out of here!" Rita Lee said, pushing Wendy towards the back of the salon. "I didn't say I was actually going to change my name. I'm just thinking about it."

It wasn't till Rita Lee was straightening up at the end of the day that the idea of a name change popped into her mind again. Wendy was right. She was feeling restless and ready for something different. Her safe, comfortable existence just didn't feel so right any more.

9

A week passed before Phil got back over to Foxville to see how the fountain was coming. There was a concrete hippo he hadn't noticed on his last visit, along with several new angels.

"Hello?" he called, dodging between an array of elves and fairies. "Anybody here?"

"This way," a voice shouted. "In the shop."

Phil skirted a pair of three-tier birdbaths and walked into a large metal building. The walls were lined with shelves stacked high with rubber and plastic molds. Concrete objects in various stages of completion took up most of the floor space. Gray-white cement dust covered everything.

"It's Phil Miller. Came to see about my fountain."

Don Johnson's head poked out from down around the hooves of an elk. "Had to do this big guy in two parts. His horns were too large for a single pour. But danged if I just didn't knock off one of his tips. Looks like I'm going to have to pour the whole rack over again."

"Too bad," Phil said, his eyes roaming the immense shop for a mermaid. "Hope you didn't have that kind of problem with my fountain."

"Your fountain is another problem entirely," Don said, wiping dusty hands on his gray coveralls. A faded blue bandana, wrapped biker-style, covered his hair. "Like I said, I've never done a mermaid this tall. The last one was for a birdbath and she was only eight inches. I've been trying to order a mold, but the biggest one I can find is about two feet. According to your measurements, she needs to be about twice that tall. Any chance you could go for a two-foot mermaid?"

"Audrey has her heart set on a fountain just like the one in the town park. So it's got to be four feet."

"Well, I'll tell you what, I'm stumped on this one. I could probably make a mold from the park mermaid, if she was here, but she isn't. I'll think about it some more, but I doubt it will do any good." Don walked toward the open door. "Let me show you the seahorses. They turned out pretty nice."

"Too bad she doesn't like rabbits," Don said over his shoulder. "I know where I can get a beautiful four-foot tall Easter bunny. Comes with a basket and eggs. I could fix it so the water squirts out of the eggs."

Phil left Foxville with a heavy heart. With all that junk sitting around in the yard at Creative Concrete, he hadn't expected any problems with a mermaid. After all, it was just an angel with a fish tail.

As he drove, Phil wracked his brain for another birthday gift idea for Audrey. He used to give his wife a bathrobe every year or two. It was easy--he found one he liked in medium and knew it would fit. But a bathrobe seemed too personal. He briefly considered chocolates, but they didn't seem special enough. Jewelry? Jewelry and chocolates? Nothing else measured up to the mermaid fountain.

By the time Phil got to the Hobart Junction turn-off, he was out of gift ideas, good and bad.

Phil hadn't felt so frustrated since back in the days he was foreman in the auto parts factory. Every so often some component of the manufacturing process would come to a complete halt because of a broken part on the line. It was up to Phil and the mechanics to figure out how to fix it and get the line up and running again. He'd always been known as a can-do kind of guy, one you could count on to come up with a brilliant solution when no one else could figure out what to do.

After his retirement, folks in town often called Phil when something broke down and they didn't know how to fix it. Getting a repairman out from Foxville or Belfort was expensive. Phil Miller was always ready to lend a hand and usually knew a way to get whatever it was working again without spending a lot of money.

But all that ended when Linda got cancer. Taking care of her became a fulltime occupation. He didn't take time for golf, even when she encouraged him to go out with the guys. He and Linda only had so much time left together and he wanted to make the most of every minute.

Phil was a different man after Linda died. His kids encouraged him to see a counselor, and he did go a few times just to make them happy. But the counselor, as helpful as he was, could only offer encouragement.

It took Audrey to bring him out of his lethargy.

When he returned from Creative Concrete and wandered out to the garden, Phil felt guilty. The roses hadn't been getting much attention lately. He pushed back old straw banked up against the tender canes to protect them during the cold winter months, absently extending the mulch to the edge of the bed while his mind circled around the fountain dilemma.

Phil did some of his best thinking in the rose garden. When faced with a particularly vexing problem at the parts plant, he usually came up with a solution while messing around among his roses. At such times, Linda used to say, "Phil's out back in the think tank."

There had to be a way to get that mermaid built. He considered and rejected a dozen ideas before it suddenly came to him.

Phil sprinted into the house and telephoned Don Johnson. "Did you say you could make a mold if you had the park mermaid there at the shop?" he asked in a rush. "What if I bring her to you?"

There were still several details to be worked out, but it could be done. The time element was his biggest concern. You couldn't steal a fountain without somebody sooner or later noticing it was gone. But if he was lucky it might only be away a day or two. The town park was on a quiet side street that didn't get a lot of traffic. And if he got the mermaid back quickly, who would know?

"You leave it all to me," Phil told Don. "Just be sure you're ready to go as soon as I roll into your yard."

He was going to need a crew for this job. Strong guys. And a truck. He flashed on Will's dented pickup. Bill and Will were pretty hefty. Them, and Jerry Beemer--that should be enough.

Will, of course, jumped on the idea. Pirating a fountain sounded like a good time. Bill was skeptical. But the more he thought about the weight of the fountain and what it was going to take to move it, the more intrigued he became. He got out a calculator and tried to remember everything Mr. Holston taught him in high school physics class about the power of pulleys.

It didn't take much to convince Jerry Beemer to join the project. He had a larcenous streak to begin with.

Since Audrey's birthday was coming up fast, Phil got his team on the job immediately. They knew the chief and his deputy were only on duty till six on weeknights. Most everybody in town was in bed by eleven. The night owls would either be down at the Pub & Grub or watching TV with their drapes closed. If his crew started at midnight, the coast should be clear.

Jerry suggested grabbing a backhoe, but Phil balked at stealing heavy equipment--taking the fountain was bad enough. He also worried about noise. If some light sleeper heard a backhoe in town park in the middle of the night, all sorts of alarms would go off.

The men strolled past the fountain right before the sun went down and carefully looked it over, keeping in mind they were about to lift it. Bill went home and got out his calculator. Jerry stopped by the Pub for a little fortification.

None of the men had been in the park at night since they were kids, and nobody remembered how dark it was. They could barely see the fountain from the parking lot. "Everybody got flashlights?" Phil asked.

"Check," Bill whispered. He was carrying a tote bag filled with crowbars and other useful tools.

Headlights off, Will backed his truck across the tender spring grass till it was close to the pool. "Stop right there," Jerry instructed in a low voice.

"You're going to have to talk louder," Will yelled out the truck window. "I can't hear you."

"Shhhh," warned three hushed voices in the dark.

Bill hauled two planks and a dolly from the back of the truck. "According to my calculations the fountain weighs 436 pounds."

"Thank you, Doctor Science," Jerry said. He took out the Coors can he had stashed in his jacket pocket and emptied it in a few gulps. "Let's go for it."

The crew crept up to the edge of the fountain and stopped short. There was two feet of water standing in the pool.

"Where did that come from?" Jerry asked, astonished. "It wasn't there before."

"Public Works must have filled it up after we left."

"No probleeemo," Jerry said. "Got fishing waders in my car. Be right back." He turned and bumped into Will. "Sorry man, didn't see you."

While Jerry went for his waders, the others walked around the pool, shining their flashlights on the fountain. "Anybody know if this thing comes apart?" asked Will.

"Only one way to find out," Phil said, and waded into the pool. Chilly water filled his shoes and soaked his socks. He tried to ignore the numbness overtaking his toes and concentrated on finding a joint between the mermaid and the shell. He gave the mermaid a hefty shove, but nothing budged.

"Think they've got the whole works cemented together," he advised.

"No probleeemo," Jerry said. He'd drained another beer back at the car and was ready for anything. His waders gave a rubbery squeak as he sloshed up to the seahorses and pushed hard. The fountain gave way a little. "Think we got her, boys."

"Whatever we're going to do, let's do it," Phil said. He was losing feeling in his feet.

The four men got behind the fountain and pushed. "Let me get a crowbar," said Bill.

After a lot of shoving and prying, the team had the seahorses loosened from the base. Jerry disconnected the hoses that kept water recycling in the fountain and climbed out of the pool. "Break time. Anybody want a beer?"

He hauled four cans out of the pockets in his waders and passed them around. "Better take it easy," Phil cautioned. "We can drink beer later."

"Righto," Jerry said, and got back into the pool. He had downed most of his beer anyway.

The others put their cans out of the way in the grass and went back to work. It required about ten minutes to manhandle the fountain into the truck. At one point Jerry stumbled, and it took every bit of strength the rest of them had to keep the fountain from hitting the ground. "Take away that guy's beer," Will said hotly. "He's had more than enough."

"Not my fault. It's these waders. The shoulder strap got hooked on one of her stars."

Once the fountain was standing up in the truck, they covered it with a large black tarp, then securely tied the whole works down. Satisfied the mermaid wasn't going to go anywhere, Will rolled the truck off the lawn. "See everybody in Foxville," he called, and sped out of town.

Chief Frank Beemer woke up in the morning with a nasty headache and a queasy stomach. He squinted groggily at the digital clock on his nightstand, then turned away. A chill shuddered through him and Frank gave a low moan.

Brenda stirred on her side of the bed. He groaned again, a little louder this time.

His wife rolled over. "Something the matter?"

"I think I've got the flu."

"What time is it?"

"I don't know, the light from the clock hurts my

eyes."

"Want some aspirin?"

"Yes, please," Frank said weakly.

Brenda climbed out of bed and reached for a bathrobe. She was glad Frank didn't get sick very often because when he did he turned into a total pity. She couldn't understand how a stalwart officer of the law could dissolve into such a baby when the slightest illness struck.

By the time she got back with the pills and a tall glass of water, Frank had his head buried beneath a pillow.

"Do you want me to call Reggie and ask him to cover for you?" Brenda asked as she handed her husband the aspirin.

"He's going to Foxville to the dentist this morning."

"Well, with you in bed and the deputy gone, there's not going to be any police presence in Hobart Junction till this afternoon. Think the town can get by without you two for that long?"

"They're going to have to," Frank groaned and pulled the blankets up to his ears.

"Could you bring me some warm milk," the chief called after his wife as she left to phone town hall.

Frank Beemer slept until noon and woke feeling quite a bit better. "I think I'm over the worst of it," he told his wife as he lowered himself into the recliner in the living room. "Could you make me a grilled cheese sandwich? I'm hungry, so I must be getting well. If I had a grilled cheese, it would help me get my strength back."

"Of course, dear," Brenda said. "Oh yes, Reggie called. There was some kind of emergency and the dentist didn't get to him till late, but as soon as he gets home Reggie is going by the office to check for messages and make a cruise through town."

"Could you fix some of your good homemade chicken soup?" Frank asked as he picked up the television's remote control. "I know it would make me feel better."

By the time his deputy called at about 4:30, Frank Beemer was bored. He wasn't used to being cooped up in the house all day.

"What's up?"

"Not a whole lot," Reggie assured him. "There were a couple of messages complaining about the Top Cats show. I don't know what they think we're supposed to do about it."

"Ummm," Frank murmured, which translated meant "No comment."

"Somebody called about a stolen bicycle; an unknown orange pickup truck was sighted cruising through the Heavenly Acres trailer park. Just your usual police calls. Nothing we can't take care of tomorrow. How are you feeling?"

"Much better, thanks."

"You gonna need for me to cover for you tomorrow tonight?"

"Nope. I'll have to take it easy, but I think I can make it okay. You go home and get some supper."

"Hello, it's me," Rita Lee called, as she opened Walt's front door. Walt was fixing dinner for her this time. "The Chief Pasta Chef," he called himself. If the smell of garlic and fresh-snipped basil coming from the kitchen was any indication of skill, then the Chief Chef was about to serve up something special.

Walt's living room was just as Rita Lee expected. Comfortable, with lots of books, a bicycle leaning against one wall, and framed photographs hanging everywhere. An extreme close-up of a delicate orchid caught her eye and she paused.

"Came upon that little beauty on a hike a few years ago," Walt explained, coming forward with a bottle of red wine in one hand and a corkscrew in the other. "They tell me it's a rare find in this area. And I almost didn't see it. Just about stepped on it and squashed it flat.

"Come on in," Walt continued, "How about a glass of wine? Hope you like red."

Rita Lee followed Walt to the kitchen. A small table was set with a blue tablecloth, candles, and a white vase of colorful spring flowers.

"How nice," Rita Lee said, a little surprised at the elegance he'd managed to achieve.

"Did it just for you. Usually I eat standing up at the counter."

Walt poured wine into two sparkling glasses. He handed one to Rita Lee and lifted his glass. "Cheers." They looked at each other and felt lightening strike. They both went quiet, the toast hanging between them.

They might have stood there forever, gazing into each other's eyes, if the water in the pasta pot hadn't picked that moment to boil over. Rolling bubbles formed and burst, liquid hit the hot burner and gave a loud sputter.

Rita Lee pulled her eyes away and glanced toward the stove. "Better check your water."

While Walt mopped up the mess, Rita Lee examined the gallery on his refrigerator door. Held in place by magnets advertising Clint Small's Ford dealership were several photographs of what appeared to be Walt's family--cute tykes sitting on Santa's lap, and an older couple (his parents?) laughing into the camera, champagne flutes in hand. Tacked beneath was a photo of people she didn't recognize sitting around a campfire. A grocery list, a months-old dry cleaning ticket, a reminder postcard from the dentist, and a game schedule for the men's slow-pitch softball team completed the assemblage. It reminded her of the refrigerator door in Teenie's kitchen, only bachelor style.

"Hope you're hungry," Walt said, pouring steaming pasta into a colander. "Think I over-estimated on the noodles. Either that or they reproduced in the pot while my back was turned."

"Noodles do that," she said with a twinkle.

Walt lit the candles and turned off the overhead light. "Dinner is served," he proclaimed with a flourish, pulling out a chair for Rita Lee.

"The Chief Pasta Chef has outdone himself," Rita Lee announced as she finished up the last of her salad. Not one morsel of angel hair pasta remained in the serving bowl. Only a few crumbs of artisan bread were left on the cutting board.

"My sister would laugh if she heard you say that," Walt said. "She declared me hopeless in the kitchen after I cooked a turkey with the plastic bag of giblets still inside. It was the first Thanksgiving after my divorce, and I invited the whole family for dinner. It seemed like a good way to pay everyone back for all the meals I'd mooched. Wouldn't have been so bad, but the marshmallows on the mashed sweet potatoes flamed out under the broiler and the green beans got scorched. Otherwise everything was fine."

Rita Lee was deeply curious about Walt's ex-wife and what led to their divorce, but since he hadn't so far brought the subject up, she didn't ask. The other thing holding her back was that he then he might want to hear about her and Jason, and she was embarrassed to tell him how foolish she'd been. It still hurt to admit she'd meant so little to Jason that he ditched her without a single word of explanation.

Better to stick to safe topics like cooking disasters.

The couple lingered over coffee, too content to move. Walt wished he'd thought to get a video--anything to keep the evening from ending. He glanced at the clock.

"How about going for a walk?"

"A walk sounds great."

Rita Lee scooped up the last of the dishes and carried them to the sink.

"I'll take care of those later," he told her. Where's your coat?"

Walt and Rita Lee strolled down Lincoln Street and turned left onto Grant. The night sky was clear, shimmering stars surrounded a waxing moon. The air smelled fresh and invigorating. The only sound was the faint barking of a neighborhood dog some blocks away. Walt slipped his hand over hers, and it felt like the most natural thing in the world. They could have been high school kids out on a date or senior citizens still discovering romance fifty years after their wedding day.

The town park came into view, a tidy stretch of green lawn with ancient maple trees and a children's play set. Crossing to a bench, they sat.

"And you never saw so many mosquitoes..." Walt was in the middle of telling Rita Lee about a canoe trip in Minnesota.

"Didn't there use to be a fountain in the park?" Rita Lee interrupted. "A mermaid and seahorses. It's been here as long as I can remember. What happened to it?"

Rita Lee jumped up and ran across the grass to the edge of the pool. "The mermaid fountain is gone!" she exclaimed in disbelief.

Two black hoses lay in a gouge in the pond. Bits of scattered concrete lined the bottom. "Looks like the work of teenagers to me," Walt observed. "Beer cans everywhere. Careful where you walk. You don't want to step on those tire tracks. They might be evidence."

"Right, a crime scene. I wonder if Frank Beemer knows about this. We should call him."

Walt didn't answer. He feared a perfect evening was about to come to a less than perfect end. Nothing like filing a police report to take the romance out of a date. But the story did have possibilities--mysterious mermaid abduction, park vandalism, cut hoses, tire tracks, 500 pound fountain gone missing.

"Tell you what," he proposed. "How about we go down to the Pub and play a game of pool. It's Friday night. Frank's out and about patrolling. He'll stop by the Pub sooner or later. We can tell him then."

"I guess this isn't like a bank robbery or anything." Rita Lee was uncertain.

"It's okay," Walt assured her. "An hour or two is not going to make any difference."

There seemed to be a lot of people in the Pub, even for a Friday night. A faint smell of clam chowder, and the sound of clinking dishes, drifted from the Grub side of the Pub & Grub. A roar erupted from the crowd watching a basketball game on the TV above the bar. Penny, the cocktail waitress, laid a round tray down on the bar and pointed to the Coors tap, signaling the bartender with three fingers. No point in trying to out-shout those guys. She gave Walt and Rita Lee a smile as they made their way toward the pool tables at the back. "Two drafts when you get a chance," Walt called to her above the din.

If there was something Rita Lee felt good about, it was her ability to play pool. There was a pool table in the rec room when she was growing up, and with nothing much in town for a kid to do, she spent thousands of hours practicing.

But tonight she couldn't hit a straight shot. She was still up by two balls, but the way things were going, Walt would close the gap quickly. Rita Lee leaned on her cue, studying her next shot. Nothing tricky here--a gentle tap a little right of center and the ball would drop into the side pocket. She could make a shot like that blindfolded.

Rita Lee groaned as the ball missed the pocket and kept going until it bounced off the far side and eased to a stop. This was beginning to get annoying.

Walt moved around the table frowning in concentration. He bent down to sight the shot, moved back a little, squinted, then slightly changed the angle of his cue.

Rita Lee held her breath, knowing exactly what he had in mind. What was this guy, some kind of hustler? She briefly glanced at his muscular butt as he leaned over the table, tempted to give him a little pat. But honor held her back. She planned to beat him fair and square.

She watched in disbelief as the eleven ball shot straight to the seven, knocked it into the hole, traveled on to catch the edge of the three and send it into the side pocket before slipping into the hole in the right corner.

"Damn fine shot," said one of the by-standers, congratulating Walt with a high-five.

"Where did you learn to do that?" Rita Lee asked in disbelief.

Right here, in this fair establishment," Walt said, reaching into his pocket for money to pay for the beers.

"Did you see that?" Rita Lee asked Penny.

"Sweetie, don't let this guy talk you into putting money on the game," the waitress advised, handing Rita Lee a beer and a small napkin. "He's a shark."

"Now you tell me."

They were even, with just two balls and the eight

left on the table. Worst of all, the shots Walt had left were relatively easy. Rita Lee gulped down her beer. Right before he bent over his cue, Walt lit up a wicked smile. The temperature in the room shot up several degrees.

It was all over in a matter of minutes. Rita Lee wiped a streak of yellow chalk off her finger.

"Mercy," she laughed, placing her cue back on the rack. "I've been brought to my knees by the Pasta Chief." She was certainly glad she hadn't bragged about her talent as a pool player. She'd be feeling mighty silly about now.

"Good game," Walt said, giving her a quick hug. "How about another beer?"

By the time they made it to the bar, the TV was off and music was booming. Dancers crowded the small wooden floor. Rita Lee was in the middle of trying to decide whether to order another beer or switch to a margarita, when Frank Beemer came through the door. He surveyed the room with a practiced eye.

Rita Lee spotted him and dodged across the dance floor. "Frank, what happened to the fountain?"

The police chief's blank look told her he had no idea what she was talking about, so Rita Lee reported their discovery in the park.

"Sounds like the high school kids have been at it again," Frank sighed. "Every spring the senior class finds some way to get into trouble. I thought I'd seen it all, but this is a new one." He paused. "Too dark to do much tonight. I'll get over there first thing in the morning." He nodded at Walt "Probably about nine, if you want to snap a few pictures for the paper."

By Saturday noon the missing fountain was talk of the town. The high school kids asked each other who stole the fountain and a half dozen names were tossed around, but each likely candidate denied knowing anything about the mischief. The mystery deepened Monday morning when the principal questioned every member of the student body, and all but two of them had plausible alibis. One who didn't was Li Ling, the Chinese exchange student. She was still struggling with English and may not have understood what Mr. White asked; the other was Bobby Epson, but he had a broken arm.

Walt prepared a story on Monday for the next edition outlining the known facts. Unfortunately, an important clue, the tire tracks, had been obliterated. Even though Chief Beemer stretched yellow crime scene tape well back from the spot, kids couldn't resist sneaking under the tape to get up close to where the mermaid used to be. Now instead of truck treads there were tennis shoe prints.

Phil Miller hesitated before going to Gretta's for breakfast on Monday morning because he feared his name was going to come up. He was relieved to hear the police chief say over the pigs-in-a-blanket special that all evidence pointed to youthful pranksters from a rival high school. As soon as he got home, Phil put in an anxious call to Creative Concrete for an update. All Don Johnson would say was, "I'm working on it."

10

While the breakfast bunch was placing bets on who would turn out to be the perpetrator of the fountain heist, Rita Lee was sorting through her lists. The final advertising blitz was well underway, and the Belfort Players had loaned a lighting system. At first it seemed music was going to be a problem. The sound at the American Legion Post was adequate for veteran's events, but when she and Teenie brought a CD player and sent rock music through the system, the result was awfully tinny.

Just in time, Teenie remembered a dusty set of speakers her brother left behind when he went off to State. They were still sitting in the back of the garage, and Teenie got her dad to help her carry them over to the Legion hall.

Accommodations for the Top Cats were reserved at Sunny Palms Motel, the nicest place in town. The owners of Sunny Palms, Del and Midge Ainsworth, were excited to be hosting real show business people, and planned to get autographs from them all. Several Legionnaires had volunteered to tend bar. She needed to call them to confirm. She also had to find somebody to stand at the door--not that she thought anybody would try to sneak in illegally--but it was a liquor control board rule. Perhaps Frank Beemer or his deputy could be talked into to doing it for a free as a favor to the fire department.

Rita Lee scrutinized her lists for items she could cross off before she went to school to read with the kids. Glasses and cups...check. Dressing room for the dancers...check.

All her early talk about how easy it was going to be to sell tickets and watch the money roll in seemed daffy now that the show was a week and a half away. Still, it was a whole lot more fun than the Valentine's Dance.

Rita Lee was searching her closet for something to wear when the phone rang. "Let's make the Legion hall into a night club. Put candles on the tables; use wall hangings; suspend balloons from the ceiling."

"Teen, forget it! I was just thinking about how nice it is not to have to decorate."

"This won't be much work. I've got loads of fabric, all we have to do it staple it up."

Rita Lee was adamant--no decorating! It took her friend almost five minutes of excited persuasion to bring her around. Teenie used words like "piece of cake" and "absolutely nothing to it" to describe her vision of the Legion Post glittering with little white Christmas lights, flickering votive candles and shining silver table runners. "Just like Las Vegas."

Rita Lee had a hunch a monster was about to hatch, but Teenie promised to take care of everything.

One more notation went on the bottom of the master list: "Decorations???!!!"

Wednesday was breathing day at the Independent. The new issue wouldn't be in the stands until about two. Phone calls were minimal, few people stopped in, and Walt had most of the day free to re-organize and re-group. Creating the newspaper was something like putting together a puzzle. In good weeks, advertisements took up a little over half the available space. Above and around the ads, news and photos were fitted into place. Certain pieces, like the letters to the editor, always went in the same spot. Other pieces changed position from week to week. The Independent was an ever-changing jigsaw.

Walt made a list of possible stories for the next issue. Beside each he made notations regarding page location and photo possibilities. At the top of Walt's list was a follow-up on the missing park fountain. Everyone was waiting for it to show up in Belfort. But so far that hadn't happened. Maybe it wasn't the work of pranksters. Maybe the fountain lay in ruins somewhere, broken to bits in an act of pure maliciousness.

He was also perplexed about the mysterious decency committee. Sylvia Crocker had stopped coming in, which was very odd. A few days ago he saw her talking to Pansy Hatfield, and Pansy was actually chuckling. Walt couldn't ever remember seeing Pansy smile, let alone chuckle. Something must be up.

Hobart Junction contained a number of well-kept secrets, but they generally centered around family: drinking problems, clandestine affairs, unruly children. Embarrassing, sad, violent truths were tucked away in cupboards all over town. A sense of "there but for the grace of God" kept such matters hidden behind a veil of silence. All other secrets got out sooner or later. Usually sooner.

That's why Walt was so surprised there was no word on the street about the decency committee or the fountain. Eventually, somebody always tripped up and let a little something slip--either by accident or design. There's nothing more gratifying than being in the know, and even better, to be in the know and have others know it. He understood how the fountain theft could be kept under wraps, since that might only involve one or two people--though they'd have to be fairly strong, considering the weight involved. But a whole committee was harder to keep mum. He knew there was a sizable contingent opposed to the male strip show so the committee might be quite large. Yet, except for the few words overheard at the lake, there was nothing to indicate the group existed. Why then did his newsman's instinct tell him a pot was boiling somewhere?

Walt pulled out the bottom desk drawer and propped up his feet, leaned back and let his mind drift. Was there a connection between the fountain and the committee? The mermaid was nude from the waist up, though her long tresses covered everything controversial. Did the committee steal the fountain to make a point about morality? If so, what was the point?

He couldn't think of one.

After a few moments of futile contemplation, Walt gave up. Let Frank Beemer do the detective work, he'd stick to reporting it. Walt slid a wire basket of press releases to the middle of his desk and started going through them, looking for anything newsworthy. He chuckled when he came to the latest press blurb about Ladies Night Out. It was obviously the work of Twila Switzer--only the owner of a bookstore would write a literary masterwork to hype six guys doing a striptease.

She could get the Pulitzer for this, he thought.

A related story on his list concerned the fire department's purchase of a camcorder and DVD player. Will Kanute had been around to proudly show off the equipment's many features and invite Walt to observe a planned burn that evening. The burn wasn't going to be much, just an old shed out by the gravel pit, but it would give the troops something to practice on and let people experiment with the new camcorder.

Fire photographs were always eye-catching. He'd try for one of Rita Lee, flames in the background, making use of the new equipment. It would be an unusual graphic to illustrate the upcoming pre-event story about Ladies Night Out.

Once the press releases were out of the way, Walt turned to the stack of newspapers on his desk. He skimmed the Belfort Bell News and the Foxville Courier for possible leads, then turned to the Farmland Herald, the county paper of record. Legal notices were a gold mine of information. The vital statistics, courthouse and county jail reports often contained nuggets pertaining to local people. Several other story possibilities were added to his list.

When he was done, black newspaper ink covered his fingers. As he soaped up his hands under warm water, he glanced in the mirror. He had to admit his hair was getting shaggy, even for him. Walt knew what a haircut from Boyd-The-Barber-No-Waiting was like. Maybe it was time to give the gals down at the Beauty Mark a try.

Turned out Rita Lee had an opening at two. Walt was a little uneasy as he walked down Main. He had an uncomfortable feeling he was just about to enter some kind of exotic female den, even though Rita Lee had assured him men came in all the time. He'd had haircuts in hair salons before, so he had no idea why this particular visit was making him so edgy.

A pleasant aroma met Walt as he pushed open the door to the Beauty Mark. Instead of the feminine frills and flounces he expected, Walt was surprised to find black styling chairs with chrome bases, two black shampoo sinks, and two whirring white ceiling fans. A heavy table made of some kind of dark wood held a variety of brightly colored hair care products. Make-up was set out on a tall white metal rack. A large black and white framed photo of James Dean decorated one wall.

"Right this way, Walt," Rita Lee said, pointing to a shampoo sink. She wrapped a thick burgundy towel around his neck and snapped on a hair clip to hold it in place. "How you been?" she asked as she gently slipped his neck into the niche in the front edge of the sink.

Deftly Rita Lee dampened his hair and worked in shampoo while they talked. He felt her strong fingers massaging his scalp and his eyes slowly closed. Already he was liking this better than going to Boyd-The-Barber. Boyd never shampooed before he started a haircut. Walt felt, rather than saw, Rita Lee reach for another bottle. He thought he smelled strawberries and coconut. He sighed with pleasure.

"Okay, Walt, time to sit up," Rita Lee told him softly when she was done.

"Right," he said, blinking back into focus. Rita Lee wrapped a fluffy towel around his damp hair and they walked over to the styling chair.

"So, tell me, any thoughts on your haircut?"

"You're the expert. Have your way with me."

I wish! Rita Lee picked up the scissors and began.

Though Walt didn't want to mention it, one reason he stopped going to hair stylists was because they had so much trouble with his curly hair. Usually he left looking like a hood ornament or the star of a television game show. But Rita Lee seemed to know what she was doing. Walt's eyes slowly closed again while she pushed her fingers through his hair. He felt himself relax, like a big lazy tom cat lying in the sun, getting stroked by its favorite human.

Walt came to with a start when Will Kanute banged in from Main Street. "Rita Lee, we've got a problem," he said, then stopped abruptly when he recognized Walt under the black cape. "Oops, sorry, didn't realize you were busy. I'll come back later."

Will prepared to turn and run. Walt immediately recognized that look of panic. A crooked politician set upon by relentless reporters had that look, so did a deer caught in the headlights of a truck.

But after an instant of confusion, Will seemed to regain composure and continued. "Bad news. Arvid had it all set up with those friends of his over in Belfort to use their theater lighting system. But today they changed their minds. Said they found out they are going to need it for some kind of rehearsal or something. Arvid thinks somebody from here in Hobart Junction got to them."

That damn committee! Rita Lee's hand jerked, and her scissors took a crooked swatch of hair out of the center back.

"Now what do we do?"

"Well, I suppose my brother Bill and I can come up with something. I think the high school has spotlights. There are those lights at the Presbyterian church they put on their living nativity scene at Christmas." He paused. "But I doubt they'll be willing to loan them to us. Some of the church people are pretty upset about this Top Cats thing."

Will paced back and forth in front of the make-up display, forgetting Walt was a reporter for the moment, and about his own role in boosting the fountain. "We're going to need to rig some sort of board so we can dim the lights and turn the spots off and on. It wouldn't hurt to wire the sound into the board too, so one person can manage the whole thing. How soon does this have to be ready to go?"

When Rita Lee told him six days, Will groaned. He grabbed a scrap of paper out of the trash basket and began to draw. "I need to track down Bill and go take a look at the stage. Wonder if Norm White over at the high school will let us rent their lights. It might take a donation to the athletic fund. Is that okay?" He continued scribbling furiously. "Let me ask Bill what he thinks about this." He scooped up the drawings and stuffed them in the pocket of his battered denim jacket.

"Don't worry, Rita Lee, we've got it covered." He was gone, leaving behind little piles of dried mud shed from the bottom of his boots.

A few minutes later Bill and Will drove by in Bill's new Camry. Walt wondered if Bill made Will take off his boots before he got in the car.

"Never a dull moment around here," Rita Lee said as she got back to Walt's hair. "There's going to be no charge for this cut." She swallowed hard, her face turning red. "My scissors slipped a bit ago, right after Will started telling me about the lighting system. I'm afraid you've got a bit of a nick out of the back."

"It'll grow back. At least it always has."

"I'm so embarrassed. I've never done anything like this before. Even in beauty school." Distressed, Rita Lee made short snips trying to correct her slip-up--a hopeless task she knew, but the only thing she could think of.

"Why not just shorten up everything else to match?"

"That would take a crewcut," she wailed.

"Go for it."

"Are you sure? Oh Walt, this is awful." The one time she wanted to do an especially good cut, and look what happened!

Rita Lee was brushing the last of the stray hair from Walt's neck when Wendy breezed in. She stopped up short. "My, oh my. New look for Walt!"

"Do you think I should have her add some blond streaks?" he asked.

For the rest of the afternoon Rita Lee found it hard to stay involved with her customers. Her mind kept wandering off to the crewcut. Walt had been so nice about it, didn't seem to mind at all that she'd totally screwed up. She didn't have many irate customers, but when things went wrong, they definitely let her know. But Walt was more than a customer, he was a friend. A good looking, sexy, funny friend.

It had been so many years since there was a man in Rita Lee's life she had almost forgotten what it was like. She was twenty-two when she married Jason and twenty-five when he left. At first she was angry; then for months she couldn't stop crying. When there wasn't another tear left, she tried dating again. That was a joke. All the guys who asked her out had three things on their minds--TV sports, beer and sex. The good men in town were taken, the rest were drunks.

It didn't help that her snake of a husband left her with a huge mistrust of every guy she ever went out with.

Finally Rita Lee accepted the fact she might remain single for the rest of her life. That was okay. If the right person came along, fine. But she wasn't going to push it. When the opportunity came up to buy the Beauty Mark, she took it. As a business owner she had the town's respect, and the curse of bad love didn't seem so oppressive.

Now there was Walt...or should she say there *was* Walt? What a mess she'd made of things.

"And then she said she was his aunt!" exclaimed Audrey Willis, who was in getting her weekly shampoo and set. Since pressure was off the community center board, Audrey felt safe to be out and about again.

"I'm sorry," Rita Lee said. "My mind wandered for a minute. Who's an aunt?"

"Edna Olson, and they say she's also Joe Spilling's step-cousin and Irene Slump's ex- grandmother-in-law."

"That's new to me, but I don't doubt it."

The relationships in Hobart Junction were complex. Years ago she gave up trying to keep track of who was related. Sometimes the only time it became clear was when Walt published an obituary.

Walt again.

She'd learned way back in junior high school to be careful about saying things about people. You never knew when that person might be a relation who was going to take offense. She remembered one girl in her senior year who married a man old enough to be her father and, through a complicated series of past marriages and divorces within the two families, was her own aunt. When her husband died, it took five long paragraphs to list all the ways he was related to folks in town.

After checking to be sure Wendy and her customer weren't listening in, Audrey said softly, "Do you have any tickets left for the Top Cats show?"

Rita Lee nodded. "You can get one when you pay for your hair."

At the front counter Audrey pulled out her checkbook. "I didn't vote for the show because of my dear husband's awful cousins. But I've decided to go. Hazel talked me into it. I'm not going to tell Phil, though. He doesn't think this kind of entertainment is suitable.

Women are supposed to be above such things, he says. Men can be so old-fashioned sometimes."

Rita Lee smiled and handed Audrey a pink ticket. "The volunteer fire department thanks you for your support."

Rita Lee glanced at the clock. Nearly 5. One kid cut left. Still to come was the fire meeting and the practice burn at the gravel pit. Rita Lee was ready for the day to be over. She wondered how many people were already talking about Walt's new haircut. Nothing like cutting a hunk out of somebody's hair to shrink customer confidence.

Two minutes later Joey Spilling arrived on a skateboard. Right behind was Lila Potter, carrying a long narrow florist box. "For you Rita Lee," she said, handing over the carton. "He ordered all I had. Must be a special day."

Rita Lee opened the box. Snuggled inside, in pale pink tissue, were nine red roses. A small white card tucked among the stems said simply, "Best haircut ever. Thanks."

"I haven't seen such a dreamy expression since Jack Baxter asked you to the prom," Wendy told her.

"That was the last time anybody sent me roses," Rita Lee replied, her nose buried in the fragrant blooms.

At home, Rita Lee searched through her cupboards for a vase suitable for the roses. Somewhere was a cut crystal vase that once belonged to her Aunt Winnie. She finally found it on the back of a top shelf, almost hidden from sight by a copper fondue pot and a covered cake plate. Gently she lifted the dusty vase down and swished hot water and detergent through it. When every facet sparkled, Rita gently took the roses from their box and arranged them in the crystal. Carrying the vase, she wandered through her house, setting them first on her bedroom dresser, then on the coffee table in the living room. Wherever she went the scent of roses surrounded her. Finally, Rita Lee returned to the kitchen. She spread a white embroidered tablecloth on the table and placed the flowers in the center.

Perfect.

She was there, gazing with private delight at her roses, when the fire signal went off. Its shrill wail reminded her of her responsibilities. The members were expecting an update on ticket sales. That thought brought her up short. She'd been so caught up in Walt's surprising gift, she'd forgotten all about the show.

The crowd at the fire hall was in full regalia when Rita Lee drove up. She heard the truck's engine turn over twice, cough, and fall silent. "She's getting close to startin'," Will called out the driver's seat window, "climb on everybody."

Three women clambered into the cab with Will. Several adventurous men boosted themselves up onto the rear of the truck. The rest piled into nearby cars and prepared to follow the fire engine and water tank truck out to the gravel pit.

Teenie opened the passenger-side door of Rita Lee's Subaru and hopped in. She was wearing the department's tall silver heat-resistant boots, and carrying leather gloves and a shovel. "How about a ride? Heard Walt sent you flowers."

"Did your nosey parker source tell you why?"

"He's in love?"

"Hardly. I accidentally cut a major hunk out of his hair. It's so bad, I had to give him a crewcut."

"So he sent you flowers. Must be a great crewcut. Pardon me for asking, but why did you butcher his hair?"

Rita Lee brought Teenie up to date on the latest

twist in the Ladies project and her suspicions that the decency committee was somehow involved "Will's working on putting together another lighting system for us, but what a hassle."

"Maybe they really did have a rehearsal or something. I hate to say it, but I think you're being paranoid about this so-called committee. So far you seem to be the only person who's heard anything about it."

"Walt heard, too," Rita Lee protested.

"And what does he say?"

They pulled up behind the other cars, parked well back from an old wooden building at the edge of the gravel pit. Rita Lee turned to her friend. "He's been checking all over town. Not a word from anybody."

"My point exactly."

Their discussion was cut short by a tap on the side window. It was Bill Kanute. He had the new camcorder in his hand. "Arvid wants everybody to gather around the engine so he can give instructions about the burn."

"Showtime," Teenie quipped, reaching into the back seat for her shovel. "Do I look okay? This is my chance for video stardom."

Rita Lee couldn't help but laugh. Teenie was dressed in her unofficial firefighting uniform: baggy hooded sweatshirt, brown twill pants that used to fit pretty well before she gained that last five pounds, and the silver boots. A shovel with her name printed in bold black letters on the handle and worn leather gloves completed the look.

"Awesome," Rita Lee told her friend, pushing the decency committee to the back of her mind one more time. "Let's go fight fire."

It was all business around the fire engine. Arvid described the plan for the burn and assigned duties. He explained that people would exchange jobs during the fire, so everyone could get experience at different positions. He stressed safety and following the chain of command. Bill Kanute was going to operate the video camera, since he was on the purchasing committee and knew how to run it.

Then Arvid explained the practice scenario--a story he'd concocted to make the situation more lifelike. "We all know the only thing this shack gets used for is kids smoking cigarettes, which is why we're burning it down--before they do. But for this exercise it's an abandoned building that's been taken over by a drug dealer." The fire chief warned everyone he'd planned a few surprises along the way, so pay attention.

Rita Lee was only half paying attention. The other half was thinking about Walt.

A few moments later, flames erupted in one corner of the decaying structure. The volunteers rolled out heavy canvas hoses and attached them to couplings on the fire engine. At a command they positioned themselves, twisted open the weighty brass nozzles and began directing water on the fire. The pressure behind the spray surprised one rookie, who stumbled, sending a shower high in the air.

Bill Kanute caught the incident on video.

Acrid smoke filled Walt's nose when he neared the training site. He'd planned on being there from the start, but just as he was walking out the door a subscriber called to complain about an incorrect bowling score in last week's paper. That led to criticism of coverage of the ladies league in general. By the time Walt finished with the call and had his camera packed, a tall gray plume of smoke was rising from the gravel pit.

Even from this distance Walt could feel heat from the fire. As he walked up there was a loud explosion and he heard someone say, "But this guy is a drug dealer.

What if it's a meth lab? I saw on TV that those things are really hazardous."

"It might be ammunition going off. That's what it sounded like to me," another argued, wiping the sweat from his face.

By their intense expressions Walt could tell no one was treating this affair as make-believe. He suspected the explosion was harmless pyrotechnics planted in advance by the fire chief, but he couldn't be sure.

Without warning, Arvid clutched his chest, gasping for air. The firefighters nearby looked on in horror as he crumpled to the ground.

Cries of alarm rose from the bystanders. Teenie fell to her knees and began yanking apart the snaps on his jacket.

"Get the guy some oxygen," someone barked.

Bill Kanute came in with the camera for a close-up.

"Oh my goodness, somebody call Ruth."

The fire forgotten, the volunteers clustered around their chief, trying to determine exactly what was wrong.

"I'm either having a heart attack or else I'm overcome with smoke," Arvid explained in his normal voice. Then he started panting dramatically again.

There was a roar behind them as a flaming wall collapsed.

"Chief, request permission to take over command," said the deputy chief. Everyone turned to stare at him. "Look, if we don't take care of this fire soon, we're going to have a real problem on our hands. It's already getting into that tall grass."

"Okay everyone, let's get back to work." The deputy ordered, assuming his role as incident commander. "Teenie, take that shovel of yours and start putting dirt on the grass fire. Tell Jerry to grab a shovel from the truck and help. The rest of you come with me."

Once water was again trained on the fire, Arvid got up from the ground. "Going well so far," he said smugly to Walt. "Had a few of them fooled there for a minute."

"That you did," Walt agreed. "Well, I came here to take pictures, so I better get to work too." He brought his camera up to his eye and peered through the viewfinder, then moved off, stopping occasionally to snap photos from one angle or another. When he noticed Rita Lee behind the nozzle of a hose, he took several dozen shots of her, using the zoom for close-ups. Drops of water rested on her cheeks, just above a sooty streak near her nose. Wisps of damp hair poked out from under a bright yellow fire hat.

Standing out of the way, Walt watched Rita Lee for a long while. It was a pleasure to behold such a fine looking woman.

A half hour later the fire was out. Soggy ashes and small bits of charred wood steamed in the fading light. When faint wisps of smoke rose from the scorched pile of rubble, the hot spots were immediately doused by the one hose still in use.

A large sweaty group stood around a bright plastic cooler of fresh drinking water. A few were off to the side smoking cigarettes

Rita Lee was there, paper cup in hand, talking to Bill, Will and Jerry about the lighting system. She told them how worried she was it wasn't going to be ready in time for the show. "We've only got a week," she reminded them.

"We've got it covered," Bill assured her.

"Teenie and I can meet you at the Legion Post on Sunday to help," Rita Lee offered.

They were arranging a time when Jerry blurted, "Are you sure we're going to be available?" Bill gave him a murderous glare.

"I thought we were waiting to hear from Phil about when we have to go to Foxville and pick up..."

Will suddenly hit him hard on the back.

Jerry spun around, fire in his eyes. "Hey, what d' ya think you're doing."

"Sorry, I thought I saw a spark hit your back."

"The fire's out, dude."

"I said I'm sorry. It's my mistake."

"Damn right."

Having established that he wasn't to be messed with, Jerry rambled away to join the smokers. "Anybody got any beer?" he asked.

As she watched, it seemed some kind of twin telepathy passed between Bill and Will which Rita Lee couldn't fathom. They'd always been like that--strangely in tune with each other. Bill raised an eyebrow, Will blinked. They both shook their heads in disbelief. That idiot Jerry Beemer had nearly given away the fountain secret.

11

Thursdays were quiet at Willow Springs Golf Club. Hardly a ball splashed into the pond near the eighth green. Quail, pheasants and ducks had the place to themselves. Only a few other golfers dotted the lush rolling landscape when Phil and Audrey, riding in one golf cart, and Del and Midge Ainsworth in another, finished the first nine holes. Since there was no rush at the turn, Audrey and Midge strolled into the clubhouse to see what they could round up in the way of snacks.

So far Audrey was just keeping score and dropping a ball to putt from the edge when the foursome reached a green, but Phil was quite proud of the progress she was making after just a couple of lessons. "You're a natural," he told her. Audrey wasn't so sure about that, but she was enjoying herself.

When the women returned, they were carrying drinks, chips, fruit and candy. "No granola bars?" Del said with mock disappointment. "Darn. I just love the taste of cardboard with a sweet sawdust filling."

As he strained to twist the cap off a juice bottle, Del turned to the others, "Anybody know why those FBI guys were in town yesterday? Saw them going into Frank Beemer's office. Two men and a woman."

"What makes you think they were FBI?" Midge asked.

"They were wearing black suits, even the lady. They had shiny black shoes and carried briefcases."

"Maybe they were Jehovah Witnesses."

"Going into the police chief's office? I don't think so. My theory is Frank's contacted the FBI for assistance on the stolen fountain case."

Audrey's eyes widened. "I didn't know the FBI got involved in little things like a missing fountain. I thought they tracked down bank robbers and terrorists."

"If the fountain's carried across state lines, they get involved," Del said with authority. "Yes sir, Frank's called in the big guys on this one."

Phil remained silent. It was ridiculous to think the FBI would come to Hobart Junction because the town fountain disappeared. Most likely the people Del saw were religious proselytizers checking with city hall to see if they needed a permit to go door-to-door. But it did point out the necessity of getting the fountain back in place as soon as possible.

With all the talk of the FBI, Phil found it difficult to keep his mind on golf when the foursome headed down the back nine. A double bogey on the sixteenth hole didn't help. He ended the day with the worst score he'd had in several years.

As soon as he got home, Phil telephoned Don at Creative Concrete. He told Don he had to get the park fountain home immediately. He was almost afraid to ask how Audrey's copy was coming, but finally broached the subject.

"She's just about cured," said Don proudly.

"Nobody's called you, have they?" Phil asked with concern. "You remember you promised not to tell a soul about this. It's a birthday surprise," he added a bit lamely.

"My lips are sealed," Don told him. "I won't even tell the FBI."

"What?" Phil gasped. The nightmare was real.

"I heard the FBI is snooping around looking for the fountain. Had a couple of ladies in here from Hobart Junction looking for a garden bench, and they were talking about it. I quick threw tarps over both mermaids. The ladies didn't see a thing. Look, I'm not going to get in trouble, am I?"

"Not if we both stick to the story we agreed to. I brought you photos and you used them to make the fountain. Right?"

"That's right. You brought me photos."

After talking a bit longer, Phil hung up. He immediately phoned Bill Kanute. An answering machine told him to leave his name and number and he'd get a call back. Another machine answered at Will's. There was no answer at Jerry's, just a long series of empty rings.

"Thank you Lord for this blessing," Berlene Goss silently prayed as she pulled into a parking space next to the entrance of the Foxville Fashion Mall. Usually the only place to park was clear in the back--and by the time she got through shopping she'd forgotten where her car was and had to hike around the lot trying to find it.

Berlene was a careful shopper--as a minister's wife she had to be. Gilford's salary was adequate, but there was little extra money left after the bills were paid. Not that she wished for anything extravagant, being quite satisfied with the blessings she received each and every day. Besides it would only start talk if she appeared to have more or nicer things than her parishioners.

It did no harm to window shop, though, and Berlene walked slowly through the mall, browsing in her favorite stores. Each time she came to the mall, she marveled at the amazing amount of merchandise. What did people do with all that stuff? It was fun to look at, but she couldn't imagine actually owning it.

There was a particular odor in the Fashion Mall that Berlene noticed every time she came. It was as if each shop's scent merged in the central hall. There was a sweet component emanating from department stores and another from shops selling chocolates and coffee. There was an odd odor which, for lack of a better description, Berlene thought of as the smell of cheap clothing. It was strongest outside shops that sold inexpensive garments made in third-world countries. She didn't know if the smell came from chemicals in the sizing or if apparel was sprayed with some kind of insecticide to keep it safe during the long transport to America.

When Berlene came to the Catherine's Cards and Candles, (which contributed its own unique scent to the mall) she went in to pick up a selection of get-well and birthday cards to send to church members. Standing before long racks of greeting cards, she wondered at the selection. There seemed to be cards for every occasion: sympathy cards for grieving pet owners, anniversary greetings to ex-spouses, congratulatory messages for neighbors with new cars.

Even the birthday section was daunting, sorted as it was by card manufacturer and then by type of birthday: grandparents-humorous, husband-loving, in-laws out of town. At the section marked "husband," she paused, thinking of Gilford. She picked up a card, read the front, and opened it. The message inside was not at all what she expected. Quickly she dropped the card back into the rack, looking over her shoulder to see if anyone had seen her reading it. Birthday cards were certainly getting explicit these days!

As she walked up to the cash register, Berlene caught her reflection in a mirror behind a display of crystal pendants. She gave her head a little shake and her hair moved with a graceful bounce. She was so glad she'd let Charity talk her into going to Rita Lee's. Getting rid of the long hair and the bun was one of the most liberating things she'd done in her life. She felt a new sense of independence--younger and more self reliant. She found she was actually quite good at doing her own hair, just as Charity had predicted. All those years of making bazaar items was finally paying off. She grinned at herself in the mirror.

Berlene's next stop was Cosgroves Department Store. But before she got to Cosgroves, she passed the food court and felt a hungry twinge. She stood for a moment surveying her choices and after considering a slice of pepperoni pizza, the Japanese chicken combo plate, and several other enticing options, settled on a warm cinnamon bun and coffee. The rolls were just out of the oven, and soft vanilla frosting still slowly dribbled down their fragrant sides.

Roll and coffee in hand, Berlene found a small table close to the edge of the food court. A newspaper sat on the otherwise empty chair across the way. Berlene picked it up and, between bites of sweet roll, thumbed through the paper looking for sales. Next to an ad for bedding plants, an announcement for the Top Cats show caught her attention.

Berlene wasn't quite sure how to feel about the

fundraiser. Her husband opposed it, and she usually went along with whatever her husband said. Not that she didn't occasionally have opinions of her own, but it didn't seem right to disagree with him in public. It might give the congregation the wrong impression. In the privacy of their own home, she sometimes spoke up, but since they were of the same mind on most issues, disagreements were rare. However, the Top Cats had set her to wondering exactly how dutiful a wife she had to be. It was all theoretical, of course, but what if her husband forbade her to go to the show? Didn't she have the right to do as she liked, as long as it didn't hurt anyone? He might claim it would damage his reputation as pastor, but his reputation should be based on who he was, not what she did.

Gilford said the show was immoral, but it didn't seem so sinful when compared to something like child abuse. What was really so bad about women watching men do a strip tease? She'd heard it said that men went to topless bars and then went out and committed sex crimes. But she'd never heard of a woman doing such a thing. It just didn't seem like something a woman would do.

Berlene thoughtfully licked white frosting off sticky fingers.

"Hello there," said a cheery voice, as an orange plastic tray with a Japanese combo plate slid onto the table. "Mind if I join you?"

Berlene looked up to see Hazel Bell pulling over an extra chair and piling up a large assortment of plastic bags. "Don't get over here too often, so I try to get a lot of shopping done when I do," Hazel explained. "Found a great sale on bath towels at Cosgroves."

"Been meaning to tell you," Hazel said between bites of teriyaki, "I like the way your hair turned out.

Rita Lee did a good job, makes you look years younger." She tore open a little package of soy sauce and poured it over the rice. "You and Charity going to see the Top Cats?"

"I'm not sure," Berlene confessed. "I know Gilford won't like it if we do."

"Dear, I learned years ago that you can't let your husband rule your life. Don't get me wrong, I'm from a generation that believes a woman should make sure her man gets fed proper meals and has ironed shirts to wear. But that doesn't mean he gets to dictate everything I do."

Three boisterous teenagers strolled by in tattered jeans and hooded sweatshirts. "Hello, Mrs. Bell," they called politely as they passed. Hazel smiled fondly and waved. "Nice kids, even though you'd never know it by those it by those goofy clothes they've got on."

Berlene sipped her coffee for a moment, then hesitantly brought up something else assailing her conscience. "I teach Sunday school. What kind of an example am I setting if I go to something like this?"

"I'm a Sunday school teacher too, don't forget. I got more than one of these gray hairs trying to keep unruly kids under control in the church basement. Those Kanute twins were the worst. Never could tell them apart, and one of the BillWills was always in trouble. Now that I see them grown up, my guess is it was mostly Will causing the mischief. But back then they stuck together on everything--let people get them confused. Since nobody wanted to punish the wrong one, the little dickens got away with murder.

"But back to your worry about being a Sunday school teacher." Hazel continued. "The best example you can set is by living the Golden Rule. It's that simple. There's always going to be somebody quick to criticize no matter what you do."

"It all seems so plain when you put it that way," Berlene said. She smiled a little.

"Well you won't be alone if you decide to come," Hazel said. "I'm going to be there with the mayor's wife. Audrey's coming, too. You're welcome to join us. We're all sitting together."

"That would work out," Berlene said, gaining enthusiasm. "Then Charity can sit with her friends and I won't embarrass her."

"Well, you won't embarrass us, that's for sure," Hazel said with a laugh. "But we may embarrass you."

Berlene couldn't imagine the women Hazel mentioned doing anything inappropriate. After all, Hazel was Citizen of the Year and Judy Small, the mayor's wife, must be dignified. Berlene felt sure her reputation was safe if she sat with them.

When the pair finished eating, they made plans to meet outside the Legion hall a half hour before the show, then picked up their packages and walked out of the food court.

As she continued on her way, Berlene considered whether she should tell Gilford that she was going to the Top Cats show. But remembering Hazel's words about not letting your husband dictate your life, she decided against it. This would be a little secret between her and Charity. If they were lucky Gilford wouldn't even find out.

There was an aura of concentration at the news office on Friday morning. Tommy sat in front of a computer trying to decode the notes he'd taken at the previous night's town council meeting. Walt was in the middle of a story about proposed upgrades to the medical clinic. The sound of footsteps crossing the wooden floor probably registered at some level, but neither looked up until Sylvia Crocker loudly cleared her throat.

"Was wondering how long it was going to take you to notice us," Sylvia said, irritated. Standing beside her was Irene Slump.

"I haven't seen you for a while," Walt said, motioning for them to sit in nearby chairs. "Wondered if you've been sick or something."

"Far from it," Sylvia said. She was wearing camouflage pants and a green long-sleeved shirt. Irene had on a brown wool skirt that fell well below her knees and a blue wool cardigan. Hiking boots and matching green day packs completed their outfits. Both had binoculars hung around their necks.

"What's up? Walt asked.

"Spring migration is underway," Sylvia reported. "We've been out at Doyle Baxter's ponds identifying birds unusual to this range." She slipped off her pack, reached inside, removed a crumpled brown bag that earlier contained her lunch and plopped it down on Walt's desk. Next came a paperback copy of Peterson's field guide to birds. "That's why we're here. We believe we've spotted a species that may be of interest to the birders who read your newspaper."

"We both saw it," Irene chimed in, just to be sure Walt understood she deserved as much credit as Sylvia for their find.

Sylvia thumbed through the bird book until she found what she was looking for. "There," she pointed, "an American white pelican. Right here in Hobart Junction."

"A pelican, you say?"

"An American white pelican," Irene corrected. "Saw it with my own eyes. It was quite a sight, just floating along as proud as you please."

While Irene and Sylvia recounted their sighting

with obvious excitement, Walt mentally tried to figure out what to do with the story. It certainly wasn't front page material, and it probably didn't fit on the sports page. Bird watching wasn't a sport as far as he knew, though bird hunting was. Too bad they hadn't shot the pelican. Then it would qualify as a hunting story, and he could foist it off on Tommy.

All at once, the news gods sent him inspiration. "Did either of you happen to have a camera with you? This would be even better if we had a nice, clear photograph to go with the story."

"You know, you're right," Irene agreed. "We also need documentation of our sighting. I can go back in the morning and take pictures. I'd like to see it again, anyway."

Walt hoped the pelican was now on its way south or north or wherever it was going, and wasn't waiting around for a picture. Or, if it was still paddling in the Baxter's pond, they'd make such a ruckus sneaking through the cattails, it would fly away. If all else failed, he'd hand the two over to Tommy. Maybe he could turn it into some sort of arts piece, photographing water birds or whatever.

"I was the one who spotted the American white pelican first," Sylvia exclaimed. "By rights I should be the one taking the pictures."

"You'll both get credit," Walt assured her.

In the editor's mind, notable bird sightings ranked right up there with vegetable oddities. Every summer local gardeners brought him strange-looking produce. One time it was a turnip that resembled Mickey Mouse. Another time it was an eight-legged carrot. Mickey made the front page. The carrot didn't. His all-time favorite was a tomato Edna Olson swore was a perfect likeness of JFK. Walt didn't want to disappoint Edna, who was very proud of her garden's output, so he dutifully photographed her holding JFK, and the pair appeared together in the following issue. Later, several readers sent admiring letters to the editor lauding the remarkable presidential vegetable.

On a hunch, Walt turned to Sylvia. "You know how much I count on your reports about what's going on in town."

Sylvia smiled modestly.

"It's hard to keep track of that show the fire department is putting on. Have you heard anything?"

There was a long stretch of uncomfortable silence. Sylvia and Irene looked at each other uneasily, then at Walt, and said nothing. Eventually Irene piped up, "No, not a thing."

My instinct was right! Walt thought as he observed the two women doing their best to look as if as if they'd never heard of the Top Cats.

"Know anything about the FBI people?" Walt inquired next.

"I heard they were in town to investigate the fountain. Hope they throw the book at those kids who took it. I'll bet you anything it turns out to be that Overstreet boy. I can't imagine why Roy lets that kid of his get away with what he does. Nothing but a juvenile delinquent, if you ask me."

"Whoever heard of boys wearing earrings?" Irene put in. "Just makes 'em look stupid."

"I did hear Arvid gave the fire department quite a scare at that practice burn on Wednesday night. Pretended to have a heart attack. They called the ambulance." Sylvia was back to her usual self-righteous self. "If you want to know my opinion, Arvid had no business doing that. What if there was a real emergency and the ambulance was out chasing after him? Somebody could have died. I don't know why they let him be fire chief."

Walt hated to disappoint the town snoop, but felt he must set the record straight before Sylvia spread more misinformation from her base in front of the post office. "Whoever told you about the fake heart attack had that part right, but nobody called the ambulance. I was there."

Sylvia wasn't going to give up on it. "He still shouldn't have pretended to have that attack. It was very childish."

Getting back to his mission, Walt had one more question for Sylvia. He tried to think of a way to phrase it to play on her vanity. "Sylvia, you're one of the town's most influential citizens. I heard a rumor there's a committee been formed to put a stop to the strip show. Have you heard anything about it?"

Sylvia abruptly rose and picked up her backpack. "It's been nice talking to you Walt, but I need to get home. What kind of film should I get for the pelican pictures?"

"Come with me," he said, rising. "I'll give you some."

"I need film, too," Irene quickly put in.

"One of my photographs won a blue ribbon at the county fair two years ago," Sylvia interjected, barely keeping her tone a notch below outright bragging.

"Didn't know you were such a shutterbug," Walt said, handing her a small plastic canister. "ASA on this is 400."

"Excellent," Sylvia responded, tucking the canister into her backpack. She took the binoculars from around her neck and stuffed them in the pack, too. The empty brown paper lunch bag remained on Walt's desk.

"By the way, I like your new haircut," Sylvia said as she strode out the door. "It gives you a handsome, military look."

"Good luck," Walt called after the birders.

"What was that all about?" Ellie asked.

"She likes my haircut. And Irene and Sylvia spotted a white pelican out at Baxter's pond."

"So?"

"So I gave them some film and told them to go take pictures." He picked up the mail and began sorting it. "That should keep Sylvia off the streets for a little while."

The good news was that the fire department was close to achieving its ticket sale goal. The bad news was that Rita Lee didn't know whether she was going to be able to pull off the show. It was 8 o'clock on Sunday morning, and she was due to meet Bill and Will in an hour. Even though Will told her not to worry, she couldn't help herself. What did Will and Bill know about stage lighting?

She wandered out into her backyard, coffee cup in hand. Clouds clotted the sky, but a steady breeze was working to send the weather east. Rita Lee had never been much of a gardener, counting on perennials to bloom without too much extra help from her. She envied the yards of her neighbors, teeming with flamboyant bedding plants and pots of colorful annuals. She always meant to put in flowers, but somehow never seemed to get around to it. A few containers of geraniums usually had to suffice.

But, for some reason, this spring was different. She stopped by the nursery to pick up petunias and pansies, lilies and lobelia. As she walked down the aisles between tall racks of flowers, other plants called out to her and soon she had filled six flats. So far the bedding plants, spaced inches apart, had tiny leaves and few buds. It would be weeks before the cheerful combination of blue lobelia, white wax begonia, yellow dwarf nicotiana and purple verbena would provide the showy display pledged by the nursery man. But she had high hopes for a flower-filled summer.

She also purchased a book with lovely illustrations entitled "The Victorian Language of Flowers" and another called "Romantic Gardens of Europe and America." However the romance of flowers was the furthest thing in the world from Rita Lee's mind right now. She felt a fresh wave of panic and nervously bit the inside of her lower lip. She walked around the yard sipping coffee and checking out her new plantings. She tried to reassure herself that everything was going to be okay, what could really go wrong after all? The light problem would get itself worked out this morning, and then it was smooth sailing until Wednesday.

The telephone's ring brought her back to the moment. She rushed inside and picked up an instant before the answering machine kicked in. She was surprised and pleased to hear Walt's voice. "My canoe's complaining it's not getting enough time on the water. I'm wondering if you want to help fix the problem. I'm thinking of taking her to Green Lake."

Rita Lee explained she and Teenie had to meet the Kanute twins in less than an hour at the American Legion hall. If they could get the lights in place soon enough, she'd love to go.

"Why don't I come help?" Walt asked. "That might speed things up some. I don't know much about electricity, but I can carry a ladder."

After they finished their conversation, Rita Lee gazed out the kitchen window at the flowers in her back yard. She couldn't be sure, but it seemed like a few more buds had opened while she and Walt talked.

"Dang it Bill, hand me some duct tape!" Will hollered from the top of a tall aluminum ladder. The extension cord he had in his hand snaked down through a collection of coffee cans, plastic pipes, aluminum foil, and cellophane spread across the floor of the Legion post.

Bill was sitting on the stage, legs dangling over the edge. He had a highlighter pen in hand and sheets of paper spread out all around him, oblivious to the commotion six feet above.

"Bill!" An angry bellow this time.

"Looks like we got here just in time," said Walt. He grabbed a roll of duct tape and handed it up to Will.

Teenie was on another ladder trying to hold a wad of black fabric in place with her left hand and staple it with her right. Additional yards of fabric cascaded out of her arms down the back of the ladder. As Rita Lee watched, Teenie got part of the drape stapled into place, but almost immediately the weight of the fabric pulled the staples out and the whole thing fell back to the ground.

"Why won't this work?" Teenie wailed in frustration.

Rita Lee was sorely tempted to say "I told you so," but resisted, barely. She'd had a bad feeling about decorations from the start. Worst of all, at this rate it was going to take hours...days...to get ready for the show. *I want to go canoeing with Walt, not hang stupid black drapes*, she thought with annoyance.

After making sure Will was set, Walt turned to Bill and his scattered pages.

"See you got a new haircut," Bill said. "That the work of Boyd-The-Barber-No-Waiting?"

"No, actually I tried to give myself a haircut," Walt lied. "It didn't turn out very well, so I had to go to Rita Lee and have her fix it. This was all she could do."

"You might want to consider wearing a hat while it grows out," Bill suggested.

"Sylvia Crocker thinks it makes me look handsome, gives me a military look."

"I guess you could say that." Bill was skeptical.

"So what have you got going here? Didn't know you were an expert on stage lighting," Walt said.

"I'm not. I went to the internet and googled stage lighting," Bill explained, as he scanned a set of instructions. "This is the best of what the search came up with. Trouble is, there's so much information, it's hard to keep track of it all." Several stray pages drifted off the stage and landed at Walt's feet.

"Here," said Bill, scooping up another dozen pages and handing them to Walt. "Look through these and see if you can find the part I marked about light filters."

Rita Lee, irritation barely in check, was handing fabric back up to Teenie when she heard a thump behind her, followed by a burst of expletives from Will. Duct tape rolled across the floor. "Get that for me, will ya, Rita Lee," Will ordered.

"She's helping me," Teenie snapped. "Get it yourself."

The two glared at each other from the tops of their respective ladders.

"I'll do it," Walt said quickly, before a bigger argument got underway. He retrieved the silver tape and handed it back up to Will.

During the next two hours the crew, following Bill's sketchy internet instructions, built a lighting system. They covered coffee cans with tinfoil, attached bulbs in each, fastened the cans to the plastic pipe and hoisted the whole works up to the ceiling. A long electric cord extended out of the light bar. Will taped it to the ceiling and then down the wall. There it plugged into another cord that went back to the control board.

Teenie and Will continued to bicker. First she covered over one of his light plugs with drapery, then he pulled down one of her drapes when it was in the way. Teenie exploded. "After all that work. Will, you know how much work it was to get that up. What a jerk!"

"Those decorations are totally lame," Will retorted. "My eight-year-old cousin could come up with something better than this. Doesn't look a bit like Las Vegas."

"It's not done yet," Teenie said acidly. "Like your light board is some kind of big time deal."

Rita Lee approached meltdown. "Come on guys, get along."

"What about the gels?" Bill broke in, noticing the colored cellophane still sitting on the floor. "You were supposed to put the gels in first, before you hung the thing up."

"Major oversight," groused Walt as he began ripping duct tape off the wall. He raised his voice, "Let's get that rig down and get it fixed. What colors are we supposed to use?"

Bill sorted through his stacks of paper looking for something that described gels. "Red and blue for sure, maybe a yellow or two. I know the directions are in here somewhere."

He glanced up from his perch on the stage. Above him, the ladder was teetering dangerously as Will stretched out into space attempting to grab hold of the rope suspending the plastic pipe. An arm flailed, a leg over-corrected in the opposite direction.

"Watch out!" Bill shouted. His warning was barely out when Will, the aluminum ladder and the lighting rig hit the floor with a thunderous crash. Light bulbs shattered, shooting fragments across the room.

"Ow!" shrieked Teenie. Blood dripped from a

ragged cut on her hand.

Will was on the floor, tangled in extension cords. Dented coffee cans hung limply from the broken plastic pipe beside him.

"Are you okay?" Rita Lee asked as she rushed over to pull the ladder out of the way.

Will gingerly sat up and slowly extended his limbs, testing to see if anything was broken or sprained. After deciding he was still in one piece, Will rose and took a few uncertain steps. He looked around at the jumble of foil and broken glass. A bit sheepish, he said, "Guess we've got to start over on the lighting rig."

Bill seemed to perk up a bit. "Maybe that's good. I've come up with a few more ideas that should make the lights work even better."

Rita Lee glanced over at Walt, who looked disgusted and ready to quit. It was obvious their canoe trip was off. She was going to have her hands full here for the rest of the day.

The project dragged on, punctuated with intermittent insults (Teenie), expletives (Will), and conflicting instructions (Bill). Finally, Walt concluded the situation might be improved if everyone had something to eat. "I'm going for a pizza," he announced. "Any suggestions?"

"No onions," said Teenie.

"Onions," demanded Will.

"Anything's okay, but no green peppers," Bill said.

"No green peppers?" Teenie protested. "A pizza's not a pizza unless it has green peppers."

"Whatever," a weary Rita Lee said. "I just need something in my stomach."

"Why don't you ride along with me?" Walt suggested to the sagging Rita Lee.

Gratefully, she took him up on his offer.

At Dewey's Drive Inn Walt ordered a supreme pizza with the works, onions on one half, green peppers on the other. Then they slumped into a booth to wait for their order to come out of the oven.

"So are you sorry you ever got into this?" Walt asked.

"That's a difficult question to answer at this point." Rita Lee looked up into his eyes. "I never expected so many problems, that's for sure. This was supposed to be easier than a Valentine's dance."

"What other problems are there beside the lights and sound?"

For a moment Rita Lee was silent. Then, cautiously, she began. "Walt, I haven't told anybody this, not even Teenie, so please keep it to yourself. I've had a couple of threatening phone calls."

"Do know who they were from?"

"I'm pretty sure one was from Irene. She tried to disguise her voice, but she didn't do a very good job."

"Have there been others?"

"Oh Walt, I don't even want to tell you."

"You need to tell someone," he urged.

After a long pause, Rita Lee spoke again. "There was one from a man. He called me a slut and a whore." She lowered her eyes in embarrassment. "I hung up on him."

"Good girl. Any others?"

"Just one. It was a woman. She said she was going to turn my shop in to the licensing division for unsanitary conditions. It's not a big deal. The inspectors will come out and see everything's fine, but it's not going to do my business any good. You know how people talk in a small town."

She sat up a little and straightened her shoulders. "But that's no big deal. I'll come out of this okay. My main concern is the fire department. They really need the money. The revenue from this show will make such a difference."

"I understand," Walt said, picking up a small shaker of parmesan cheese that stood in the middle of the table. "But that doesn't mean you should have to put up with creepy phone calls." He banged down the jar. "That's got to stop."

"Being called a slut by some heavy-breathing moron is pretty awful."

"If it gets too bad, you should go stay with Teenie. I'm concerned about you being there alone."

"It's not that bad. A few crank phone calls don't scare me."

A young man wearing a white paper hat came up to the table carrying a large flat box. "Pizza's ready, folks."

"Just keep in mind what I said," Walt reminded Rita as they got up to leave. "If ever you don't feel safe, don't try to be a hero. Go stay with Teenie till this is over."

Nothing much seemed different when they got back to the Legion hall. Teenie had a few more drapes in place. Bill and Will were huddled over a drawing. Rita Lee felt broken light bulb crunch under her shoes and wondered what happened to the broom.

She was just starting to sweep up when Jerry Beemer, tool belt in one hand and a half-rack of beer in the other, came trooping in.

"Hi guys. Saw your cars parked outside and thought you might need help. Guess I was right." He surveyed the disarray in the room.

"No probleemo, Ree. I'll get you fixed up in no time."

12

"Really Rita Lee, you should have told Jerry to leave the minute he got there," Teenie complained the next morning. "All he did was drink beer and get in the way. I don't think he did a lick of work."

Teenie lifted her coffee cup with a hand wrapped in white gauze. "Thank goodness for Walt."

They were sitting in Rita Lee's kitchen going over lists. Rita Lee's usual Monday volunteer stint at the elementary school was cancelled because the third graders were on a field trip to the Belfort Historical Museum. That gave her all day to tie up loose ends before the Top Cats show on Wednesday.

Sunlight through a partly open window fell on twenty-seven signatures written in newly-learned cursive on a "Thank You Ms. Taylor" banner attached with bird magnets to the front of the refrigerator. A half-empty pot of coffee and a container of French vanilla creamer stood next to the microwave.

Both women looked like they could use another cup of coffee. Teenie's decorations were in place and looking good by five, but it was close to midnight before the crew finally got the lights back up and working properly. Walt had hung in until the end, which was the only thing that prevented Rita Lee from totally losing it. She didn't want him to see her screaming like a banshee, which is what she felt like doing a couple of times.

"Did anyone ever figure out why the breakers kept cutting out?" Teenie asked.

Rita Lee squeezed the bridge of her nose, hoping the twinge she felt wasn't the start of a headache. "Walt says everything's under control, but I'm still anxious. The breakers are working okay now, but what if they decide to kick off again during the show? What if people want their money back?"

"This is a fundraiser, Ree. People aren't going to ask for their money back. Worse comes to worse, the Top Cats can dance by candlelight while everybody sings. It'll be fun no matter what happens."

Rita Lee was not so certain. Ticket sales were going so well. She really didn't want to have to hand out refunds because of a whiplash piece of work by BillWill and Jerry.

"It was nice of Walt to help," Teenie said, looking closely at her friend.

"The plan was to go out in the canoe after we got everything done," Rita Lee said morosely. "Obviously that didn't happen."

"Thank goodness Walt was there. If we had to depend on BillWill and Jerry, we'd still be standing around in the dark. Wouldn't the decency committee just love that!"

Rita Lee was instantly alert. "I thought you said the

decency committee doesn't exist."

"I don't think it does, but if it does..." Teenie's voice dropped off into silence. After a long moment, she got up and refilled her coffee cup.

"So what about Walt and you? You guys got something going?"

"Not really. We're just friends, that's all."

She wasn't aware how forceful her denial was until she saw Teenie's startled look. "Just friends," she repeated, slowly and quietly this time.

"Looks like more than 'just friends' to me," Teenie said, stirring two teaspoons of creamer into her coffee. "You two seem like a perfect pair."

"Teenie, you're such a matchmaker. Don't you ever give up? Not one of the guys you've ever tried to hook me up with has ever worked out."

"I'll admit a few tries turned disastrous." Teenie started to giggle. "Remember that hardware salesman, Larry's cousin from Belfort? How was I supposed to know he was gay?"

"A nice guy though," Rita Lee said with a small measure of regret. "At least he and the guy he picked up at the bar were nice enough to bring me home before they went on with their evening."

Teenie lifted the lid of the cookie jar and pulled out a handful. "A little stale, but all the better to dunk, my dear." She crossed back to the table and piled a half dozen oatmeal cookies in the middle.

"I'm not going to even bring up the drug dealer," Rita Lee said, taking a hard cookie and dipping it into her half-filled cup.

"Don't remind me," Teenie groaned. "I thought he had all that money because he was top salesman at Clint Small's. How was I to know it was the perfect place to peddle drugs? People stop by to look at Fords, he takes them out to the sales lot, and under the hood of a car the goods change hands."

"He did offer me a good deal on pot, though."

"For that guy, I apologize," Teenie said.

"You could go into business," Rita Lee teased. "Call yourself 'The Nightmare Dating Service.'"

"I refuse to believe Walt Billings is a nightmare date," Teenie protested.

"No, you're right," Rita Lee agreed. "Truth is, I've been trying real hard not to even think about him too much."

"Why ever not?" Teenie regarded her friend with puzzlement.

"Because I'm scared," Rita Lee confessed, pain mixing with distress. "Walt's too nice a guy. I just don't have that kind of luck with men. If I let myself get involved, something bad will happen. I've got a good life and great friends. Why take the chance on getting my heart broken again?"

Teenie was thoughtful for a moment. "Because by taking that chance, you could find true love."

Rita Lee went still inside. "True love." Words from a romance novel or fairy tale. It seemed unlikely that they applied to her, a thirty-four-year-old hairdresser from Hobart Junction. She shrugged. "Well maybe. But first I have to get through Ladies Night Out. Then I can think about Walt Billings."

"Just give him a chance," Teenie pleaded.

Mayor Small usually tried to spend at least part of the day on Monday at town hall. He began by meeting with Louise Bird, the town clerk, to get an idea of his schedule for the week. Louise actually ran Hobart Junction on a daily basis, and Clint was first to say so. "Worth her weight in gold to this town," he often remarked.

Next to a tall vase of yellow tulips, a candy dish sat on the counter that separated the citizens of Hobart Junction from the town paperwork and files. Clint helped himself to a couple of Hershey's kisses and walked over to his desk in the corner. Town hall wasn't big enough for a private office for the mayor and a meeting room for town council. Since council members approved the budget, they had their meeting room and the mayor made do.

That was okay with Clint. If privacy was needed, he moved into the meeting room and closed the door. The chairs were more comfortable in there, anyway.

Clint Small was a good-looking man and a sharp dresser. His friendly manner and uncanny ability to remember names and faces contributed to his success in automobile sales and to his three terms in the town's top elected post. He always made it a point to look people straight in the eye, especially when negotiating the price of a used car.

"What's up?" Clint asked the clerk, who was frowning at her computer screen.

"Just checking on that grant application we put in to the state. Public Works says the water main leak is getting worse. It's gone from a trickle to gallons a day. I got a call on Friday from a delegation from Orchard Heights. They asked to be put on the agenda for the next council meeting. They're coming to complain about lack of water pressure."

"Anything else?" Clint asked bleakly.

"There's a proclamation for you to sign recognizing School Bus Drivers Week, and a couple of letters that need your signature. I've been working up a preliminary budget for next year, and if you've got time this morning, I'd like to have you look it over. It's underneath the letters to sign."

"Anything special I should be looking at?"

"Well, Public Works and the Chief of Police get raises."

"I thought the chief wanted a new patrol car."

"That's in there, too," Louise said, shifting in her chair. She was wearing a flowered dress that kept creeping above her knees. Hastily tugging her hem, Louise searched for a red pencil to hand the mayor. "This is just preliminary, you understand, but we've got to start somewhere."

With a sigh, Clint slipped the budget off the stack and began reading through it. Sometimes being mayor wasn't all that much fun.

"Don't think so," he harrumphed when he reached the figures for Public Works.

"Dream on," he snorted at the increase for the police department.

Unless they discovered gold beneath Main Street, this budget was so far out of line the town would be broke by March. The mayor picked up the red pencil and started to slash.

Clint looked up with relief when the door to town hall opened. It was Doyle Baxter, his long-time friend and campaign manager. Clint greeted Doyle warmly. "Any more signs of that pelican out at your place?"

"No birds, but hundreds of birdwatchers tromping everywhere. I expect a tour bus to show up any day now. Last weekend my grandkids made $15 selling pop and cookies to the crowd."

Clint chuckled as he dropped the budget down on his desk. "Can I buy you a cup of coffee?"

"Yep, but first we need to talk about something. How 'bout we step back into the meeting room?"

Clint raised his eyebrows.

"Politics," Doyle said, tilting his head toward the back room.

Clint couldn't imagine what Doyle had in mind, but led the way.

"Better close the door," Doyle suggested.

"Well?" Clint asked, once they were both seated.

"We need to talk about that show the fire department is putting on down at the Legion hall."

"Don't remind me" Clint groaned. "There's hardly been a minute of peace around my house in weeks. Every time I get things calmed down, Gracie or Irene calls and gets Mother stirred up again. Then Judy gets on the phone with her buddies and starts talking about how much fun they're going to have--just to irritate my mother.

"Mom's started eating meals in her room--which isn't all bad. At least they don't argue at the table any more," Clint said.

"Well, I'm here to tell you your mother isn't the only one in town who's upset. There's a big block of voters talking about a recall if you don't take a stand against this thing."

"A recall? You're kidding!" Clint wouldn't have been more amazed if Doyle told him Judy had grown a second head.

"Sorry to say, it's no joke." Doyle went on to explain how a committee had been secretly working for weeks to put a stop to the show. It was now all-out war, and the heavy artillery was aimed at the mayor. "They want you to go to Judge Potter and get an injunction."

"Why me?" Clint protested. "Why don't they go themselves?"

"You're the one they elected."

"Well, I'm not doing it," Clint said flatly.

"They claim they've got enough votes for a recall.

And when you're gone, they plan to put Boyd in as mayor."

"The barber?" Clint couldn't believe what he was hearing. "The guy with all the knock-knock jokes? He'll ruin the town."

"You don't need to tell me," Doyle said glumly "Boyd's a booster club member. Talks a blue streak, never gets anything done."

Clint laid his head on his arms. Nearly sixteen years of civic labor was about to be sent down the tube by a knock-knock joker. He thought of all he'd been through in the endeavor to make Hobart Junction a better place to live and work--all the late-night council meetings, all the hours spent listening to citizen complaints, all the times he'd entered that stupid three-legged sack race at the Strawberry Festival just so voters would think he was a good sport.

He thought of projects still on the books--the leaking water main, an upgrade to the sewer plant, and his pet project, new picnic tables for town park.

What did Boyd-The-Barber know about running a town? He could barely come up with a decent hair cut.

"Do you think they're really serious about the recall? "And who are 'they' anyway?"

"Mostly it's women who are doing the organizing. Pansy Hatfield, Sylvia Crocker, Irene Slump. They've rounded up a bunch of church folks and people like your mother. Nothing beats a fight against evil to get people riled up."

Clint dropped his head back down on the table.

"Boyd told them when he's mayor he's going to build an addition on to the senior center. And pass an ordinance to ban liquor sales within town limits."

"He can't do that," came a muffled protest.

After a long silence, Doyle spoke. "There's more."

"What?"

"They're prepared to organize a boycott of Clint Small Motors."

A groan escaped from the heap on the table.

"It's up to you, Clint. The way I see it, most of those people don't drive Fords anyway. So I wouldn't expect you to lose much business--if you even care. But Boyd-The-Barber is another matter. The man's an idiot."

Clint looked up. "They have to have a lawyer to get an injunction. Who's paying for the lawyer?"

"Pansy has some ambulance chasing cousin over in Belfort who's agreed to represent them."

Clint looked down the council table and beheld a vision of Boyd-The-Barber-No-Waiting sitting in the very chair he'd occupied for sixteen years. In his vision, Boyd was about to veto the vote on new picnic tables. Clint couldn't stand it. Shoulders sagging, he turned to Doyle. "Do you have Judge Potter's phone number?"

13

"Easy there, easy," Phil Miller cautioned. It was nearly one in the morning and an almost full moon illuminated the "Welcome to Belfort" sign.

It was Jerry Beemer's idea to drop the park fountain there. "That's where people expect it to show up. No point in disappointing everybody."

Phil worried about the exposure involved, but was hard pressed to come up with a better plan.

They carried both fountains from Concrete Creations over back roads to Belfort. Now they were slowly lowering the park fountain out of the back of Will's pickup.

"Careful, Jerry," Will warned in a low voice.

"You don't need to whisper," Jerry said loudly. "Nobody's listening. This burg closes down at ten. Can't even find a drink this time of night."

"Just the same, keep your voice down," Will said.

"Righto," Jerry said, in an exaggerated whisper.

Once the park fountain was out of the truck and sitting behind the welcome sign, Phil got out a rag and carefully wiped it off. "No point of leaving fingerprints," he explained

"Good thinking," Bill agreed. "One more fountain to go. Let's hit the road."

An hour and a half later, the conspirators rolled up in front of Audrey's garden. Phil insisted Will turn off the truck lights a block away. "Not a sound out of any of you," Phil ordered. "This fountain is supposed to be a surprise for her birthday tomorrow. You know what to do here. So just do it, without waking her up."

Unloading the second fountain went considerably faster. Phil's main concern was that no flowers be destroyed in the process.

"You want us to hook this thing up?" Jerry asked, a green garden hose in hand.

"No. I'll take care of that later," Phil told him.

"Whatever you say," Jerry said, dropping the hose into an expanse of yellow and white pansies.

"You going to wipe the fingerprints off this one, too?" Will asked.

"Hadn't thought about it," Phil said, perplexed. "You think I should?"

"Can't hurt," Will advised.

The Tuesday morning breakfast special at Gretta's Good Food Café was blueberry waffles, three slices of bacon and orange juice. The special came with homemade blueberry sauce or Vermont pure maple syrup. "No use in ruining a perfectly good waffle with fake syrup," Gretta told her regulars.

Things were a bit hectic in the kitchen. Jerry Beemer showed up for work a half hour late, looking like he'd missed way too much sleep.

"Hung over?" Gretta queried solicitously, watching him slowly tie a clean white apron round his waist.

"Not to speak of," Jerry said. "Just a late night. Way too late."

Gretta's eyes twinkled. "Was there a young lady involved?"

Jerry considered the mermaid, with her long cement tresses, but decided she didn't qualify. "A lady would have been nice, but this time I was working on a job, and it took longer to get done than I thought. Cut into my sleep time."

He walked to the cooler to retrieve the blueberries. "How about we try a different waffle special some Tuesday--say pecan waffles with applesauce. I'm getting tired of blueberries every week."

"Not a bad idea," said Gretta, fondly. "You know, you've got a real talent in the kitchen. Ever thought about going to culinary school?"

"How's that?"

"Chef's school."

"Would I get to wear one of those tall white hats? How much does it pay?"

The sound of the front door opening interrupted Gretta's reply. "You're on your own back here," she said, wiping her hands. "Try not to fall asleep."

Glancing out the pass-through, she saw Walt, Frank, and Phil enter the cafe, just behind a couple of contractors. The breakfast rush was on.

The chief of police walked up to the counter, a green thermos in hand. "Haven't got time for breakfast," he told Gretta. "Any chance you can give me a fill-up?"

"Want a doughnut or two to go with the coffee?"

"Only one doughnut. I'm on a diet."

"What's your big hurry, Chief?" Gretta asked, lifting the clear plastic lid that covered the plate of doughnuts. "Never seen you pass up blueberry waffles before,"

Frank Beemer hitched up his pants. "I just got notification they found our mermaid fountain over at Belfort. Right behind the welcome sign at the edge of town. I've always said it was going to turn out to be a prank. Looks like I was right."

"Is everything okay? Is the fountain broken?" Gretta asked as she handed Frank a frosted doughnut wrapped in a square of wax paper.

"From what Chief Wilcox told me, she seems to be just fine. Course we won't know for sure until Public Works gets her back in place and runs some water through her."

"Any indication who did it?" Walt asked.

"Not at this time," Frank said, turning to head back out to his patrol car. "Of course Elroy Wilcox will be in charge of that part of the investigation, because the fountain was found in his jurisdiction. But I'll be working closely with him, since the perpetrators are probably from here. Unless it turns out the perps are from Belfort. I wouldn't put it past those kids over there. Couple of bad apple types in that senior class may well be responsible."

The police chief got as far as the door and stopped. With a doughnut in one hand and the thermos in the other, there was no way to open the door. After a second of confusion, Frank carefully balanced the doughnut on the lid of his thermos and reached for the knob. In a loud, firm voice he declared, "One way or another, we're going to find out who did this, and when we do, we're going to throw the book at 'em."

Back in the kitchen, Jerry's devil-may-care attitude went south without him. He ducked out of view, even though his uncle wasn't looking his direction. Jerry was thoroughly sick of jail and didn't want to be back in there any time soon. He sure as hell hoped Bill and Will kept their mouths shut.

A worried Phil Miller was thinking the same thing about Jerry.

From the start Phil knew it was going to be difficult to explain the appearance of a second, nearly identical fountain in Hobart Junction. When he conceived the plan, he assumed the park fountain would be back in place long before Audrey's birthday and his story about taking photos to Creative Concrete would ring true. Now, however, the tale seemed a little farfetched. Would people believe him?

Walt was conferring with Gretta, probably giving her his order for blueberry waffles. After an instant of panic, Phil decided, what the heck, he might as well jump into the deep end and let fate decide if he was going to sink or swim.

"Morning, Walt," he said, passing up his usual chair at the retiree table. "Mind if I join you?"

Phil was wearing a wrinkled golf shirt that looked like he'd slept in it--which he had. After the fountain deliveries were completed, he drove home, dropped onto his sofa and that was it until morning.

Gretta flipped to a new page in her order book while Phil slouched in across from Walt. "What's it going to be? You want the waffle special?"

"And a cup of coffee, please."

Gretta liked Phil. He was always polite and left a decent tip, unlike some of the other retirees. She was lucky when that old tightwad Burley Spilling left a quarter. "Back in a jiffy," she promised.

"Big news about the fountain," Phil ventured.

"And right before deadline, too. I hope the Henrietta Club doesn't come after me when they find out their

95th anniversary party got bumped off the front page."

After a slight pause, Phil launched a headlong dive. "You know, the funny part is there's now two mermaid fountains in town."

"Really? Where's the second one?"

"In Audrey Willis' rose garden. I gave it to her as a birthday gift. Her birthday is today."

Phil rushed on before Walt could ask any questions.

"Audrey always told me how much she loved that fountain, so I took some pictures of it over to Don Johnson at Creative Concrete in Belfort and had him make me one just like it. A lot of it was constructed from molds he already had on hand. The rest he made after he studied the photos. It's pretty amazing what a person can do with just a dozen photographs. You should write a story about that guy some time."

Phil paused to catch his breath. He hoped he wasn't over-doing it.

"That's a pretty special gift," Walt said, showing no marked interest. "I'll bet Audrey was surprised."

"She hasn't seen it yet. That's why I came in for an early breakfast. After I eat, I'm going home to clean up and then head over there."

Since Walt didn't seem to be particularly suspicious, Phil decided to plunge a little deeper. "Do you think I should put a bow on the fountain?"

"Don't see why not," Walt said, shifting silverware so Gretta could put a mug of piping hot coffee in front of him.

"Let me know when you want a refill," she advised Phil. "You look awfully tired, dear,"

Walt took a sip of coffee. "Heard anything about a boycott of Clint Small Motors?"

"Not a word," Phil answered, relieved the editor wasn't questioning his fountain story. "What's up? The environmentalists protesting green house gases again?"

"Gretta was just telling me about it, but she doesn't know very much."

"Give me a sec. I'll go ask the contractors what they've heard." Picking up his coffee, Phil slid out of the booth and walked across the room. In a few minutes he was back.

"They say it has to do with Ladies Night Out. Pansy and Irene and that crowd are trying to force the mayor to get an injunction."

"Hey Gretta," Steve Bryson called. "What about that bet, the one that Andy won't go see the Top Cats? Does it say what happens if the show gets cancelled?"

"The bet is in the drawer under the cash register. You know where it is, go look it up." Gretta glanced at her watch. "I'm going back to see what's going on with Jerry. It shouldn't take him this long to cook up a batch of waffles."

"What does happen if the show gets cancelled?" Phil wondered. "Does it mean the fire department has to give all those women their money back?"

In the kitchen, Jerry was scraping the last of a batch of waffles out of the waffle iron into the garbage can. The air smelled of burnt batter and a thick layer of gray smoke hovered above the grill.

"My goodness Jerry, what's going on?" Gretta, hands on wide hips, glared at her breakfast cook.

"I'm sorry, Gretta," Jerry apologized, uncharacteristically repentant. "I closed my eyes for just a minute, and I guess the waffles got a little burnt."

"Hey, the smoke's getting pretty thick out here," Steve Bryson shouted. "You got a kitchen fire going? Should we call the fire department?"

"No, just open the front door," Gretta called back. "Jerry was resting his eyes and charred the waffles."

Coming out of the kitchen, Gretta picked up two menus and fanned the air. "It's a good thing I like that kid. He sure can be a trial sometimes.

"Anybody like more orange juice or a coffee refill while we're waiting for Jerry to get his act together? It's going to have to be pancakes, since he ruined the waffle maker."

"Where's the fire?" asked Arvid Smiley, hurrying in the front door.

"No fire," Gretta told him. "Jerry just overcooked the blueberry waffle special."

Arvid rolled his eyes. "So what else is new?"

"An injunction." This from Steve Bryson. "Will Rita Lee have to give the money back?"

"I must have missed something," the volunteer fire chief said, scanning the group in confusion. "I thought we were talking about burnt waffles. What's this about an injunction?"

Walt brought Arvid up to date on what little he'd learned about the latest attempt to stop the fundraiser.

"I don't get it," Arvid brooded. "Ruth told me she's sitting at a table next to Judy Small. So is Clint sticking with his mom on this one? That's not like him, he usually sides with Judy."

"Maybe he thinks decent women should be protected from those lowlifes," Phil put in, expressing his personal view on the matter.

"More likely it's the threat of a boycott." Arvid absently picked a mug from the tray and poured himself a decaf. "But that's not like Clint either. He's always been his own man. That's what makes him such a good mayor."

"It's going to be a darn shame if this thing gets called off," Gretta said. "The Legion boys have already picked out the new pool table they're going to buy with their share of the money. They showed me a picture of it just the other day."

A ding from the pass-through bell signaled the first plates of pancakes were up.

Walt glanced at his watch. It was nearly seven. He wondered if it was too early to call Rita Lee.

"Phil, Walt, you get the first batch, since you were here first." Gretta set two heaping plates before them. "I had Jerry cook up some fresh bacon."

Another ding notified Gretta her cook was trying to make up lost time. "He's on a roll now," she told everyone.

Two middle-aged women entered from the street. "Take a seat anywhere," Gretta advised. "Be with you in a jiffy...soon as I get these pancakes spread around."

"No hurry," one of the ladies told her.

"We're in town for a couple of days to do a little fishing and to go to the Top Cats show," the other explained to Walt and Phil.

"Can you recommend a good fishing hole?" the first woman inquired over the top of the adjacent booth. "We're from Foxville," she continued, by way of explanation. "The rest of the group is coming over tomorrow for Ladies Night Out. There's a whole bus full."

Arvid blanched. He imagined the thousands of dollars that were just about to slip away from the volunteer fire department. "I'm going to go make a few phone calls," he announced to no one in particular. "Maybe this whole thing's just a bad rumor."

"Let me know what you find out," Walt called to the exiting figure. "I'll be at the news office all day."

The editor slowly poured a puddle of blueberry sauce onto his plate. He wondered if Rita Lee was aware of the latest development, and if she knew, how she was holding up.

"Time I got on to the office," Walt said unexpectedly, pushing his half-eaten breakfast to the side. "Tell Audrey happy birthday for me."

"Will do," Phil responded, amazed that Walt hadn't even questioned his fountain alibi. Maybe he could pull it off after all.

As Walt hurried toward the news office he barely noticed the early morning joggers and dog walkers he passed on the street. He was astonished to find that Rita Lee had become much more than the subject of a front page story. She crowded into his thoughts when he least expected it. Brushing his teeth, the memory of her heart-stealing smile had a way of sneaking up on him. Stuffing a load of dirty clothes into the washing machine, he wondered where Rita Lee was and what she was doing.

It had been a long time since a woman had affected him that way, and he wasn't quite sure he liked it. He had a comfortable life and a satisfying job in a community he'd grown fond of. A woman had a way of changing things, even though Rita Lee would probably make things better.

"Am I falling in love with her?" Walt wondered with some consternation. "Well maybe. But first I have to do what I can to make sure Ladies Night Out doesn't get cancelled. Then I'll think about Rita Lee Taylor."

Through the window of the Beauty Mark, Rita Lee watched Walt walking back to the news office. He must have gone to Gretta's for the blueberry waffle special she speculated. She was in the midst of a crazy daydream about Walt and breakfast in bed when the phone rang.

"Ree, don't panic. I'll be right there."

"Panic?" Rita Lee asked a dead connection. Whatever was Teenie talking about?

"Have you heard about the injunction?' Teenie

asked, sweeping into the salon a few minutes later. She wasn't wearing make-up, which was remarkable for Teenie, who never appeared in public without at least mascara, eyeliner and lipstick.

"No," said Rita Lee slowly, dreading what she knew was coming next.

"The decency committee hired a lawyer in Belfort. They've gone to Judge Potter to try to stop the show."

"I thought you said there wasn't a decency committee."

"Well, I was wrong."

"Is there anything we can do?"

"Pray."

14

Phil Miller pulled up in front of Audrey's house half-expecting to see Frank Beemer standing beside his patrol car with handcuffs. Instead, an excited Audrey ran down the walk to greet him. She was still in her blue chenille bathrobe and worn scuff slippers. "Phil, the most amazing thing has happened. There's a mermaid fountain in my garden."

"Happy birthday," he said with a wide grin

"I just knew it was from you," Audrey said shyly. "I guessed it as soon as soon as I saw the fountain."

"I was going to put a bow on it, but I didn't have time."

"It doesn't matter," Audrey said, and gave him a hug. "This is my best birthday present ever."

"Maybe we should go inside," Phil suggested. "You might not want the neighbors to see you in your bathrobe and slippers."

"My gosh, you're right. I'm so excited about the fountain I forgot all about my bathrobe. Do you want a cup of coffee or tea?" offered a flustered Audrey. "You look real tired."

"Tea would be great," he said, following her into the house.

"I never dreamed I'd ever have a real fountain," Audrey said, as she poured a pot of English Breakfast into two delicate pink cups set with saucers on floral place mats.

"Glad you like it," Phil said. "I had it made over at Creative Concrete in Belfort."

"The one close to the golf course?"

"How do you know about that place?" Phil asked, startled. His cup clinked against its saucer.

"I was there with Hazel Bell not too long ago. She was looking for a concrete bench to put in her garden. That Don Johnson is a little strange. He started throwing tarps over some of the statues, and it wasn't even raining. There wasn't a cloud in the sky." Audrey shook her head. "I don't know about that guy...though he has some cute things in his yard. Did you see those darling angels?"

"Must have missed them," Phil murmured.

They sat for several moments in companionable silence. A lonesome corner of Audrey's heart was filled with a joy she never expected to experience again after her husband died. To be given such a romantic birthday gift took her breath away.

"Looks like that rotten strip show is off," Phil said, by way of making conversation.

"Oh no, I was looking forw..." Audrey caught herself just in time. "What happened?"

"Some lawyer went to Judge Potter to get an injunction."

"Oh, poor Rita Lee. She's put so much work into this."

"It was a bad idea from the start," Phil grumped.

Audrey sipped her tea and secretly wondered if a phone call to Judge Potter might help. It wouldn't hurt to ask Hazel and Louise to call, too. If the judge knew the whole story, she was sure he wouldn't grant the injunction. Phil might not approve, but it seemed a shame to for the fire department to lose all that money.

Audrey lifted the pale green ceramic pot shaped like a cabbage head and sweetly inquired, "Another cup of tea?"

For once, Walt was heading toward deadline a little ahead of the game. This was good because he needed the extra time to get through to Judge Potter and talk to him about the injunction. He thumbed through his rolodex and picked up the phone.

"Judge Potter's chambers."

"Hi, Polly," Walt greeted the bailiff. "It's Walt Billings at the Hobart Junction Independent. Wonder if I might speak with the judge."

"I'll put you on the list," she said in a weary voice. "I gotta warn you the list's getting pretty long."

"Would any of those calls have to do with an injunction to halt an all-male dance review?"

"Most of them," the bailiff confirmed.

"Is there a chance I could sneak in close to the top of the list? I've got a deadline today, and it would really help if I could talk to His Honor soon."

"Right now the judge is in conference with a couple of trial lawyers, but I'll see what I can do when he gets finished," Polly promised.

It was almost eleven when Judge Potter finally telephoned. "Let's go off the record for the time being," Walt suggested. "I'm hearing a lot of rumors about an injunction, and I need to get the facts before I write the story, but I don't want to interfere with your job."

"Sounds good to me." The judge trusted Walt, who never misquoted him and was known for his fair and honest reporting.

"Have you received a request for an injunction?"

"I have."

"What are you going to do about it?"

"Haven't decided. Truthfully, I've been so busy with this darn trial, I haven't had time to really study it."

"Got any thoughts on the matter?" Walt tapped the eraser end of a pencil on his desk.

"There doesn't seem to be any local law that applies in this case, so I'm not sure what the grounds are for an injunction. I'll have to read the filing more carefully. Looking at the list of phone calls I've got in front of me, there may be some community standard that's being violated. So far, though, I'm not convinced. Clint Small seems pretty certain the show needs to be stopped. He's an excellent mayor and I have to respect his views."

"Did he tell you about the boycott?"

"No, he didn't. What's that all about?"

"There's a group been threatening him with a boycott of Clint Small Motors."

"Can't imagine him buckling under to something like that," the judge observed.

"Me either," Walt agreed. "Something's fishy somewhere."

"Sorry to have to cut you off Walt, but Polly's waving at me. I've got to get back to the courtroom. What's your opinion of this show?"

"Pretty harmless as far as I can tell. About the same as the female mud wrestlers the guys brought in a few years ago. Of course I'm always in favor of free speech no matter what form it takes. Comes of being a newsman, I guess."

"I understand," the judge said. "Sorry I can't give you an answer before your deadline. Hopefully I'll get an opportunity to get to the injunction request late this afternoon, but that won't do you any good."

"I'll make it work, Your Honor. Thanks for taking time to talk to me."

Walt pushed his chair back from the desk. He wasn't sure if his call to the judge had made a difference. But he'd done his best for Rita Lee and the fire department. Now he had a newspaper to get out.

By noon Rita Lee was ready to lock the door of the Beauty Mark and go home. The phone wouldn't stop ringing. Everyone had heard rumors the show was about to be cancelled. Some wanted to know if they could get their money back. Rita Lee defiantly told one and all that as far as she was concerned the Top Cats would appear at the Legion Post at 8 p.m. on Wednesday. "I'll see you there," she assured them.

Privately, she didn't know if she should phone the Top Cats and cancel or hold tight. If she cancelled, the fire department would lose its $500 deposit. However, she hated to see the dancers drive all the way to Hobart Junction, only to have to turn around and go back to wherever they came from.

But as involved as she was personally, some people didn't care one way or another about Ladies Night Out. They expected to get their hair done, and, stressed or no, Rita Lee knew she had to stay put in the salon to take care of her customers.

Time seemed to slow to a crawl. The second hand on the clock moved at a fraction of its usual speed. Rita Lee had to grit her teeth to keep from screaming when a giggling Sissy Hatfield told her all about cheerleader tryouts. When Grandma Spilling carried on about bingo at the senior center, she was tempted to snatch a handful of those sweet old gray hairs and give them a yank.

Steady there, girl, she counseled herself.

About four, Teenie came in, two youngsters trailing behind her. "My sister went to Belfort to shop and I volunteered to look after her kids," Teen explained. Heard anything about the injunction yet?"

Rita Lee opened her arms in a don't-ask-me gesture. "Not a word."

"Why don't you give Walt a call? He'll know." Teenie grabbed at her four-year-old nephew, who was happily pulling brushes off the lowest shelf of the white metal display rack. "Honey, put that stuff back."

Teenie next diverted her niece, who was going for the make-up display. "Sweetie, keep an eye on Tucker, will you? I need to talk to Auntie Ree."

"Call Walt," Teenie urged. "I want to know whether to go over to the Legion hall and finish up decorating."

"I hate to bother him when he's trying to meet deadline," Rita Lee said. "If the judge's decision goes against us, it's going to be so awful, and one part of me wants to put off hearing it as long as possible."

"I'll call then," Teenie said, picking up the phone. There was a short pause while she keyed in the number. "Stop that!" she yelled at Amy, who was rocketing Tucker around in a circle in Wendy's chair.

"Oh, sorry Ellie, I didn't mean you. I was hollering at the kids. Is Walt there?" Another pause.

"Walt, it's Teenie. Rita Lee and I are dying to know. What did Judge Potter say?"

Rita Lee watched enthusiasm drain from her friend's face. The news must not be good.

"Okay, sorry to bother you." Teenie dropped the receiver back into its cradle. "He says the judge hasn't even gotten to it yet. He's in the middle of some big trial. It's probably going to be tomorrow morning before we know anything."

"Oh super, now what do we do?"

"Tell you what I'm going to do. I'm going to get these kids out of here before they wreck the place." Teenie grabbed Tucker out of the way of Estelle Conroy, arriving right on time for her weekly appointment.

Amy and Tucker, we're leaving. Put those magazines back...now!"

Pushing the children ahead of her, Teenie gave Rita Lee a few final words of encouragement. "It's all going to work out. I feel it in my bones."

"Then I'll see you at the Legion hall at nine in the morning," Rita Lee told her. "We still have to put together a dressing room for the Top Cats."

Estelle hung her jacket on the wooden rack in the corner and planted herself in the chair at Rita Lee's station. "Such a hubbub. Last time there was this much talk was when the chamber of commerce got into the rhubarb with town council over who was going to pay for toilet paper in the public restrooms."

"If I remember right, "Rita Lee said, draping a mauve cape over Estelle, "the Chamber felt it was the town's responsibility, and the council contended that it was mostly out-of-towners who used the toilet paper, so the chamber should pay."

Estelle began to laugh, a hardy rumbling from deep in her chest. "Sylvia Crocker appointed herself to count the number of tourists using the restrooms. They say she also measured how much paper each person consumed, don't ask me how.

"In the end, the council budgeted a set amount each year for toilet paper. After that the chamber pays."

Estelle begin to laugh harder. "It's a good thing this show is at the Legion hall. You know how much toilet paper the women are going to use up. It could break the town and the chamber both."

"Speaking of women," said Estelle, as Rita Lee worked shampoo through her hair. "They say Frank Beemer's called in the reserves to handle the crowd. He's going to be real disappointed if the judge cancels everything."

Rita Lee felt tears of frustration about to spill and blinked hard to push them back. It was difficult to imagine people actually believing such foolishness--rioting females, indeed! She pictured Judge Potter and the pressure he was facing to shut down the Top Cats. If he believed a story like that, it might turn the tide against the show.

What other false tales had he been told?

Rita Lee spent a nearly sleepless night worrying about Ladies Night Out. At one point, she put a coat on over her nightgown and wandered, bathed in moonlight, among her recently planted flowers.

What had she been thinking...bringing male strippers to Hobart Junction? She'd let down the fire department and her business faced ruin.

Well, maybe that was a bit of an exaggeration, she conceded, but things weren't looking good.

Rita Lee tried every trick she could come up with to induce sleep. She drank two cups of chamomile tea and then went back to bed and counted backwards from 100...three times. She tried deep breathing, thinking "re" on the inhale and "lax" on the exhale. She considered getting up and soaking in a soothing tub of lavender scented water. But she was too exhausted to go through the motions of filling the tub. So she laid there as the hours crept by, tossing, turning, worrying, wishing she was asleep.

Rita Lee wasn't the only one on edge. Berlene Goss lay next to her husband, eyes wide open, pondering a conversation at the dinner table. Gilford was scooping out a second helping of round steak casserole made with cream of mushroom soup and crispy fried onion rings when he brought up Ladies Night Out.

"I called Judge Potter today, to let him know I support an injunction against the strip show. I thought it might help since I'm a member of the town's religious community."

Belene smiled benignly and quickly changed the subject. She was afraid if the conversation continued, she might confess that she'd also spoken to the judge during the day. Audrey Willis encouraged her to make the call and even gave her advice on what to say. Berlene was reluctant at first, but when Audrey told her how certain people were blackmailing the mayor, she was outraged. It's not that she cared that much about the show, but she didn't like the idea of poor Clint being shaken down, undoubtedly by members of her own congregation.

Now, in the dark of night, she shifted uneasily. She was having second thoughts about going to the show. Gilford planned a trip to Foxville to attend a mens dinner and Bible study, so the coast was clear. But her conscience was bothering her. In daylight her newfound independence was exhilarating; at midnight freedom mingled with fear.

She forced her eyes closed and said a little prayer for strength and wisdom.

At the other end of town, Pansy Hatfield slept soundly, snuggled beneath a plush purple comforter. She went to bed confident that in a few hours the impious would get their just reward when Judge Potter called off the stripper show. She was sorry the Legion and the fire department wouldn't be getting the money they needed, but they shouldn't have picked that kind of fundraiser in the first place. Her conscience was clear.

15

Wednesday morning, nine a.m. Rita Lee and Teenie let themselves into the Legion building. They had no clue what the day was going to bring, but whatever happened, they wanted to be prepared. Before long, six dancers and their master of ceremonies would arrive, expecting to rehearse. Right now, there wasn't a dressing room for them.

Arvid Smiley and several other fire department volunteers were in charge of building the dressing room. At first, it was assumed the Top Cats would use the men's restroom to dress, but then Rita Lee learned they were bringing a dozen costume changes for each dancer. Starr Glitter, who acted as mistress of the revels, was bringing nine full-length sequined gowns and as many wigs.

"Be sure there's plenty of space for the costumes," their manager instructed Rita Lee during one of the initial conversations. "The dancers make changes in under four minutes while Starr tells jokes, so the back stage area has to be well organized. She changes while they do their numbers. The timing is split-second."

With this in mind, the building crew came loaded with two-by-fours, tools and wide sheets of black plastic. Within two hours they erected a makeshift dressing area for the dancers to the left of the stage.

Meanwhile, Teenie finished decorating. She smoothed white cloths over each table and centered votive candles in silver holders along silver runners. Shiny silver ribbons curled in and out among the candle holders.

She illuminated the bar area with miniature white Christmas lights, and put additional strings around the entrance door. Taking in the effect, Rita Lee was glad her friend had been so insistent about decorating.

Bill Kanute ran one last test of the sound and light system before the cast arrived. And by some miracle, everything seemed to work. Nevertheless, he and Will promised to bring tools in case there was a failure during the show.

Standing in the center of the room, Rita Lee gave directions and answered questions, all the while trying to ignore the knot in her stomach. When the building crew needed more screws, she drove to the hardware store. She showed the liquor store delivery man where to stack cases of wine and beer, and then counted plastic cups to be sure they had enough. One by one she crossed off items on her day-of-the-show list.

Every once in awhile a sharp pain snatched at her midsection. What was taking the judge so long to make his decision?

Rita Lee was just about to go to the drugstore for something to settle her stomach when Walt came through the door.

He was smiling.

"You're a go, girl."

A cheer rang through the room. Rita Lee rushed to give Walt a huge hug. "Oh thank you, thank you," she gushed, holding him tight.

Walt enjoyed the close contact as long as he decently could. "Hey, it wasn't me. Thank Judge Potter."

"What did he say?" Teenie wanted to know.

"I haven't seen the written ruling yet, but in essence what he said over the phone was that he couldn't find law to back up an injunction. He mentioned the importance of freedom of speech, even in the face of opposition by some community members."

"Why did it take him so long?"

"He spent a lot of time doing research of other cases; he considered all the phone calls and messages. I think Judge Potter wanted to be sure he made the correct decision...which is what judges are supposed to do."

As the group enjoyed a moment of triumph, a 1976 Bluebird motor coach pulled up outside. In its first years, the bus had transported a big league baseball team up and down the east coast; then it was passed on to the farm club. When maintenance costs got too high, the bus was sold to a third-rate rock band, which folded and leased it to a Wisconsin polka band. Eventually, the vehicle came into the hands of Max Picklebaum, manager of the Top Cats.

After a few minutes, the Top Cats descended into the sunlight. The young men were dressed in jeans and tight-fitting T-shirts, most displaying bar or beer logos. Some of the guys appeared to be seeing sun for the first time in weeks. They shaded their eyes, which were already protected with sunglasses, from the glare.

Last to emerge was a tall thin man with a blue-black stubble, high cheekbones and fine features. His name was Jeffrey Constantine. Women knew him as Starr Glitter.

"My God, Max, where are we?"

"It's called Hobart Junction."

"There's got to be an easier way to make a living," Jeffrey moaned, and turned around and climbed back into the bus.

Max and the dancers gazed dejectedly at the Legion hall. Max shrugged. "You get paid the same in Chicago or Hobart Junction. This may not be the big time, but you gotta start somewhere. Get a little experience and maybe the Chippendales will be next."

The young men, most of them in their early twenties, accepted the advice of their manager. They'd heard about paying dues. It was all part of show business. If that's what it took to get to the top, they were willing.

"Let's go in and check it out," Max suggested. "It can't be as bad as it looks."

Rita Lee watched the Top Cats enter, six head-of-the-line specimens of the male half of the species. Well-built, she observed, not my type, but definitely cute. Except for that one older guy with the paunch. He must be the manager.

Gathering herself together, Rita Lee greeted the dancers, who were staring in disbelief at the black plastic dressing room. "Welcome. I can't tell you how glad I am to see you, and how glad I am that you'll be performing here tonight. This is such a thrill. "You don't know what we've been though."

One of the dancers looked Rita Lee over closely, as if he suspected insanity.

"Glad to be here," Max answered, forcing a hearty tone. "The boys have been looking forward to performing in Hobart City."

"Now if you'll just lead the way to the dressing

room," Max continued, walking right on past the black plastic, "we'll get our costumes unloaded."

"That's it." Arvid Smiley said, stepping forward, and indicating the recently completed project. "Me and the boys from the fire hall just finished it."

"That's it?" Max squeaked.

"Yep, we put the whole thing up in less than two hours. If you need something changed, just let us know. We got all our tools right here."

Looking skeptical, Max traipsed behind the plastic and surveyed the space. The dressing room appeared even worse from the inside, but they'd have to make it work. "Oooookay," he muttered, shaking his head in disbelief.

Max stuck his head out from behind the shimmering black wall. "Where's Shotgun? Tell him to get the costumes out of the bus. Rehearsal and sound check in a half hour. Warm-up starts in ten minutes."

The Top Cats shook off their stupor, all the while sizing up the guys from the fire department...who were, in turn, sizing up the Top Cats.

"Nothing like a little testosterone to stir things up," Rita Lee commented to Teenie. She walked over to Arvid, who was vainly attempting to keep his gut sucked in. "Don't you wish the guys in the department were in as good shape as the Top Cats?" she teased. "There would be a lot less huffing and puffing at fire practice."

Arvid was still trying to think of a snappy comeback when the first costume trunks rolled by, balanced on a dolly guided by a burly man with stringy black hair and a beard. "Where do these go?" he shouted.

"This way, Shotgun. Behind the black plastic," came Max's muffled voice.

"Awesome," Shotgun observed, the first to truly appreciate the dressing room. "Looks like the set for a

Mega Doom concert."

Shotgun served the Top Cats as roadie, driver, sound man and sometimes cook. He'd been with Max for seven years. The dancers usually didn't last more than one tour. The ones with talent moved on to better paying gigs. The others usually left because they were sick of living in cramped quarters, eating bad food, and never having a chance to spend the money women tucked in their G-strings. Life as a Top Cat wasn't nearly as sexy as they thought it was going to be when they auditioned for a spot in the line-up.

The adoration of an all-female audience and their appreciative screams were intoxicating while they lasted--during the two hours of the show--the other twenty-two hours were mostly tedium.

Still, there were occasional high moments. This was one of them--running through warm-ups looking like professional football players, while the local hayseeds stood around gaping in awe.

Shotgun propelled the empty dolly toward the door. He respected the dancers because he knew the time and effort they invested in staying in shape, but he had no desire to change places. He was content to drive the bus.

Enough of this, Rita Lee told herself after watching the Top Cats warm up for a minute or two. She turned and searched the room for Walt. She wanted to hear more about the judge's ruling.

Before she could track him down, Bill Kanute showed up. Rita Lee switched gears and steered Bill over to Shotgun. "Bill and his brother put together the lights and the sound system for the show," she explained.

Shotgun looked dubious. "You fellas have anything to do with the dressing room?"

"No," Bill protested. "That's Arvid's work. I got all my information from the internet."

Shotgun wasn't sure he got what Bill was telling him, but hoped for the best. "They're going to start rehearsing in just a few minutes. It'll give you a chance to get everything set."

While Bill demonstrated the sound system for Shotgun, Rita Lee got back to her search for Walt. He wouldn't leave without saying good-by, so it was only a matter of finding him.

She glanced at her watch. Five hours until curtain time. Too bad there wasn't a curtain.

She finally found Walt outside, standing beside the tour bus, talking to Charity and the tall, thin man who needed a shave.

Red lettering on the side of the bus proclaimed,

THE TOP CATS....ENTERTAINING
AMERICA'S WOMEN ONE DANCE AT A TIME.

"Rita Lee," Walt hailed. "Come here and meet Jeff Constantine. Turns out he knows my cousin Marty, the one who owns the Sunset Club in San Diego. They play there all the time."

"Welcome to Hobart Junction," Rita Lee said, extending her hand. "A lot of women are looking forward to your show tonight."

"We'll give them a good time," Jeffrey promised.

"It's a small world," Rita Lee said, "you knowing Walt's cousin and all. My roommate Kitty moved to San Diego. Wouldn't it be total Twilight Zone if you knew her, too?

While Jeff and Rita Lee discussed Kitty's whereabouts, Walt scrutinized activity across the street. Two men and a woman wearing black suits and shiny shoes were passing by, casually surveying the tour bus.

"Aren't those the FBI people," Charity asked.

"Wonder why they're still in town, since the fountain's been found."

"The FBI was only a rumor," Walt told her. "They're church people going door-to-door."

"I don't think so," Charity said. "My mom invited the lady to come to Christian Women's Society, and the lady told Mom she hadn't been inside a church in ten years."

"Well then, I don't know who they are. But I'd bet money they aren't FBI."

Shotgun hurried up to the group outside the bus. "Jeff, they're ready for a sound check."

The show's emcee reluctantly turned to the entrance. "How bad is it in there?"

"The stage is okay, but the dressing room's a joke."

"Are we in the basement again? Are there leaky pipes? If there are I'm going to dress in the bus, I don't care what Max says. The last place just about ruined my gold gown."

"You'll be okay," Shotgun assured him.

"My dear, I hope so," Jeff said, slipping into his Starr persona. "Please God, let the sound be adequate. All I ask for is adequate." He lifted long-lashed eyes upward, hands to together in supplication. "That's not too much to ask, is it?"

"Are those lashes real?" Charity asked Shotgun, once Starr made her dramatic departure.

"You bet, with a little help from her beautician. But wait till you see her tonight. She's a real knockout."

"How long have you been in show business?" Charity asked, endowing Shotgun with her most brilliant smile.

"I've been with Max for seven years. Before that I was a roadie with a band called "The Toothpicks."

"They were good," Charity said. "What ever happened to them?"

"Booze and drugs," Shotgun answered sadly. "Sometimes I was the only one sober for weeks on end."

"That must have been a drag."

Shotgun basked in her solicitude. "Can I offer you a soda or juice or something? We've got plenty in the bus."

"I'd love some juice," Charity said. "I've never been in a tour bus before."

"This one isn't much. Nothing like the one The Toothpicks had. But I'll be glad to show you around."

"Oh, cool," Charity said, following him up the stairs into the bus.

Walt slipped his arm around Rita Lee's waist and drew her close. "Got a minute?"

"Sure do," Rita Lee said, leaning into him a bit. They drifted over to the shade of a maple tree. "Mind if we sit down? I've been on my feet for hours."

"Be my guest," Walt said with a flourish, indicating the grass at their feet. Rita Lee gratefully slid down and leaned back against the tree.

"You going to make it?"

"Oh sure," Rita Lee said, brushing off her fatigue. "I'm just glad all this work wasn't for nothing. Tell me again what the judge said."

They hadn't been sitting for more than two minutes before Bill hurried out and frantically scanned up and down the street until he spotted Walt and Rita Lee under the tree. "Oh good, I found you. The stage lights stopped working. The manager is about to lose it."

"Tell you what," Walt said as he gave Rita Lee a hand up off the grass, "how about tomorrow we forget all this madness and go on a day-trip with the canoe? You're going to need a break when this is over."

"Sounds like heaven to me."

As it turned out, heaven was more than a day away.

16

Charity barely made it home in time to change for the show. "I thought you'd be dressed by now," she chided her mother. "We don't want to be late."

"I've decided not to go." Berlene told her daughter.

"Of course you're going. Dad's out of town, and there's a place reserved for you at the table with Audrey, Hazel and Judy."

"I'd be deceiving your father," Berlene said, hugging her arms close to her chest.

"He didn't say you couldn't go," Charity protested as she wiggled into a form-fitting sheath than appeared to be made almost entirely of Lycra.

"He says the Top Cats are immoral."

"Mom, letting little children go hungry is immoral; allowing factories to pollute the air we breathe is immoral; waging war so fat cats can get even richer is immoral."

"But I know he wouldn't like it." Berlene nervously twisted her wedding rings.

"But he'll get over it." Charity slipped into strappy three-inch heels. "Tell me this: if you go to the show, how do you think it will change you? Are you suddenly going to become evil? Will you start telling lies and being mean to people? No, you're going to be the same sweet person you've always been."

"I just don't think it's an appropriate place for a pastor's wife."

Charity walked into the bathroom and swiftly applied make-up remover. Once her face was clean and dry, she started over. From inside the bathroom she called, "Besides Mom, there's someone I want you to meet."

"At the Top Cats show?" Berlene couldn't imagine who that could be.

"He's the coolest guy. His name is Shotgun. He's the roadie."

"Roadie?" Berlene felt a little faint.

"That's the guy who looks after the equipment, and drives the bus and stuff. He's not in the show, Mom."

"Does he attend church?"

"Mom, how should I know? I just met him this afternoon." Charity brushed a liberal amount of pale lavender eye shadow on each lid and followed up with black liner. "His real name is Bobby Phillips. Shotgun is a nickname."

"Is he from around here?"

"No, he grew up in Miami." Charity came out of the bathroom to face her mother. "And here's the best part. Shotgun introduced me to Max Picklebaum, the Top Cat's manager. Max is looking for a production assistant. I might be getting a job with his company."

"Oh, honey, do you think that's a good idea?" Berlene could hardly believe what she was hearing. Her daughter was leaving home to join a troop of striptease artists. Where had she and Gilford gone wrong?

"Mom, just come and meet Shotgun and Max and the rest of the Top Cats. They're decent people...you'll see."

Berlene gave up. Her daughter's destiny took priority over her husband's anger. As Charity said, he'd get over it.

She went to put on something dressy.

Frank Beemer's office was small. Fliers, posters and bulletins covered the walls, which needed painting. Two gray metal desks, one for him and one for his deputy, Reggie, took up most of the room. There was barely enough space for a couple of file cabinets and an extra chair or two. It obviously wouldn't do for the briefing he had planned.

"We'll use the council meeting room," he instructed the group squeezed in around him, and led everyone across town hall.

"Make yourselves comfortable," the police chief said, indicating the padded chairs. Frank took a spot at the head of the table, and the rest settled down either side.

"A few introductions before we move on to tonight's operation," Frank began. He pointed to the fellow on his left. "This is Reggie, my deputy. Next to him are David and John from the state liquor control board. Across the table there's Alice, also from liquor control, and officers Williams and Bonner from Foxville. They'll act as back-up."

Each of the uniformed cops was fully armed, with at least thirty pounds of extra gear hanging from their belts. The three liquor control board representatives were dressed in black suits and shiny black shoes.

"There should be close to three hundred women tonight," Beemer went on. "I can't provide exact numbers because there's no way of knowing how many tickets the fire department's going to sell at the door." He looked around the table to be sure everyone was paying attention. "There could be some men show up, too. I know of at least a couple of dares and a bet or two that's ridin' on this thing."

"David, John and Alice here," he nodded in their direction, "contacted me because they got warnings there's going to be a lot of under-age drinking at this event. The state doesn't like it when that happens. You want to tell us about the warnings, David?"

"Well, yes." David cleared his throat and slicked back his hair. "The calls have all been anonymous, but there's been enough of them to cause concern. There's one woman who phones every day--we've discounted her as a crank--but the rest sound legitimate. For example, one female reported she overheard a group of teenagers talking about buying tickets through an older friend. Another caller told us several of her high school friends planned to attend and were going to buy wine."

"Age isn't our principle concern here," John broke in. "As long as they don't drink, it's not our problem. But as soon as they consume an alcoholic beverage, we're going to get involved."

Alice frowned and raised an eyebrow. "What John means to say is, alcohol will be served at this event and no one under twenty-one is admitted. But if we find in checking IDs that a person is under-age, we won't automatically have her arrested. She has to be a minor in possession first."

"Are you saying we're going to be the ones arresting these women--not you?" Reggie wanted to know.

"Only the minors in possession," David confirmed. "John will pose as an assistant bartender, and watch out for over-generous pouring. Alice will mingle among the crowd, observing suspicious activity and making note of people under legal drinking age. She'll notify the chief, and then you'll move in."

"What about you? Where will you be during all this?" Officer Williams quizzed. He wasn't so sure Chief Beemer made a good decision bringing in outsiders.

"I'll be outside monitoring activities in the parking lot."

"Yes, well," Frank said loudly, trying to take back leadership of the meeting. He held up a sheaf of papers. "I've got a detailed operations plan that I'd like to pass around at this time."

Backstage at the Legion Post, the Top Cats prepared for the show. They'd performed together so many times, each man knew exactly how every other man moved, and they seldom bumped into each other in the dressing room, even in the closest conditions. It was a different version of the dance they did on stage. No bumps and grinds to be sure, but the same nimble footwork and attention to space.

Costumes were always placed in the same order, in the same relative position to other dancers' costumes. Make-up and hair products were spread out between stand-up mirrors on portable tables. Everybody knew which dancers carried certain products they weren't willing to share. The rest borrowed from each other constantly.

One area was set apart for warm-up and stretching. Since space was at a premium, the men worked in shifts. Some of the exercises were straight out of ballet. Others came from the football field.

Starr occupied her own corner. She had a personal table with a lighted mirror, a custom make-up case, and plenty of room to spread out the creams, powders, glosses and lotions that transformed her into a fabulous diva. Wigs, from jet black to platinum, stood on individual stands above each of her glimmering garments. Matching shoes were in place below.

"Does anybody have eyelash adhesive?" she asked, plaintively.

Two dancers doing push-ups in the corner snorted.

"Sorry dear, I'm all out," someone responded.

The general atmosphere was less boisterous than usual. They were trying to keep the noise down, since black plastic wasn't much of a sound barrier between them and the women filling the hall. "Watch you language back here," Max warned. "This is supposed to be a high-class act."

Finally, one of the dancers went out to the tour bus for a portable CD player. The pop music drowned out the men's backstage banter and ramped them up for the coming show.

As curtain time neared, the dancers rubbed themselves down with oil developed by professional weightlifters to create body sheen and accentuate bulging muscles. They donned the first costume, stepping into custom-padded thongs designed to give them the manly look they imagined all women wanted. The layering continued, most of it held together by Velcro for easy removal later. At last, they were ready: six dandies in white tails, top hats and their signature bow ties.

Outside, a line of women snaked down the side of the building and out into the parking lot. It was the Foxville contingent. Their rented school bus stood empty at the edge of the lot.

The evening air was thick with feminine laughter. Ticket holders greeted friends, sharing warm hugs, careful not to mess up each other's hair and make-up. They were dressed for a night on the town, wearing outfits and jewelry that only came out on special occasions like weddings and New Year's Eve. Twinkling lights around the entrance announced a good time inside, and the crowd was ready to party.

Audrey Willis, who usually didn't like to be late, lingered in her car, self-conscious about walking up to the entrance. What if one of the neighbors saw her going in? She was just about to turn around for home, when she recognized a woman who lived down the block, a silver-haired matron several years her senior. At least she wasn't going be alone in sending the neighborhood to the dogs. Audrey stepped out of the car, hung the strap of her velvet evening bag over one shoulder, and set off to find her friends.

She joined the end of the queue feeling out of place, but was soon caught up in the excitement, chatting with two friendly visitors from Belfort in line in front of her. At the card table in the vestibule, she handed Teenie her ticket and stepped forward into a silver world lit by flickering candles. "Oh my," she breathed. "How elegant."

"Yoo hoo, Audrey, over here," hailed Hazel from a table on the left side of the room. "We saved you a spot."

In the room's dim light, Teenie's black fabric drapes were difficult to distinguish from the black plastic dressing room walls. They blended together to create a strange, exotic setting, nothing at all like the Legion hall Audrey was used to. The portraits of past commanders were nowhere in sight; faint smoke from sweetly scented candles filtered details at the edge of the room. The provocative beat of music drifting from behind the black plastic caught her off-guard.

"I was just about to go get a glass of wine," Judy Small told Audrey as she walked up to the table. "Want me to get one for you, too?"

"That would be nice," said Audrey, still taking in the decorations and the crowd of well-dressed women. "White, please," she added, slipping her handbag onto the table. She was a little surprised to see Berlene sitting beside Hazel, being she was the pastor's wife and all, but decided if Berlene was there, it was okay for her to be there too, and relaxed a bit more.

Rita Lee was the last woman in Hobart Junction to get dressed for Ladies Night Out. She arrived home to change ten minutes before Starr Glitter was scheduled to open the show. Up until then she was attending to details, making sure the dancers had what they needed, the bartenders were set, and the volunteers at the ticket table could handle various situations that might come up.

Rita Lee felt she'd done all she could do to make the event a success, and now it was time to enjoy the Top Cats along with everyone else. Only she was so exhausted she was tempted to forget the show, go to bed and sleep for two days. Rita Lee doubted anyone, except perhaps Teenie, would miss her if she didn't appear. It took genuine determination to stand upright and focus enough to select something to put on.

"You'd think this was a big deal--deciding what to wear," she said outloud. "It's not like I have a whole closet full of party clothes to choose from." Rita Lee placed her index finger along side her jaw and feigned puzzlement. "Let me see, shall I wear my little black dress or my little black dress?"

"No question," she mocked. "I'll wear my little black dress."

After the dress came the shoes. "I don't think so," she said, dismissing the stiletto heels she usually wore with the dress. What she wanted, what she needed, was comfort. At the back of her closet were old black pumps that fit like well-worn gloves.

"It's party time," she told the shoes that had been with her at more functions than she cared to remember. "You may be senior citizens, but there's life in you still."

Rita Lee sat down heavily on the edge of the bed. "I must really be getting rummy," she sighed. "Now I'm talking to my shoes."

When Rita got back to the Legion hall, there seemed to be even more vehicles in the parking lot than when she left for home. The last drivers had parked every which way, blocking early arrivals. She didn't want to even venture a guess about how long it was going to take to untangle the mess and complete an orderly exit at the end of the show.

The lot was remarkably quiet considering how excited and noisy it had been just a short while before. The only movement came from a man Rita Lee didn't recognize who was creeping between cars. He had his head down and appeared to be peeking into the front seats of vehicles he passed. Rita Lee worried he might be a car thief, and hurried forward to alert someone to come outside and keep an eye on him.

As she neared the entrance, Rita Lee heard a shout from inside. "Take," yelled many female voices. "It," hollered others. "Off," screamed a third group.

"Come on, girls," a deep, throaty voice was saying as she opened the door," you can do better than that. Remember, the group that makes the most noise gets the Top Cats for the first number."

On stage a striking brunette in a low-cut cherry red evening dress pointed her lacquered nails at one side of the room. "Group one..."

"Take"

"Oh my, that was awfully good. The rest of you are going to have to be very loud to beat group one. Now, let's hear it, group two."

"It," the middle section shrieked.

Starr Glitter put her hands on her hips and swished her shoulders. "Oooooo, good. Group three, you've got your work cut out for you. So give it a try." She pointed to the women seated to her left.

"Off," the third group screeched as loud as they could.

Starr placed both hands on her sexy chest. "I think we have a tie. I'll have to hear you again, all together now." She raised languid arms above her head and then pointed at the audience.

"Take it off!" the excited women roared.

The cheer echoed through the room.

"Ladies and gentlemen," Starr Glitter purred, pointing in the direction of the dressing room. "Please give a great big welcome to the Top Cats."

The crowd went wild.

17

A steady, primal beat filled the room. Pulsating pop music followed on its trail. The stage lights came up to full brilliance, illuminating a bare stage.

Berlene held her breath, fearful of what she was about to see, but excited at the same time. Next to her, Judy brought two fingers to her lips and blew a whistle loud enough to bring in every dog within blocks.

As if in answer to her call, the Top Cats strutted on stage. They twirled and leaped with the precision of a male cheerleading team. Their movements were suggestive without being low down. They were proper gentlemen in snow-white tuxes, top hats and tails come to entertain the ladies on their night out.

The opening dance routine consisted mainly of thrusts and shakes they'd picked up watching boy band music videos, with a few dance sequences from the Chippendales thrown in. Back in New Jersey, the tour had started out with an official choreographer, but he was long gone. His complicated routines had been slowly replaced by easier moves the guys could remember and execute smoothly.

The top hats came off first, to become containers for the gloves. Next to go were the jacket sleeves, leaving the dancers in spangled vests, which in due time were unzipped to reveal brawny chests. During the first few minutes of the show, audience members confined themselves to whispers, "Oh my word, look!"..."Can you believe this?" Then one brave woman let loose with a wolf whistle. The audience began to cheer, and in no time at all the music was barely audible over the laughter and squeals.

On stage, the Top Cats warmed up to the audience. They were still performing their synchronized routine, but individual personalities were beginning to emerge. One dancer remained aloof, a mysterious stranger. A second assumed the role of a kid brother, harmless and full of fun. Another winked salaciously at a lady in the front row.

"Take it off!" screamed a woman in the back.

The Top Cats did as they were told.

"Looks like those young fellas are doing okay," Harry Bell observed to a fellow Legionnaire. They were stationed behind the makeshift bar, watching the Top Cats bump and grind among the tables, collecting dollar tips as they went. Traffic at the bar had been steady all evening, and in their mind's eye the Legionnaires were already playing pool at their new table.

"Hey look, isn't that Gretta stuffing money down that dancer's shorts?" asked Carl, one of the bartenders, sounding a little shocked.

If you can call those dinky little things they got on

shorts."

"I'm trying not to look," Harry admitted. "I'll probably see my wife doing it next."

"Those ladies are getting a little personal, don't you think?" Carl asked the man standing next to him. The guy was from out of town, a "special deputy" Frank Beemer brought in through a side door shortly before the show started.

"John's here to make sure nobody drinks too much," the police chief explained before disappearing again.

Harry wasn't sure what Frank was implying, since Rita Lee held a meeting with the bartenders ahead of time and instructed them to watch out for anyone who looked like she'd had enough to drink. "We don't want anyone driving home looped," she warned.

Did Frank think the Legion bartenders were such nitwits they couldn't tell if a woman was drunk or not? Harry continued to stew as he poured another round of drinks.

After a final thrust of hips, the Top Cats swaggered back to the dressing room, the music faded and the lights dimmed to black. Out into a single spotlight slinked Starr Glitter, this time clad in a shimmery aquamarine gown with flames of silver sequins. "Aren't the Top Cats just too cute?" she cooed. "They make me sooooo hot," she panted, fanning herself.

"But let me tell you about my ex-boyfriend Dudley," she began, launching a comedy routine that kept the audience in stitches while the guys changed costumes. She made fun of Dudley's ego, his lousy bedroom technique, his reluctance to help around the house. She was just getting started on his mother when the resonant beat of tom-toms flooded the hall. As the laughter died, Starr turned toward the dressing room and gasped in mock terror. "Run for your lives...Wild Indians!"

For their second production number, the Top Cats emerged in fringed leather buckskins and feathered war bonnets. At the middle of the stage, red-orange light from a fake campfire began to flicker. The Indians danced around the fire in a routine almost identical to the one they'd performed during the previous number, but nobody seemed to notice, especially after the war bonnets were tossed aside and the dancers stripped down to tan leather loincloths.

"Six white wines," Gretta told Harry, coming up to the bar. "I'm here on a booze run for my table." She turned her back on the bartender to watch the strippers.

"Are you sure you can carry all these?" Harry dubiously asked, as he filled the last glass.

"Are you kidding? This is nothing compared to toting six prime rib dinner platters."

"Good luck," Harry called after her. "Watch out you don't spill wine down one of those Top Cat's pants."

"Quite a show, isn't it?" Walt Billings said, stepping into the spot recently vacated by Gretta. He had a camera hanging from a strap around his neck.

"Are you talking about the Top Cats or the women?" asked Andy, slipping out of the shadows where he was trying to remain as inconspicuous as possible. "I see you have your camera with you. Any chance you can take a picture of me and the bartenders--just to prove to those jokers down at Gretta's I was here?

"Sure, glad to. Go stand there next to Harry and Carl." Walt noticed the stranger lurking back behind the bar. "You might as well get in this, too."

"No, that's okay," the man said, sliding back even further.

Walt took a closer look. He recognized the man as one of the FBI agents who'd been hanging around town.

"Don't I know you from somewhere?"

"This here's John, a special deputy Frank put in with us," Harry informed him. "Maybe Frank's afraid we're going to pocket the fire department's money or something."

The special deputy looked uncomfortable but said nothing.

Before Walt had a chance to ask anything more, there was a boom from the direction of the stage. Purple fog began to swirl toward the ceiling, until the whole front of the stage was enveloped in a thick purple haze. From out of the fog emerged six wizards in black swirling robes and pointed hats with peacock feathers tucked in the bands. They wore tall leather boots and carried staffs topped by silver dragons that shot out radiant light.

"Boy howdy, would you look at that!" Harry gasped, thunderstruck.

The applause was deafening.

By now Berlene had completely forgotten to keep an eye on Charity and Shotgun. She was whooping and laughing along with everybody else. She couldn't believe how much fun she was having. When the Top Cats threw off their flowing capes to reveal sleek snakeskin singlets that stretched over bulging chest muscles and rose high on slim hips, Berlene cheered as loud as her table mates.

Then the dancers shed their reptile skins and Berlene was in for another surprise. Now they were down to black satin thongs printed with stars and moons. The lights went out, revealing a gyrating glow-in-the-dark galaxy.

"This is quite artistic," she reassured herself. "Gilford wouldn't mind."

When the lights came back up to dim and the Top Cats snaked among the tables, Berlene reached into her purse and got out a dollar. As one of the dancers paused to swivel his pelvis invitingly in her direction, she reached out and tucked the bill into the thin strap that crossed his hip. It was the most daring thing she'd done in all her life.

The young man bent, gave her a quick kiss on the cheek, and danced away. As his body came close, Berlene caught an exotic scent that remained for a moment after he moved on. She closed her eyes trying to identify the elusive fragrance, but it faded away too quickly. She was left with the sensation of a steamy evening in a foreign port, where spice and musk eternally mingled.

"Did you get a look at that enormous crotch?" Judy whispered from across the table.

Berlene's face turned bright pink. In truth, she tried not to look too close when she tipped the dancer. She felt reckless enough as it was.

"Looked like a lot of padding to me." Hazel was skeptical. "No man's that well put-together."

"You'd know," Judy sniggered, but her words were drowned out by applause as the Top Cats exited and Starr Glitter returned to the spotlight.

At the back of the room, Rita Lee tried to count the crowd. It was difficult to keep track however, because so many women were on their feet, either changing tables, or heading for the restroom or bar.

"Quite a success," Walt remarked. She hadn't heard him come up behind her, and his warm breath so unexpectedly near her ear sent her insides fluttering.

"I was trying to get a body count, but it's impossible. It's a wonder Starr doesn't tell everybody to sit down and shut up."

"She's used to Las Vegas audiences," Walt reminded her.

"Just the same, maybe we should go outside to

talk," Rita Lee suggested. In truth, she hoped for a few minutes alone with Walt.

"It's hard to believe that person on the stage is the same guy we saw getting out of the tour bus a few hours ago," Rita Lee said in disbelief once they'd slipped out into the fresh evening air.

"Amazing what make-up and attitude can do," Walt observed.

"I just wish Sylvia and Pansy were here right now so they could see what a good time everyone's having."

"I doubt they'd see it the same way we do," Walt replied, resisting a strong urge to take Rita Lee in his arms. "To them it's only further proof Satan's set up shop in town."

"Do you really think there's such a thing as the devil?" Rita Lee asked, her eyes round and serious.

Walt thought for a moment. "Well, in the news business I've encountered a lot that seemed pretty evil, but when I looked into it, I've often found in the background there was an abusive parent or misguided religion or some other human failing involved. Maybe for some it's easier to blame the devil than to accept responsibility."

A raucous roar erupted from inside the hall, reminding Rita Lee where they were. "I'm sorry," she said, flustered. "I didn't mean to get so serious."

"I like occasional seriousness in a woman," Walt said huskily, and gathered Rita Lee in for a long hug.

Rita Lee closed her eyes and leaned against Walt's chest, but the electricity thrilling through her was muted by exhaustion. She pressed hard, hoping to absorb enough of Walt's forceful energy to get her through the rest of the evening.

After a long moment, Rita Lee drew her head back, eyes sparking. "Don't I remember you saying you were going to give this event a miss?"

"Couldn't stay away," Walt admitted, reluctantly releasing her soft body. "Besides someone had to be here in case the lights go out."

"Oh gosh, don't even think the thought!"

If all else fails, you can call Jerry Beemer," Walt advised.

"No probleemo," Rita Lee quickly fired back, and then started to chuckle. "I thought Teenie was going to kill him on Sunday. I truly did."

As the couple watched, Frank Beemer's police cruiser came slowly around the corner and past the Legion hall. Trailing closely behind was a cop car from Foxville. "Looks like Frank's called in extra officers," Walt noted. "Nice to know the town is so well protected in case some woman decides to hold up the bank or something."

"I hope he's checking out that man sneaking around in the parking lot," Rita Lee said with some heat.

Walt gave her an inquiring look, and she explained about the stranger she'd seen earlier.

His eyes followed the police cars as they disappeared from view. "Was the strange guy in the parking lot wearing shiny black shoes?"

"Didn't notice," Rita Lee said absently. "I suppose I better get back inside." She turned and gave Walt a shy smile. "Thanks for the hug." Then she was gone.

Walt watched Rita Lee hurry back to the entrance. When she opened the door, a swell of funky music surged out. He watched her shoulders begin to move in time to the music as she stepped inside.

He thoughtfully recalled her last words. It seemed a curious thing--to say thanks for a hug. His usual experience with women was they either demanded attention, or they were like his ex-wife, who needed no attention at all. Walt was still thinking about Rita Lee and how unlike most women she was, when he noticed the two patrol cars ease to a stop in the fire lane. He gave Frank Beemer a friendly wave, then headed back in to see what the Top Cats were up to.

Across the hall, Audrey Willis found her attention wandering. She'd enjoyed the show so far, but the dances were getting a little repetitious. And after two glasses of wine, she was feeling sleepy. She glanced toward the door, thinking about leaving early. Her gaze settled on a woman sitting by herself who seemed to be taking notes of some kind. Was there a new reporter working at the Independent?

On stage, the Top Cats launched a number with the group dressed in navy blue coveralls and billed uniform caps. The lights went down to dark, and the dancers twirled glowing red-tipped flares in unison. She guessed they were supposed to be airport workers directing a plane into a parking spot. The whole routine seemed silly. The waving flashlights reminded her of camping out with the cub scouts.

Everybody else seemed to be enjoying the number though. The noise level in the room had been steadily rising during the past hour. Some of the most restrained women Audrey knew were now laughing uproariously and cheering the Top Cats' every move. As liquor loosened inhibitions, the most adventurous jumped out of their seats for a risqué bump and grind with the near naked entertainers.

"Time for me to go," Audrey told herself.

Without warning, the overhead lights came on, illuminating the room with hard, stark brightness. Several in the audience screamed in confusion. The dancers continued on for about a half minute, then one by one came to a stand-still, bewildered.

Starr Glitter, just zipping herself into a long amber evening gown with gold bugle beads, peered out from the black plastic dressing room to see what was going on. "Oh my god," she exclaimed, spotting the police. "It's a raid!"

Near the bar, Walt Billings picked up his camera and patted his pocket to be sure he had plenty of film.

Flush-faced spectators blinked and squinted against the sudden glare. In the harsh light they swiveled around in their chairs, mystified. Was this part of the show?

Rita Lee's first thought was somehow the lighting system had malfunctioned and turned on the overheads instead of the spotlights. Then she saw Frank Beemer and knew better. She quickly wove her way between tables to reach the police chief. "Frank, what's the matter? Are you the one who turned on the lights?"

"Yes, ma'am," he told her with an official bark. "We have a report of underage drinking, and we're here to check IDs."

"This is a joke, right Frank?"

"No, ma'am. We're here on official police business." Beemer hitched up his pants and placed a hand on the handle of his revolver. The other hand gripped a mace can hanging from his black leather belt.

"Frank, we had someone at the door checking ID," Rita Lee pleaded. "Please don't make a ruckus."

"Sorry, Ms. Taylor, but we're only doing our job, the job taxpayers pay us to do."

Rita Lee took a deep breath and held her tongue, with supreme effort. "So how can I help you?" she asked, resisting the impulse to roll her eyes. When Frank called her "Ms. Taylor" she knew there was no hope.

The police chief turned to his deputy. "Reggie, check in with the liquor control people. Alice has been taking notes and will tell us where to start."

"Frank, you need to tell everyone what's going on," Rita Lee advised.

"You tell them," Frank said shortly. "You can do that."

"What shall I say?"

"Nobody leaves till we check her ID."

It took everything she had not to explode. "Look at these women, Frank. You know most of them are way past twenty-one."

"Rita Lee," the police chief said with what he considered ultimate patience, "the state has stepped in. It's out of my hands."

"If you say so," Rita Lee growled between clenched teeth. She angrily turned her back on the police chief and marched up to the stage.

Along the way, attendees called out, asking what was happening. Rita Lee could only shake her head in fury and keep moving.

"Ladies," she announced from the front of the stage. She didn't need a microphone, the hall had suddenly hushed. "This is hard to explain, but some people from the state liquor control board are here, and they seem to think there's underage drinking. They say everybody has to show ID."

A roar of tipsy laughter burst forth, especially loud from the over-forty group. Estelle Jones let out a delighted cackle as she pulled out her driver's license. "My children say I'm too old to drive," she told the lady sitting next to her. "They're trying to take my license away. But you see, I need it to prove I'm twenty-one."

"I know it sounds like a joke, but Frank Beemer is serious." Rita Lee pointed to the chief, who shifted uneasily.

"Hey Frankie," Hazel Bell called out. "Thanks for

the compliment. Been around fifty years since anyone checked my ID."

"Hazel, you're not that old," someone hollered.

"I remember when Frankie was born," Hazel announced.

"Me, too," yelled a slurred voice. "Remember that pointy little head he had? His poor mama was afraid he was never going to look normal."

Frank heard the Foxville officers snicker and felt his ire begin to rise.

"People, please" Rita Lee called out, striving to keep the peace. "This shouldn't take very long, then we can get back to the show. Right, Frank?"

Three hundred twenty-seven pairs of woozy eyes glared in Frank's direction. He, in turn, glared at John and David, the liquor control boys. They shrugged their shoulders, no help at all.

"I guess," he finally said, after some consideration.

"Then let's get this over with," Rita Lee urged.

"I'm from Foxville," came a protest. "I rode on the bus. Nobody told me I had to bring my driver's license."

"Yeah, what about people who didn't bring ID?" screamed another angry voice.

Frank Beemer turned to Alice, who was now standing next to him, notebook in hand. She was wearing a stern gray suit and no make-up. "Case by case," she murmured in his ear.

Grateful for support, Beemer thundered forth, "It will be decided on an individual, case-by-case basis by a representative of the state liquor control board." He motioned for Alice to step forward.

"Booooo," the women howled.

The Top Cats, sensing the mob's resentful mood, drifted off toward the dressing room, trying not to call attention to themselves. So far there had been no mention of public lewdness, but they weren't taking any chances. They dressed in jeans and jackets as quickly as possible. All had heard tales of unfortunate guys, only trying to make a living in the dance business, being busted by hick cops. It was every stripper's nightmare to end up spending a night in jail with nothing on but a G-string.

Starr took a long swig from the bottle of bourbon sitting next to her make-up mirror. Turning back into Jeff Constantine involved removing a lot of make-up and padding. If there was a chance the show might go on once the ridiculous ID check was over with, it made sense to stay in character and costume.

"How does it look out there?" she asked one of the dancers.

"Fairly ugly. I'm glad I'm not that stupid police chief, who's just about to get himself lynched by a mob of pissed off women"

Walt, watching the ID check get underway, was thinking much the same thing.

The officers from Foxville stationed at the exit were standing at attention, feet spread, hands clasped behind their backs, ready in case someone's grandma tried to escape. At a nearby table, a lady picked up an empty plastic cup and lobbed it at them.

Her companion grabbed a cup and zinged it toward her sister-in-law sitting two tables over.

"In-coming!" called out an alert bystander in a jungle print pantsuit.

The cup flew past its intended victim and hit someone else in the back of the head. The unintended target happened to be a former girls all-state softball pitcher. "Honey," she yelled, "that was the wrong thing to do."

She stood up and with a powerhouse arm hurled her half-filled cup back across the room.

It bounced off the black plastic and ricocheted onto the stage, joining a bra tossed there earlier.

"Beer fight," called a laughing woman in the front row, picking up her own plastic glass and chucking it over the heads of the audience.

At the next table, a young grandmother from Foxville took dead aim.

The cup hit Alice square in the chest. Red wine splashed down her suit and dripped off the notebook, blurring her accusatory notations. The crowd cheered like fans celebrating a rookie's first shut-out.

"Officer, arrest that woman," Alice ordered.

"Who? Who threw it?" Frank wanted to know, watching cups fly in all directions. By now the audience had dissolved into gales of laughter. "Arrest that woman. Arrest that woman," they mimicked. Soon the whole room had taken up the chant.

David and John rushed up to assist their compatriot. "Look, Chief, either you get this crowd under control or I'm calling in the SWAT team," David snarled

Frank Beemer saw his career in ruins, twenty-two years of public service shot down in a volley of plastic cups. Desperately he searched the crowd for Rita Lee until he finally spotted her at the edge of the stage.

"They're going to call in the SWAT team," he yelled frantically,

"Okay, Frank, I'll see what I can do," Rita Lee promised. "Ladies, ladies," she shouted. "Can I have your attention. Please."

Slowly the audience shushed itself down enough to hear Rita Lee. "There's only one or two more tables of IDs to check and then we can get on with the show. Can I ask your patience for just a few more minutes?"

The group was low on cups anyway and didn't mind settling down, giving everyone time to catch their breath. A couple dozen spectators headed for the parking lot, initiating a traffic jam that took hours to straighten out.

Harry and Carl held a private conference behind the bar. They knew all about brawls, having participated in a few back in their wild oat days. More trouble was brewing they agreed, and they began stashing the booze down out of the way. Before long a line formed in front of them. "Bar's closed," Harry announced, rapping his knuckles on the counter.

"Till when?" the first woman in line demanded, red-faced.

"Uh, well, uh..." Carl stammered, "until things quiet down and the show starts again."

"Oh, please," she pleaded, giving him a wide-eyed, innocent look. "Just one little drink, just a half glass of red wine."

"Come on, Carl," the woman behind her cajoled, "give Netta a drink. She promises to be good."

"Can't do it. If I serve one of you, I'll have to serve you all, and the line is getting pretty long."

"Well, just remember I'm first in line," Netta ordered. "What's up with those liquor people anyway? Oh, would you look at that!"

She pointed to the chief of police, flanked by the three state officials, now standing at the table occupied by Hazel, Audrey, Judy, and Berlene. "Give me a break. All of those gals are old enough to be my mother."

Maybe it was because she was a little drunk, or because she'd known Frank since he was a baby, or because she had a stubborn streak in her, but Hazel refused to show her ID. When the trio from the liquor control board got to her, she folded her arms close to her chest and said, "No."

"Hazel," Audrey implored, "show the lady your

driver's license."

"I'm not showing that bitch anything," Hazel declared.

"Watch your language," the liquor control lady brayed.

"Bitch!" Hazel repeated, defiantly shoving her purse beneath her on the chair and sitting down hard.

"Let's just get this over with," Alice growled, snatching Hazel's purse out from under her and opening the clasp.

"Give my purse back," Hazel demanded, the gray hairs on the back of her neck beginning to rise.

"As soon as I check your ID." Alice stood her ground, knowing she had the power of the liquor control board behind her

"Over my dead body," Hazel snapped, and grabbed for her pocketbook. By design or accident, Hazel punched Alice mid stomach.

Alice yelped, but held fast to the handbag.

"Give Hazel her purse back right now," Berlene demanded, jumping into the fray.

"You stay out of this," John yelled. Berlene turned around and slapped him.

Audrey, seeing her friends in trouble, lost her timidity and elbowed David as he moved in to assist Alice.

Judy took up her own large leather handbag and hit Alice alongside the head.

Alice reeled and would have fallen if Frank hadn't caught her.

"Nazis," a shrill voice howled from the crowd.

Behind the black plastic, Starr Glitter couldn't stand it one minute longer. She had to see what was going on. Taking one last swig from the bottle of bourbon, Starr kicked off her pumps and waded into the crowd.

Walt stood to one side snapping photos as fast as he

could. His lens caught the angry faces of indignant audience members; the police chief looking down perplexed at the wine soaked woman in his arms; and Starr Glitter, platinum wig askew, just as she slugged Reggie.

The deputy swayed for a moment, then slid to the floor, out cold.

"That's it!" Frank roared. "You're under arrest. The whole lot of you."

He handed the dazed Alice off to John and detached handcuffs from his belt.

"Williams, Bonner," Frank instructed his back-up officers over the loud protests of the on-lookers, "handcuff these women. They're going to jail for interfering with a police officer, disturbing the peace, and public drunkenness."

"Her too?" Bonner asked doubtfully, pointing to Starr.

"Especially her," the police chief declared.

He began reading the women their rights.

"Wait a minute, Frank," Rita Lee entreated. "Let's talk it over. Are you sure you want to do this? How about if we just have everyone apologize. Things got a little silly for a few minutes, but none of these women meant any real harm."

Ruth Smiley stepped in to reason with him. "It's certainly not going to help the volunteer fire department to have them arrested. Remember this is all for a good cause--a fundraiser to help out the town."

Frank looked up from snapping the cuffs on Audrey's wrists. The veins on his neck were bulging dangerously and one eyelid had developed an angry tick. "I don't care if the money is for the sainted Mother Theresa. These women are going to jail!"

18

Rita Lee watched aghast as the four women, plus Starr Glitter, were led out bound at the wrist from the Legion hall. The hilarity of just a few minutes before had vanished. In its wake was indignant buzzing.

"This show is over," Alice announced triumphantly. "We're officially closing it down for administrative violations of state liquor laws."

"What laws? You didn't find one under age drinker in the whole group." Rita Lee couldn't believe what she was hearing.

"The law is very clear," Alice said. She held up her hand, one finger sweeping the air. "Dancers are not to perform within six feet of patrons." She held up a second finger. "Dancers are not to allow themselves to be touched." A third finger joined the others. "Dancers are not allowed to simulate certain sexual acts as outlined in Nebraska Revised Code, Section 77.1.c."

A flash went off as Walt photographed Alice waving her fingers in Rita Lee's face.

"Move back or I'll have your film confiscated," Alice threatened.

The editor, well aware of his rights, clipped off two more shots with accompanying flashes.

In the harsh light, the Legion hall revealed itself, devoid of its previous enchantment. Half-congealed wax puddled around malformed candle stubs and dotted the silver runners, askew on stained tablecloths. Plastic cups littered the floor. Torn black plastic revealed the innards of the hastily constructed dressing room. Only the fabric Teenie had so arduously stapled into position remained intact, though its edges were frayed.

The reek of purple smog and spilled booze mingled with the redolent aroma of wilted perfume and burning wicks as the last of the scented candles flickered out.

By contrast, most of the audience had recovered from the shock of watching four of the town's most prominent women hauled out in handcuffs and were cheerfully finishing off their drinks and gathering up scattered belongings. A few hopefuls traipsed back to the bar on the off chance they could talk the Legionnaires into one more refill.

It crossed Rita Lee's mind she should get up on stage and apologize, but before she could, Twila and Trixie descended upon her. They looked ready to strangle someone.

"Who called in those liquor people?" Trixie demanded to know. "I'll bet you anything it was that awful Sylvia Crocker."

"Her and Pansy Hatfield," Twila insisted.

"We don't know that," Rita Lee said, her mind racing in multiple directions. Was anyone asking for a refund? Where were the Top Cats? What was happening to the arrested women?

She barely heard Twila's complaints about Pansy's meddling in her selection of books at the Cozy Corner.

"I'm going to file a complaint with the state." Trixie exclaimed. "They have no right to storm the building with armed officers and interrogate and intimidate innocent citizens."

Rita Lee closed her eyes and took a deep breath. How was she to get away without being rude? She didn't want to be impolite, but she had things that needed taking care of.

Rita Lee was rescued, if rescued is the word, by Teenie. "Ree, is there anybody you can get to help us out in the parking lot? It's total gridlock. Walt and Carl are directing traffic, but they could use more help."

"No point in calling the police department," Rita Lee sighed. "We know they're too busy."

"Oh mercy," Twila said. "My car is right in the way. I parked behind Billie Jo and Ronda and blocked them in. They're probably madder than hops."

"I wonder what happened to Gloria Spilling," said Trixie. "I think I was supposed to give her a ride home." She looked vaguely in the direction of the exit. "Maybe she's outside looking for my car."

"Come on, Hon," she said to her friend as she took Twila's arm. "It's time for us to go home."

"Thanks for the great night, Rita Lee," Twila called over her shoulder. "The town's going to be talking about this one for years."

"Teenie, what am I going to do?" Rita Lee moaned, sinking into a folding chair and covering her face with her hands. "The fire department's never going to speak to me again."

"They will when you give them a check for twenty-one hundred dollars, plus their half of the booze take."

"Did we really make that much?" Rita Lee looked up, despair vying with elation.

"We did...at least that much, and it could be even more once I do a really accurate count." Teenie crowed. "Not one person asked for their money back."

"What happened to the Top Cats? Where are they?"

"Well, you know where Starr Glitter is. I'm not sure about the rest of them. Did you try their dressing room?"

"Hello?" Rita Lee called out. "Top Cats, are you still here?"

There was no response. So Rita Lee ducked behind the black plastic. But all she found was an empty bourbon bottle, racks of costumes and six navy blue G-strings scattered on the floor.

"Looks like they left in a hurry," Teenie observed, picking up a jar of foundation sitting in front of Starr's make-up mirror. "Cover Girl, I wondered what products that guy uses. He sure is gorgeous, isn't he?"

"Well, they've obviously left," Rita Lee said, ignoring Teenie.

Turning to leave, she bumped headlong into Charity and Shotgun.

"Have you seen the Top Cats," Rita Lee asked, after everyone was again steady on their feet.

"They're out in the bus. They called Max and he's on his way with a lawyer."

Rita Lee moaned.

"This guy's good," Shotgun assured her. "Max keeps him on retainer, just in case."

"Does this happen often?" Rita Lee eyes widened.

"Once in a while," Shotgun admitted.

"How does it usually work?" Rita Lee asked, not entirely sure she wanted to know.

"Usually, the guys spend the night in jail, and in the morning they go before the judge, who gives them a lecture and a fine, and everybody gets back on the bus and goes on to the next gig."

"That's what happens to the Top Cats. What happens to women in the audience?" Teenie wanted to know.

"Depends," Shotgun said. He gathered up the shoes scattered in Starr's corner and put them back in place on the rack. "Sometimes the judge lets them go, sometimes he sets bail."

"Bail? Who pays that?"

"Usually it's the lady's husband or boyfriend. Once in a while, her father or a girlfriend. In a pinch, Max will do it." Shotgun began sorting make-up and putting it in cases. "Tell those guys that came up with the light system that they did a great job. Never seen anything quite like it, but it worked good."

"Bail! Oh my goodness, Charity. Your mother was one of the women arrested. Have you called your father?"

Charity paused in folding a wizard cape. "Not yet," she replied, refusing to look in Rita Lee's direction.

"Why ever not?" Teenie was aghast.

"Well, he's not home right now. He went to men's Bible study in Foxville."

"She's hoping Max can get the whole thing straightened out before her dad finds out," Shotgun explained. "No point in getting the reverend excited if we don't have to."

"A whole busload of women are on their way back to Foxville," an exasperated Rita Lee told the young woman. "How long do you think it's going to take him to find out his wife's sitting in jail?"

Charity couldn't help herself, she started to laugh. "My mother, the Mrs. Reverend Gilford Goss, hauled off to the slammer. Along with the mayor's wife, the Citizen of the Year, and Audrey Miller, one of the sweetest people in town."

"Don't forget Starr Glitter," Teenie added, with a chuckle.

"You guys, this is a disaster! Rita Lee corrected. But a second later she, too, was convulsed with laughter. Exhaustion had unexpectedly caught up with her. She couldn't stop laughing if she tried.

"Frank Beemer's in trouble now," she gasped, as another paroxysm left her quivering.

At town hall, the chief of police looked around the over-crowded room wondering where he was going to put everyone. The purple rage that had sent his blood pressure close to max-out only a half-hour before was settling back to near normal level. Rational thought had returned and with it the realization he was in a tight spot. Hobart Junction was a small town with no serious crime to speak of. There were two small holding cells next to his office, each large enough for two people if the prisoners didn't move around much. Which is usually what happened. The drunks flopped down on the bunks and slept till morning. The guilty party in a domestic violence situation either remained until he or she calmed down enough to go home and apologize, or was sent off to the mental health center for counseling.

True criminals went straight to the county jail in Belfort, which had the resources to deal with them.

When Starr took off her wig and morphed back into Jeffrey Constantine, Frank Beemer's problems multiplied. Now he had two genders to house, which meant the man in the gold evening dress had one cell to himself, and the four women were going to have to go in the other. Considering the prominence of the individuals involved, Frank had to be mindful of how he treated them. He didn't want to be accused of violating anyone's civil rights. Finally, after careful deliberation, Frank decided to lock the female arrestees in the town council meeting room.

"I'm going to get the paperwork done on Constantine first," he informed the women as he switched on the light in the meeting room. "Take a seat, ladies, and I'll be back in a while."

"What about the restroom, Frank?" Hazel asked.

"If you need to use the restroom, knock on the door and call for Reggie."

Hazel deliberately walked to the open door, snorting with disdain as she passed the police chief. She pounded loudly on the frame with her knuckles. "Reggie," she bellowed, "I need to use the ladies room."

Reggie, who had spent several years in Hazel's Sunday school class as a youngster, automatically jumped to attention at the sound of her voice but wasn't sure what to do next. "Is it okay, Chief?"

"Accompany the prisoner to the women's restroom, Reggie."

"Right, Chief." The deputy gave his superior a small salute. "Mrs. Bell, you come with me."

As Frank turned to follow Reggie and Hazel out of the room, Judy Small spoke up. "Please sir, can we have water?"

"When Reggie gets back, ask him to bring you some," Frank wearily answered.

"Thank you, sir," Judy mocked.

Beemer, sensing revolt fermenting in the mayor's wife, quickly left, locking the door behind him.

"What about my phone call? I want to call a lawyer," Judy hollered through the door.

"Is he going to fingerprint us?" Audrey asked, her voice tumultuous.

"Oh, probably," Judy confirmed, slouching in one chair and pulling up another for a foot rest. She kicked off her heels and began rubbing sore arches. "I should have known better than to wear these shoes, they're natural born killers."

Judy's offhand attitude surprised Audrey, who was at once terrified and mortified to be where she was. All she knew about jail was what she'd seen on television-- tough female convicts in baggy dresses and stretched-out sweaters smoking cigarettes and giving each other evil looks. She prayed nothing like this was about to happen to her.

Audrey's dress was wrinkled, her hair a mess, her make-up splotched...and the next thing that was going to happen was a mug shot. Now she understood why people in wanted posters always looked so horrible.

Berlene wasn't feeling any better. Guilt gnawed at her like a beaver at an aspen tree. She'd deceived her husband, laughed at dirty jokes, touched a stripper's G-string (not to mention his naked skin), and even let him kiss her. Worst of all, she'd done nothing to protect Charity from that dreadful hippie roadie person. Which is why she had come in the first place.

From watching TV, she knew she was allowed only one phone call. But who should she call? She couldn't call Charity, who was off with Shotgun somewhere. She briefly debated telephoning one or another parishioner, but rejected them when she thought about the talk it would cause. There was her sister in Omaha, a great person for most matters, but too far away to be any immediate help. That left her husband.

"Anyone else need to use the restroom?" Hazel cheerily called to her fellow prisoners when the deputy let her back into the room.

"Reggie, honey, bring us water," Judy beseeched.

"We're dying of thirst,"

When the deputy hesitated, Judy slid further down in her chair and feigned dizziness. "The Chief told us you'd bring us water as soon as you got back."

Reggie, who wasn't in any mood to wait on a roomful of women, decided it was time to get tough. "Okay, but that's it. I've got a job to do."

"Isn't taking care of prisoners part of your job?" Judy pointed out.

"I guess so," Reggie admitted, and then exited before someone else wanted to use the restroom.

"I'm disappointed," Hazel told the others. "I was really looking forward to being behind bars. This just isn't the same."

She looked scornfully around the room. In the center was a long table and well-padded chairs. At the far end, a coffee maker and a wicker basket filled with packets of sugar sat on a low cabinet. An antique car calendar, courtesy of Clint Small Motors, hung close to the secretary's chair.

"This is entirely too comfortable," Hazel complained. "It's not even going to fill up one page of my memoirs."

"You could lie on the hard floor instead of sitting in a cushy chair," Judy suggested.

"True, but I might never get up off the floor."

"You're in good shape. I saw you dancing up a storm at the senior prom last Saturday."

"But I sure was sore on Sunday. Teenage dances are hard on the hips. It's almost enough to make me give up chaperoning." Hazel settled in a chair and looked over at Berlene, who seemed ready to cry.

"Quite a predicament we're in." Hazel said sympathetically to her fellow inmate. "Remember that day in the mall when we talked about going to this thing?" Her eyes gleamed. "Who would have guessed I was sending you to the slammer?"

"You're so...so...relaxed about all this." The minister's wife remonstrated. "I don't understand how you can take it so lightly." Two tears welled up and ran slowly down her cheeks.

Audrey opened her evening bag, extracted a lace handkerchief, and passed it over to Berlene.

"Poor Rita Lee," Audrey said. "She went to all that work, and then we got arrested and they stopped the show. The fire department's probably going to lose a lot of money."

The comment added to Berlene's already heavy burden of guilt and she began to weep in earnest.

Judy marched over to the door and pounded on it. "Hey Reggie, we've got crying going on in here. Bring us some tissue."

Frank Beemer, who was busy filling out the paperwork on Jeff Constatine, wondered if it was a violation of civil rights to refuse to bring Kleenex to a bunch of bawling prisoners.

"Tell 'em to look in the cabinet," he advised his deputy.

"Look in the cabinet," Reggie yelled in the direction of the locked door.

"What did he say?" Judy asked the others. "Reggie, I can't hear you. You've got to come in here."

The deputy got up from behind his desk and shuffled half way through the clerk's office. "Look in the cabinet," he repeated in the voice he usually used to chastise umpires at basketball games. When no new demands were forthcoming, Reggie returned to his arrest report.

Judy located the tissue and placed it next to Berlene. "So what about Rita Lee and Walt?" "Are they going together?"

Audrey spoke up. "I heard he sent her flowers...red roses."

"They'll make a good couple," Hazel noted. "If they get together, two broken hearts will be mended."

"I didn't know Walt had a broken heart." Audrey said. "How did that happen?"

Hazel happily filled the others in on what she knew of the editor's former life, mostly gleaned from conversations they'd had over the years since Walt moved to Hobart Junction...how his wife was way more interested in getting ahead with her career than she was in having a husband. How they drifted apart until they hardly saw each other. How she finally told him she'd found someone she thought could make her happier, and how being married to a newsman wasn't doing her career any good.

"He doesn't like to talk about it very much."

"That's understandable," Judy said, "especially considering how much people gossip around here."

The reminder of what was going to happen when word of her arrest spread through church sent Berlene into another fit of tears.

"Think of what Rita Lee's going through right now," Audrey said, giving Berlene a comforting pat. "It makes our worries seem small."

For Berlene, it was scant solace.

19

"Can you believe it's only 10:15?"

Rita Lee and Teenie sat at an untidy table in the empty Legion hall. Both had their shoes off. Off to the side, they could hear Bill and Will arguing about the best way to dismantle the lighting system.

"I don't even know what I should be doing now," Rita Lee confessed. "I thought I had everything covered, but there's no check-list for this." She absently picked at a spot of hardened candle wax on the tablecloth.

"How about starting with a glass of wine?" Teenie suggested. She crossed to the bar in her stocking feet and rummaged around till she found the cache on the floor behind the bar. She filled two plastic glasses to within a centimeter of their rims and carried them back without a spill. "Can you believe they sent in undercover agents? It's too bad Starr Glitter decked Reggie instead of the liquor control bitch."

Rita Lee sipped slowly as she reviewed the moments before the melee. She tried to think back to see if there was anything she could have done to prevent the arrests. Nothing came to mind.

"Do you think it would do any good to go down to the police department," she asked.

"First, we have to get out of the parking lot. Where's your car?"

"I really have no idea. I gave my keys to someone, I can't even remember who it was, right after the gridlock started...maybe it was Carl."

Teenie stood up, glass in hand. "Let's see how it's going out there. We can check on the Top Cats at the same time."

Outside in the dark parking lot, exhaust fumes hung in the air like the aftermath of a stock car race. Several dozen automobiles stood abandoned, left behind by owners who decided to let designated drivers ferry them home. Walt backed an older vintage Pontiac across the lawn and through a low ditch at the edge of the road, its owner standing to one side directing him with none too steady hand signals. It was difficult to tell if it was alcohol or inexperience that caused her to oscillate both arms in opposing directions.

"That woman needs help," Rita Lee declared, and hurried to assist.

Teenie walked over to the Foxville school bus, whose occupants appeared to have brought along fortification for the return trip. One lady reached out an open window with a bottle of tequila and a slice of lime. "You look like you could use a drink," she told Teenie.

"Thanks, but I'm fine," Teenie said, indicating the half-filled glass in her hand.

Carl directed the last vehicle blocking the bus out of the way, and the bus driver revved its engine to life.

"Thanks for the excitement," the lady called out the window. "Give the Top Cats a good-by kiss for me."

Oh sure, Teenie thought as she waved the big yellow bus out of the parking lot. She glanced across to the silver tour coach. Dim light filtered out at the edge of drawn shades. No sound or movement came from that direction.

"I don't know how that lady ever got her car back in there," Walt said, shaking his head in disbelief. "There's a pool of oil on the grass where she parked. Hope she makes it home before the engine blows."

"Think we finally got it," Carl stated with satisfaction as he walked up to join the others. "Biggest traffic snarl I've ever seen. There's nothing worse than a bunch of women drivers. Must have left all their good sense at home."

Rita Lee opened her mouth to defend her sex. Instead she yawned.

Two bright headlights rounded the corner and pulled into the parking lot. In the glare, it took everyone a second or two to recognize Jerry Beemer's black pickup rolling to a stop near the Legion hall entrance.

"Heard they shut down the show," Jerry said, leaning out the window of his truck. "Some lady slugged my uncle?"

"Actually, one of the Top Cats punched Reggie, but you're close," Teenie told him.

"Heard those Top Cats put on quite a show," Jerry went on. "Did Andy show up?"

"Stayed through the whole thing," Walt confirmed.

"Dang, wish I'd been there," Jerry said with regret.

"You missed a good one," Carl chimed in. "You should have seen Gretta. It's her birthday, and one of those dancers got her up on stage and sang to her. She gave him this big passionate kiss and just about smothered him." Carl chuckled, recalling the young, muscular dancer clutched in the arms of the over-sized birthday girl.

"There's quite a few cars down at town hall," Jerry said, as he slid out of his truck. "How many people got arrested?"

"Sounds like we better get down there," Walt said. "Rita Lee, you want to ride with me?"

Teenie, recognizing a matchmaking moment when she saw one, grabbed Jerry's arm. "Bill and Will are inside taking down lights. Can you help Carl pack up the bar?"

Jerry, recognizing a chance to cadge a few free drinks when he saw one, happily acquiesced.

"You two go on," Teenie said. "We'll get started on the clean-up."

It took only a few minutes to drive to town hall, and it was as Jerry reported--all parking spots along both sides of the block were filled.

Walt scooped up his camera and put two rolls of new film in his jacket pocket. As he and Rita Lee walked up the street, Irene Slump came from the other direction. She carried a notebook and two pens.

"Evening, Irene," Walt greeted her when they met at the door. "I'm surprised to see you out and about at this time of night."

"I see you got word they arrested those strip dancers," Irene gloated. "I told you something like this was going to happen."

Walt held the door open so both women could enter. Irene went first, and Rita Lee made a face behind her back. It was childish, but it made her feel a little bit better.

Town hall was jammed with people. Sylvia Crocker and Pansy Hatfield were there, gossip vultures circling easy pickings. Irene triumphantly joined them. An indignant Harry Bell sat in the clerk's chair. Various members of Stitch and Bitch perched on the edge of the mayor's desk, on hand in case the arrested women needed moral support. Bobby Spilling, the senior class president, and several other civic-minded teenagers lounged along one wall, ready to put in a good word for Hazel, their favorite school dance chaperone.

The door leading to the police chief's office was firmly closed.

When Judy heard the growing clamor outside in the clerk's office, she wanted to know what was going on. "Reggie," she shouted. "I need to go to the bathroom."

The throng in town hall exchanged quizzical looks. "That sounds like Judy Small," Irene said.

"Frank has the women incarcerated in the meeting room," Harry angrily explained.

"Women?" Irene asked, her eyes glittering. "How many women got arrested?"

The room went suddenly quiet.

"Reggie," yelled the voice behind the door, louder this time.

Sylvia took it upon herself to bang on the police department door. "Hello in there, someone's calling for Reggie."

After a time, the heavy wooden door opened a crack and Reggie peered out.

"Someone, it sounds like Judy Small, has to use the restroom," Sylvia reported, excited to be part of the action.

Reggie looked over the crowd, which had grown considerably since last time he checked, and swiftly closed the door.

A short while later Frank Beemer came out, a grim look on his face. "I'm sorry folks, you all have to leave.

Town hall is closed until tomorrow morning at nine."

"I'm not leaving my wife," Harry Bell heatedly told the police chief.

Beemer was adamant. "Then you're going to have to wait outside."

"Reeeggie," whined Judy's voice again.

All eyes turned toward the meeting room door.

"Where is the mayor?" one of the Stitch and Bitch contingent wanted to know.

"He's on his way," said Frank. The apprehensive officer wasn't looking forward to the arrival of the man who signed his paychecks, and certainly didn't want the meeting to occur in front of this mob. "Like I said ladies and gentlemen, you're going to have to leave. Now!"

"Any comment for the newspaper?" Walt asked, pen poised.

"No comment at this time."

"When will the prisoners be released?"

"That's up to Judge Potter."

"I told you, didn't I tell you, those Top Cats would be the ruination of Hobart Junction," Sylvia said to no one in particular. "A town like ours wasn't meant to have something like this go on. We're good people here."

"And the people who got arrested aren't good people? Is that what you're saying?" the senior class president asked in confusion, thinking of Mrs. Bell.

"Well, they're in jail, aren't they?" Sylvia sniffed.

Watching her from across the room, Rita Lee was put in mind of a crotchety banty hen, feathers rumpled, beady eyes blinking.

Frank Beemer looked anxiously at his watch. "You're going to have to continue this discussion outside, folks."

Reluctantly, after a lot of crabbing, the crowd disbursed, until only Walt, Rita Lee and Harry Bell remained inside.

"Frank," Harry said, trying to reason with the police chief. "You were there when the chamber of commerce named Hazel as the citizen of the year. In fact, as I remember it, you were the one who nominated her. I was right there behind the bar. I saw the whole thing happen. My wife didn't do anything but sit on her pocketbook. It was that undercover agent who caused the ruckus. The chamber is going to look like idiots if Hazel is turned into a criminal."

"I've got to uphold the law, you know that," Frank said, standing his ground. "If Hazel didn't want to get into trouble she shouldn't have gone to the show in the first place. I don't care if she is citizen of the year. The law has blind eyes."

He hoped Walt was getting all this. It would make an excellent quote in the next week's newspaper.

Beemer turned to Rita Lee, who was now sitting at the clerk's desk, chin cupped in her hands, eyes half closed. "Everybody in town is blaming me, but you've got to take some of the responsibility here. It's your fault all this happened." He pointed an accusing finger in Rita Lee's direction. "If it wasn't for you, none of these women would be in jail."

The words hit like sharp stones.

"Now wait a minute, Beemer," Walt objected.

Rita Lee held up her hands, too fatigued to take exception. "That's okay. Like the police chief says, he's only doing his job. Let's just go." She rose and picked up her coat. Walt took it from her and held it while she slipped her arms into the sleeves. He gently drew the coat over her shoulders and adjusted its collar.

Without a word, he put his arm around the dejected Rita Lee and steered her out the door.

Not much was said on the drive back to the Legion

hall. Rita Lee let her head drop back on the headrest and shut her eyes. She tried to blank out the words and images swirling through her brain. Despite her willed intention not to think any bad thoughts, the police chief's accusation would not be banished. Because of events she put in motion, the reputations of four women were permanently tarnished.

The Top Cats' tour bus was no longer in the dark parking lot. Rita Lee supposed they had moved on to the Sunny Palms Motel to wait for Max and the lawyer. Walt pulled his car up next to Rita Lee's Subaru and turned off the engine. She drew her coat close and reached for the door handle.

"Do you want to spend the night at my house?" Walt softly asked. "I could scramble eggs or something, if you're hungry."

Rita Lee slid back into the seat and let his words flow over and through her. She knew Walt was offering more than refuge from distress for a few hours. He was welcoming her into his life. It had been so long since she'd shared any kind of intimacy the thought left her wonder-struck. A man she enjoyed as a friend and respected as a person was offering her a place in his kitchen and, she instinctively knew, his bed. But she couldn't accept. Not now. She didn't want to come to him because she was feeling needy, and she didn't want him making the offer because he felt sorry for her.

With supreme effort, she crammed her soul's longing back into the safe protected corner of her heart where it couldn't be hurt. She stared out the windshield, not wanting to meet his eye for fear she would give in. "I'm really tired, Walt. I think the best thing for me to do is just go home."

Walt, caught in a surge of conflicting emotion himself, allowed the moment to pass without further comment except to say, "You know you're welcome any time."

"That's nice of you," Rita Lee said, aware of how wooden her words sounded, but unable to say more. She quickly opened the car door and jumped out before she made things worse.

Walt waited to see her safely inside her Subaru, then left for home. For the first mile or so, he felt relief, like he'd dodged a bullet he'd foolishly aimed at his own heart. But as he turned the corner to home, it struck him how quiet and lonesome it was without Rita Lee. He was just about to go back, bang on her door and declare his devotion, when that dodged-a-bullet sensation came back and he kept on driving.

The jangling ring of the telephone assaulted Rita Lee when she stepped into her living room. She couldn't imagine who would be telephoning at such a late hour and decided to let the answering machine screen the call before she picked up the receiver.

Rita Lee self-consciously listened to her voice instruct the caller to leave a name and number. There was a long pause, then a muffled male voice came through, low and threatening. "You think you're so smart because you made a lot of money for the fire department. Well, little lady, you did a lot more harm than good, as you'll soon find out. You just wait. It's not over yet."

There was another heavy pause and then the machine clicked off.

Overcome, Rita Lee dropped her coat on the floor, kicked out of her shoes, and crawled into bed. She pulled the covers over her head. Her last thought was of Walt.

20

"Chief," Reggie said hesitantly, eyeing his dour superior. "I didn't want to say anything before, what with the crowd and whatnot, but why don't we switch the prisoners around? You could put the ladies two apiece in the holding cells and put the guy in the meeting room. The ladies would be more comfortable if they could lie down. They're looking pretty tired sitting up in those chairs. And I could run home and get a camp cot for the guy to use."

His deputy might not be the brightest bulb on the string, but Frank had to admit Reggie was thinking much better than he was at the moment. If the women had a place to lie down, maybe they'd shut up and go to sleep--that would be a bonus.

Frank was getting up to make the switch when loud pounding on the front door drew his attention. "Don't answer that," he warned Reggie. "Probably Irene or somebody else wanting to put in their two cents worth.

The banging became more insistent. Finally Frank gave up. "Go see who it is and get rid of them. Tell 'em town hall opens at nine in the morning and to come back then."

Reggie cautiously peered through the front window trying to determine who was creating the racket before he opened the door. "It's Charity Goss and some hippie. They have a duffel bag with them," Reggie reported. "Maybe they plan to spring the prisoners."

"I seriously doubt it. But they're not going to stop until somebody talks to them, so see what they want."

Reggie returned after a few minutes carefully carrying a black sports bag. "I did a thorough contents check before I brought this in," he assured the chief, "but maybe you better look it over too, just in case I missed anything. There doesn't appear to be a bomb, but you can't be too careful. At the police academy they showed us all kinds of stuff that looks totally innocent but will blow up big time." He gingerly laid the gym bag on Frank's desk.

The police chief, showing a foolhardy lack of concern as far as Reggie was concerned, unzipped the duffel and dumped out a pair of jeans, underwear, socks, a leather jacket and a pair of loafers. "You say these came from Charity?"

"She said they're for the guy in the gold dress."

With a dyspeptic grimace, the chief pushed the garments across the desk. "Take 'em in and tell him to change. Then walk him to the bathroom and have him get rid of that make-up...especially the fake eyelashes. Tell you the truth, looking at him the way he is now gives me the creeps."

"I know what you mean," Reggie agreed. "A man's head on a woman's body--it sort of reminds me of a scary movie I saw one time." He stuffed the clothes back into the bag.

"Maybe while I'm getting him straightened out, you can move the women prisoners into the holding cells," Reggie suggested.

With a distinct lack of enthusiasm, Frank headed for the council meeting room. For not the first time that night, he cursed the liquor control board and every one of their officious enforcers. If only he'd kicked those three out the first time they stepped into his office, he'd be home in bed right now getting a good night's sleep.

Using his knuckles, the chief rapped on the meeting room door to let the ladies know he was coming in. He felt rather like he was warning a box of rattlesnakes that he was just about to lift the lid.

But the scene inside was remarkably calm. The aroma of fresh-brewed coffee filled the room. Obviously someone had taken it upon herself to fix a pot of coffee using the council's supply--probably Judy Small, who didn't mind helping herself to town property.

Audrey was sound asleep, sitting up in the mayor's chair. Little snuffles of air occasionally puffed from her lips in a very ladylike snore. Berlene had a box of tissues in her lap and a half-filled trash basket beside her. Her terrified look made Frank wonder if he'd turned into some kind of fiend.

Hazel, stretched out on three chairs with a cup of coffee on the table next to her, was working on a crossword puzzle.

"We're going to move you all into the holding cells; you'll be more comfortable there," he explained to the drowsy group.

"Wonderful," Hazel beamed, her gray head bobbing, "I get to be behind bars!"

The prisoners were half way across the clerk's office

when a key turned in the lock and the front door swung open. It was the mayor, Clint Small.

"Honey, I'm so glad to see you," Judy said, running over to give him a hug. "Tell this idiot to let us go. We didn't do anything and he knows it."

Her husband gave her a quick hug in return and then stepped back. "Well, Judy, it's like this. I've been thinking this whole thing over ever I heard Frank brought you down here. Mother got a call from Sylvia right after it happened and told me all about it. In this case, I have to agree with Mother. As much as I know you don't want to hear it, I've got to say, 'You made your bed, now you lie in it.'"

Judy's broad smile faded. "Your mother wasn't anywhere near. She doesn't know what happened. She's just trying to cause trouble, like always. Why do you even listen to her?"

"The second consideration involves policy," Clint went on, ignoring his wife's angry outburst. "Frank and I get along just fine, and I'll tell you why. We have an agreement. The police chief doesn't interfere with town hall business, and I don't interfere with police business."

"Clint," Judy wailed. "Why are you doing this?"

Hazel took Judy by the arm and led the angry woman off toward the holding cells. "Forget it. We don't need him," Hazel advised. "We ladies got into this together, and we'll get out of it together."

Rita Lee let water run through her fingers until it was as hot as she could stand, and then stepped into the shower. As the steamy warmth cascaded over her, she felt her tired body gradually return to life. She stood for several minutes, eyes closed, barely moving, all thought subdued in the soothing rush of water. She lazily raised one arm, then the other, before slowly turning to let the shower's reviving flow fall on her back.

With major effort, Rita Lee suppressed anxiety over last night's pandemonium and what might be going on right now at town hall, ordering herself to stop thinking about it until after she finished her shower. But Walt was another matter.

As hard as she tried, she couldn't stop his final words from sneaking in to torment her. "You know you're welcome any time." She wondered if he truly meant it, or if it was something said in the heat of the moment...though "heat" might be an exaggeration, considering her zombie condition and the lack of real passion on his part. Maybe she'd misread the whole scenario. Most likely all he was offering was a late-night plate of scrambled eggs. Rita Lee abruptly felt silly for not accepting.

She didn't understand her shifting emotions. Last night going home with Walt seemed absolutely wrong. This morning she wondered if she'd made one of the biggest mistakes of her life. Here she was, thirty-four years old, married and divorced, feeling like a teenager with her first crush. No, that wasn't right. Her first crush, on senior football star Jack Baxter, hadn't been near this confusing...or as daft.

As she toweled off, an insistent rumble in her stomach reminded Rita Lee she'd missed dinner, and maybe lunch, the day before. She tried to remember. Did she pick up a sandwich during one of her afternoon runs to the hardware store? No matter, her stomach was letting her know in no uncertain terms it was time to eat now.

Wrapped in a bathrobe, Rita Lee slid a cup of water into the microwave for tea. She fished a couple of cookies out of the jar and walked over to the window. The sun was nowhere in sight. Gray clouds punctuated the skyline, dull indicators of foul weather ahead. She returned to the counter and shuffled through a canister of assorted tea bags. What was it going to be this morning? Something herbal like lemon blush or a black tea like Earl Gray? Silly question. She was going for caffeine.

Rita Lee was barefoot, but otherwise presentable, when she heard a loud knock at the front door. She padded over and, after a moment's hesitation, turned the knob. Outside an impatient Max Picklebaum paced her porch. He was dressed in a dark blue suit, set off by a paisley silk tie and fourteen-karat gold cuff links. Standing to one side, out of his way, was a fellow of about forty-five dressed in a gray pinstripe suit. A slightly scuffed briefcase was balanced on the porch railing beside him.

"Ready?" Max asked, his words sounding more like a command than a question. He pointed a finger in the direction of his companion. "This here's my wife's cousin, Benny Wonderland. Funny name for a mouthpiece, but he's one of the best in the business. Gotten me out of more jams than I care to talk about. Soon as I saw Jeff was on his way to jail, I got on the horn to Benny and made arrangements to bring him in. One thing for sure, he knows how to deal with small town judges."

"Please, come in," Rita Lee invited. "Have you talked to the police chief to find out when everyone goes before the judge?"

"Tried calling down there, but all I got was an answering machine," Max reported in disgust.

"Frank Beemer may be over at Gretta's eating breakfast," Rita Lee guessed. "Or he could have gone home to change clothes."

"I hope no one sticks up the mini-mart before he gets back," Max cracked.

Benny Wonderland laid his battered briefcase on the table, opened it, and took out a yellow legal pad and a gold ballpoint pen. "I'm still not sure exactly what happened, though Max tells me it had nothing to do with the show itself. Can you fill me in?"

While Max paced, Rita Lee gave the attorney her version of the previous evening's events. By the time she got to the part about the flying cup of wine landing on the liquor control lady, Max couldn't stay out of it any longer.

"Direct hit, boom!" he declared, slapping himself on the chest. "Lady who threw it has quite an arm."

"Go on," Wonderland told Rita Lee. He turned to his brother-in-law, "Max, you shut up."

She continued, with occasional loud outbursts from the Top Cat's manager.

"So Jeff was still dressed as a woman when this happened," the counselor confirmed, once the tale was complete. "That's great. First thing, we'll file a counter complaint against the deputy for sexual harassment." He slapped the table in delight. "That'll shake them up."

"In this case was the deputy harassing a man or a woman?" the confused manager asked.

"Haven't figured that part out yet." Benny tapped his pen on the edge of the table. "The deputy isn't gay by any chance?"

"Not that I know of."

"Too bad. There was a case a few years ago where a gay deputy harassed his ex-boyfriend's mother. Could be some precedents there."

Rita Lee was getting a bad feeling about Benny Wonderland. Max claimed his wife's cousin was the best in the business, but she wondered how much of Max's enthusiasm was based on the family discount he was getting on attorney fees. She noticed the cuffs of Benny's pinstripe suit were beginning to fray. Hardly a sign of financial success, especially in someone who was supposed to be so good at what he did.

Maybe all his other suits are at the cleaners. Rita Lee wanted to believe, but she knew it wasn't true even as the thought skittered around her brain.

"Do you know who the prosecutor's going to be?" Benny inquired.

Oh, golly. Rita Lee tried to remember who the county prosecutors even were. She read their names in the newspaper once in a while, but couldn't remember any of them specifically. She thought there was a chief prosecutor and one or two deputy prosecutors, but beyond that she didn't know.

"No matter. By the time we get through with this case, the guy will wish he'd never heard of the Top Cats and Benny Wonderland."

Rita Lee wasn't so sure. An awful premonition crept into a corner of her mind. What if this so-called lawyer really didn't know what he was doing? What if he made things worse and everyone had to serve jail time?

"Or, how about this? We claim mistaken identity. I've used that defense plenty of times and it always works."

Mistaken identity? Whatever was he talking about? She stared at the lawyer, baffled. As if in answer, Benny Wonderland jumped up from his chair and began to pace the kitchen, enthusiastically detailing the legal niceties of the mistaken identity defense. Rita Lee's concentration drifted. Visions of the Top Cats' brawny bodies gyrating before the crowd of appreciative women whirled by. She heard the applause and cheers, and remembered the fun everyone was having...right up to the minute the police stepped in. Rapidly the picture in her mind changed to the melee and the sight of four women being marched out of the hall. She thought of Walt and the opportunity for love she'd foolishly brushed aside. A fog of depression settled on her heart, making her listless and blue.

She was pulled back to the present by a sharp bark from Benny.

"I'm sorry. I guess I lost you for a minute there. What did you just say?"

"Don't worry about it," Max assured her. "He was just saying a few words about small-time sheriffs."

"Frank Beemer is chief of police, actually," Rita Lee corrected.

"Doesn't matter. They're all the same." Benny dropped his legal pad and pen into the briefcase and snapped the lid closed. "Pretty open and shut case, I'd say. Time I got down to see my client." A happy idea struck him. "Do you think any of those ladies are going to need representation? I'll give them a group rate, if they do."

Whatever initial faith Rita Lee had in the attorney had rapidly deteriorated, and she certainly wasn't going to recommend him to anyone. After a long pause searching for a tactful response, she finally said, "I guess that's up to them."

"See you in court," Benny said, smiling broadly as he adjusted the knot in his necktie. "We'll have everybody out in an hour."

Rita Lee, who didn't have near as much confidence in the attorney as he obviously had in himself, hoped he was right.

Frank Beemer, dressed in a fresh uniform, sat at his desk drinking coffee. The half-empty sack of glazed doughnuts before him was clear evidence his low carbohydrate diet was done for. His wife, usually his staunchest supporter, hadn't even gotten out of bed when he slipped home to change clothes. She only raised her head from the pillow long enough to say, "You hauled in the mayor's wife. Good going. Say good-bye to a raise this year."

He didn't need to be reminded.

It had been a long night, what with the female prisoners crying, traipsing to the restroom, and making continual demands. It was almost three in the morning before the last of them, Judy Small, finally fell asleep. Now it was nearly seven, and he could hear low talk in the holding cells. Frank knew it was only a matter of minutes before the whole routine started up again.

A glance at his watch told him it was still too early to call the prosecutor's office. Lucky for him and his prisoners, it wasn't an election year. The last thing they needed was Winston Buscrut, the prosecutor, up in front of the judge grandstanding before the voters. Most of the time, he and Winston got along just fine, seeing as they both had the same objective--putting the bad guys behind bars. But this was a special case, one Frank fervently wished would quietly fade away. If the prosecutor decided to make examples out of the women, the police chief's life was going to get a lot more difficult. As it was, he didn't imagine Gretta was going to be slipping him a free slice of apple pie any time soon.

The chief was reaching into the sack for just one more doughnut when the phone rang. The blinking red light indicated a call on the direct line from the county dispatcher. He quickly wiped the sticky glaze on his fingers onto his pant leg and reached for the receiver.

"Chief Beemer, we just got a call from a Reverend Gilford Goss, who called 911 to report his wife and daughter missing. He's from Hobart Junction so I assume you know who he is. I told him you'd get back to him as soon as possible."

"Thanks, Jenny." He exhaled loudly. "Just so you'll

know, Mrs. Goss isn't missing. I've got her here in a holding cell. My guess is the daughter, Charity, is over at the Sunny Palms motel. I'll give Gilford a call right away."

Frank found the phone number in Berlene's paperwork and after stalling for a few minutes put through a call to Reverend Goss.

"Hello," came a frantic voice. It was evident the pastor expected to hear the demands of a kidnapper.

Frank identified himself and explained the situation as best he could. This was the first time he'd talked about events with someone who wasn't an eyewitness, and even he had to admit his actions appeared precipitous. When Reverend Goss wanted to know how much Berlene had to drink, Frank had no answer. When he asked what she'd done to disturb the peace, Frank couldn't pinpoint anything in particular. Someone hit one of the liquor control agents with a purse, but he couldn't remember for sure if it was Berlene.

Finally, with some asperity, Reverend Goss asked to speak with his wife.

Frank told him he wasn't sure she was up yet.

"Then get her up," Gilford Goss ordered.

Reluctantly, Beemer opened the door to the holding cells. All four women, looking worse for wear, sat on their bunks glaring his in direction. "Berlene," he said softly, "your husband's on the telephone. He called you in as a missing person."

"Tell him I'm okay," she said grimly, "and I'll talk to him later."

There was a flinty look in Berlene's eyes he'd never seen before. The tissues were nowhere in sight. Folding her arms obstinately across her chest, Berlene gave Frank a dark look. "As far as I'm concerned, the ladies got into this together, and we'll get out of it together. If that means serving jail time, so be it. You can tell my husband that, too."

Shuffling back to his desk, Frank Beemer silently cursed Rita Lee Taylor and the entire membership of the Hobart Junction Volunteer Fire Department. What an unholy mess!

The Thursday morning special at Gretta's was biscuits and sausage gravy. The place was packed. Walt wasn't sure if the throng was there for Gretta's light-as-a-feather biscuits, which were legendary, or for the lowdown on last night's show and arrests. He supposed it was some of both.

Andy went from table to table collecting bet money and retelling the story, adding fresh details at every table. When he described the wizard costumes and how the Top Cats stripped down to glow-in-the-dark G-strings, some of the men scoffed.

"Tell them, Walt. You were there."

Walt confirmed the story but said little more. His mind was on Rita Lee. It was apparent she didn't share his tender feelings--but he could live with that. In fact, it was probably better. They would just be friends and avoid a lot of the unnecessary emotional strain that always seemed to accompany a romantic relationship. It was easy enough to back off, give her room, if that's what she wanted. But he still worried about Rita Lee and wondered how she was faring this morning. He was tempted to call, but decided to hold off. He didn't want to be a nuisance.

Walt only half listened as Andy described the confrontation leading to the arrests, "By that time, ol' Frank was pissed. Hazel was sitting on her purse, refusing to move and Frank was getting madder and madder. Then somebody shoved one of the liquor control agents and the fight was really on. Next thing I saw was Starr Glitter--who's actually a guy--come out from behind the dressing room and join in swinging. When she...or he...decked Reggie, Frank just lost it. Next thing you know, he had Hazel, Berlene, Judy and Audrey in handcuffs and was dragging them out of there, plus that Starr Glitter guy."

Phil Miller, sitting in his usual spot at the retiree table, went pale. "Are you saying Audrey was arrested?" he asked in shock. "Not Audrey Willis. She wasn't even there."

"Sure looked like Audrey to me--unless she's got a twin sister I don't know about."

"Audrey would never be at something like that," Phil protested.

"Say what you will, she's sittin' in jail right now," Andy insisted, pocketing the last of his winnings. "She's in good company though. The mayor's wife, the pastor's wife, and Ma Bell are in there with her."

"Exactly what did she do to get arrested?"

Phil was still having trouble believing the woman they were talking about was his Audrey.

Andy scratched his head. "That's a good question. But I can't give you a good answer. I don't remember her doing anything."

"What about Rita Lee?" Phil inquired. "Did she get arrested?"

"No. She and Ruth Smiley did their best to talk Frank out of taking anybody in, but he was too mad to listen."

Phil whipped the napkin off his lap and quickly wiped his lips. "Audrey's going to need a lawyer," he told the others. "I don't want her in court facing Winston Buscrut without representation. That guy would throw the book at his own mother."

Phil scooped up his USA Today and hastily left the restaurant.

Andy turned to Walt. "Looks like you're not going to have any problem coming up with front page news this week."

"Better print extra copies," advised Steve Bryson, who was sitting at the counter gulping down a four-biscuit order of biscuits and gravy. "Everybody in town's going to want one."

"I suppose so," Walt said, making a listless stab with his fork at food turning cold. For some reason, the biscuits and gravy didn't even taste good this morning.

"If you want to get some quotes from a man's point of view--from an eyewitness who was there--I'll be happy to give you an interview," Andy eagerly offered.

"Coward. You were hiding in the back," Gretta accused. "You should have been sitting up front with me." She gave him a poke with her order pad. "That's where the real eyewitnesses were."

As his gravy turned grey, Walt once again considered calling Rita Lee, but finally rejected the idea. She probably wasn't interested in talking to him. His doubts multiplied until they were replaced with incipient anger. She'd been leading him on, letting him think she cared when she didn't. He'd been a fool to let himself get so involved.

Walt's furious reverie was interrupted by the appearance of Reggie, who nervously surveyed the café patrons, anxious about the reception he was going to receive. He made his way between tables until he was standing directly in front of Gretta. "I'm here to pick up breakfast for the prisoners," the deputy announced, keeping his voice low, but official.

"So how's it going over at the jailhouse?" Steve Bryson asked between bites. "The ladies doing okay?"

Reggie relaxed; he was among friends. "There's a couple of guys in suits over there, the Top Cat's manager and a lawyer. When I left, the lawyer was waving a fistful of papers in the chief's face and saying a lot of things about sexual harassment and mistaken identity. He was talking fast and using lots of long legal words I didn't understand."

"Mistaken identity, huh? Is that how you got that bruise you got there," asked Joe Spilling, staring at the purple splotch on Reggie's cheek.

"Happened last night." The deputy didn't elaborate.

"Heard you got knocked out by a woman," Joe said, looking over at Andy and winking.

Reggie became defensive. "Nah, I didn't. I might have fainted or something, but I didn't get knocked out."

"Are you going to tell the judge that?" Walt asked, surprised about this new development.

A look of concerned confusion spread across Reggie's face. "Do you think I should?"

"Well, you're going to be asked to put your hand on a Bible and swear to tell the truth. And I'm sure you'll do what's right."

While Reggie was thinking that one over, Walt posed another question. "What time is the hearing going to be?"

The query jogged Reggie's memory concerning the mission he was on, and raising his voice the deputy called in the direction of the pass-through. "Hey Jerry, how are those breakfasts coming?"

In response, the cook placed several plastic sacks filled with styrofoam containers on the shelf. "Here you go."

The deputy scooped up the bags in both hands. "The ladies are going to eat well this morning. This smells great." He wished he'd had the chief order breakfast for him, too.

"Got to get these back to the police department before they get cold," Reggie told the regulars. "I don't want Judy Small crabbing at me."

"Giving you a bad time, huh?" Steve Bryson asked sympathetically.

"You have no idea," Reggie groaned. He was losing all interest in a return to the holding cells. "I sure hope the judge gets them out of our hair this morning."

Pushing Rita Lee out of his mind for good, Walt took a last, quick gulp of coffee. "Wait up a second Reggie, while I pay my bill. Think I'll take walk over with you, and check out what's happening."

Monroe Street seemed cold and empty as Rita Lee trudged to the salon. The curtains in most homes in the neighborhood were still drawn tight. The only creature out and about was Edna Olsen's dog, and he gave her a low growl as she passed. The morning air was colder than she'd expected when she left home. After walking only a block, Rita Lee shivered and pushed her hands deeper into her jacket pockets.

As she rounded the corner onto Main, she spotted Walt and Reggie coming out of Gretta's. Rita Lee panicked and dodged out of sight. She didn't want Walt to see her--afraid of what he might say, afraid of what he might not. Her pulse pounded and the tips of her fingers tingled, as they always did when she was alarmed. All confidence drained away; she spun around, and keeping her head low hurried back toward home.

About halfway down Monroe Street, Rita Lee slowed to catch her breath. What was she doing, letting some man grab hold of her heart to the point she couldn't even walk downtown to her own shop?

Forget that! she told herself angrily, changing direction once again. Still, she was filled with relief when she came around the corner for a second time, and Walt was nowhere in sight.

21

Rita Lee slid into one of the chairs at the front of the salon and exhaled with relief. She felt a lot better just being there. She smelled the familiar aroma and it gave her comfort. So many memories were immersed in this place. Laughter and gossip with friends, shared confidences with clients. Tragedies, travesties, and tales of hope and redemption confided by women and men shrouded by a plastic cape. Rita closed her eyes and took a deep steady breath. No matter what happened with Walt or the volunteer fire department, she still had the Beauty Mark.

She took another breath and let it out slowly. Her life wasn't so bad, even if did get dull at times. Getting to know Walt had been fun while it lasted, but that was over now. Which didn't really matter, because the relationship probably wouldn't have worked out anyway.

She slowly opened her eyes and gazed morosely

around her beloved salon. What she saw made her want to burn the place down. The shelves were dusty and she could barely see out the front windows because of the greasy film. The make-up display was beyond boring; the furniture in the waiting room needed rearranging immediately. Rita Lee jumped up, hung up her jacket and rolled up her sleeves. It was time for a spring cleaning.

She began with the front windows and used up almost a whole roll of paper towels before she was satisfied every single streak had been eliminated. Then she started in on the furniture. After shoving the chairs to the other side of the room, Rita Lee decided the hair products display was going to have to be moved if the chairs were going to fit where she wanted them. She dumped all the jars and bottles in a corner, then slowly started pushing the heavy rack across the salon. The rack's feet gave out a clattery squeal as they scraped across the tile floor, but Rita Lee kept on shoving until the rack blocked the front entrance. She briefly stopped to catch her breath and spotted the stack of hair magazines. Out of date, out of style, out they go. The magazines landed with a dull thud in the wastebasket.

Already Rita Lee's mind felt clearer and like she was more under control.

Leaving the display rack where it stood, Rita Lee ducked down behind the counter. She sat cross-legged on the floor, pulled everything out, and began rearranging the lowest shelf.

That's where Wendy found her some time later.

"Got caught in tornado, did we?" Wendy commented, taking in the jumble at the front of the salon.

"This place is a mess!" Rita Lee declared, tossing a bottle to one side.

"Well if it wasn't before, it sure is now. You expecting the customers to come in the back way from now on?"

Rita Lee gave her a blank look.

"The display rack's pretty much blocking the front door," Wendy pointed out.

"I'm going to move that as soon as I clear out all the junk. Why are we saving this stuff anyway?" She pulled over the wastebasket and began unloading the shelves.

"Ree, are you okay?" Wendy regarded her friend with concern.

"Of course I'm okay. I just want to get the salon straightened around."

"Well, you're certainly doing a fine job."

Wendy picked up the appointment book and put it back on the counter. "Heard anything about what's going on over at the police department?"

Rita Lee sagged like a deflating balloon, every ounce of frantic energy leaving her in a whoosh. "Max, the Top Cats' manager, and a lawyer named Benny Wonderland stopped by my house first thing this morning. The lawyer said not to worry, but I'm not sure if the guy knows what he's talking about or not. He seems pretty sketchy to me."

"What does Walt think?"

"I haven't talked to Walt," Rita Lee said with a distant stare.

Before Wendy could ask more, there was a sharp knock at the front door. Arvid and Ruth Smiley were standing outside, alarmed. "You have a break-in?" Arvid shouted through the glass.

"Nope, just Rita Lee doing spring cleaning. Go around to the back, it's open."

"Spring cleaning...today?" Ruth bustled in, Arvid on her heels. "I don't think this is a good time for that, dear. Don't you have to go to court?"

Ruth was dressed in one of her nicest pantsuits. Arvid had on clean shirt and his shoes were polished. They obviously planned on an appearance in the courtroom.

Rita Lee got up off the floor with a slightly bewildered expression. "I...I...just got this urge to clean."

"It happens," Ruth said, taking in Rita Lee's disheveled appearance. "But now we'd better get things back in order. Arvid, help Rita Lee move that rack away from the door."

Once the rack was back in place, Wendy and Rita Lee re-arranged the shampoos, gels and mousse. They were just about done when Teenie breezed in, balancing her coffee travel mug on top of a metal cash box.

"Arvid...cool...I'm glad you're here. I tried to call you at home a bit ago. Wanted to give you a financial report." Teenie looked as if she'd just been notified by the bank there'd been a large mistake in her favor.

"The fundraiser was huge success--even more than we thought it was going to be. With the department's half of the liquor sales, we netted over three thousand dollars." Teenie opened the cash box to reveal neat stacks of bills, sorted by denomination and bound with rubber bands. At the bottom was a wad of checks. "I can hardly wait for the bank to open," she gloated.

"Let's get Walt Billings to take a picture for the paper of Rita Lee presenting a check to Arvid," Ruth suggested. "That should shut a few people up."

"Not just me," Arvid objected. "We need to get the fire captains in the picture, too."

"Don't deposit the money just yet," Rita Lee glumly reminded the elated Teenie. "We may need it to post bail."

Teenie's face fell. "Do you think?"

"Has anyone heard when the hearing's going to be?" Arvid inquired

"I'm sorry," Teenie said. "I should have told you first thing, but I was so excited about the money I forgot. The judge has some sort of big trial going on, and they're finishing up final arguments this morning. He told the prosecutor, who told Frank Beemer, he can't get to our case until late in the afternoon."

"So everyone's going to have to spend another day in jail?"

"That's what I heard." Teenie took a sip of coffee and handed the mug to Rita Lee. "Want some?"

"I'll make a fresh pot," Rita Lee said. "I think we're going to need it."

Frank Beemer stared into the murky brown liquid in the bottom of his cup. It was only 9:30, and already his nerves jangled and his mouth was sour from too much coffee. He thought about his wife and wondered what she was doing right now. He wished he was home, making himself a fried egg sandwich while she loaded the washer and folded clothes from the drier. His small windowless office felt stuffy and oppressive. Ordinarily he didn't notice, since he seldom spent time there except to read mail and fill out paperwork. Most of the police chief's working day was spent in his cruiser or out in the community. But for now he was stuck behind a dusty desk, staring at dull gray walls. It was going to be a long day.

The Tops Cats manager and his loudmouth lawyer were out of the way, but Phil Miller and another attorney were due soon. He sincerely hoped that was going to be the last of them. Frank wasn't sure how many more lawyers he could put up with.

He heard the town clerk out at her desk answering the phone again. The two lines into town hall had been swamped ever since the office opened. She was fielding all calls, leaving Frank available in case an emergency occurred that required immediate police attention. When she put down the receiver, Frank left his desk and walked out to ask how it was going.

"Mostly calls from concerned friends and relatives inquiring about the prisoners. Four people phoned to say you're a chump--my words, not theirs, which were worse. Four others say you did right thing. So the popularity contest is dead even right now."

Frank picked a chocolate kiss out of the bowl on the counter and began stripping the foil. A cheerful whistle came from behind the locked meeting room door. Evidently, whatever Benny Wonderland said to Jeffrey Constantine during their brief private conference had left him a good mood.

"Quite a canary you got in there," Louise said, tipping her head toward the auxiliary holding cell.

"Just be glad you don't have to listen to Judy Small squawk."

"Good morning," a cheery Pansy Hatfield greeted Frank and Louise as she pushed open the door to town hall. Her arms were loaded with books and a large brown purse hung off one shoulder. "I'm here representing the Library Oversight Committee. Our group feels a responsibility to lift the spirits of those unfortunate women arrested last evening."

She peered avidly in the direction of the police department door. "Are they here? I'd like to speak to them and present these books and pamphlets in person."

"I'm afraid that's not going to be possible, Pansy," Frank said, and reached for another piece of chocolate.

"I assure you I haven't slipped a hacksaw blade in among the books," Pansy protested indignantly, blood rushing to her face.

"I understand, but the official policy is no visitors

except legal counsel."

"Clint Small was here. Irene told me so."

"Clint Small is mayor," Frank explained, speaking in the tone of voice he used with six-year olds. "His office is here. All he did was stop by to check messages. He didn't speak to his wife."

Pansy didn't for a minute believe a word of it, but couldn't think of what to say next. So she shoved the books at him. "Is there a policy against edifying reading material?" she challenged.

"No, ma'am. I'll make sure the prisoners get these books, and I'll tell them where they came from."

Partially mollified, Pansy sorted through her handbag. "Give them these pamphlets, too."

After the woman left, Louise took the books from Frank's arms. "What have we got here?"

She spread the books out and examined the titles. "Finding Serenity: A Woman's Guide to Living a Virtuous Life by Reverend Pamela Ditmerr. They'll love that one. And here's When You've Sinned Greatly, also by Reverend Ditmerr. I'm sure that's uplifting, too. You want me to check for contraband before you pass them out, Chief?"

Frank gave her a morose look and drifted back to his desk to wait for Phil Miller and the next attorney.

An hour later, the excited prisoners were questioning Audrey, just returned from a conference with her new lawyer. "Tell us everything he said," Hazel demanded. "When are they going to let us out of here?"

"We have to go before the judge first. That will be around three this afternoon," Audrey explained. "The prosecutor will tell the judge about the charges against us. And Frank and Reggie will describe what happened and why we were arrested. And then the judge will decide if there's enough evidence to hold us. My lawyer says either the judge or the prosecutor can decide to drop the case, and that's what he's hoping will happen."

"What if the case doesn't get dropped?"

"I guess they decide on a trial date and set bail."

"Bail," Berlene groaned. "How's Gilford ever going to raise bail? I'll die of embarrassment if he has to go to the church board."

"Did your lawyer give you any idea how likely it is the case will be dropped?" Judy asked. She lounged on her bunk, a pillow propped behind her back.

"He said the prosecutor's pretty tough, but the case has some holes in it...like we're each charged with public drunkenness, and none of us had more than a drink or two. Also, Phil heard Reggie say at Gretta's that he wasn't knocked out, he fainted. But Reggie might have said that to save face in front of the guys. Who knows what he'll testify on the stand. The other thing is the prosecutor could decide to press the case just to keep his name in the media."

The four prisoners went silent, imagining their lives if the media became involved. A picture on the front page of the Independent was bad enough, but that was nothing compared to TV reporters camping on their lawns.

Nobody said a word for several minutes, mired in images of destroyed flower beds and angry neighbors.

Judy looked depressed. "Ever notice how slowly time passes when you're not having fun?"

Their moody reverie was disturbed by Charity Goss, who sailed in, arms loaded with clothes.

"Ladies, your personal shopper is here. No longer will you have to wonder about what to wear into court today." She dumped a stack of garments out next to her mother and gave her a quick hug. "One more load to go, I'll be right back."

"Thanks, Charity," Judy called. "Bring makeup."

Berlene sorted through the pile, locating all items with her name attached. "Thank you Heavenly Father for giving me such a wonderful daughter," she uttered softly.

"And thank you for Frank," Hazel added. "I'm sure he's breaking the law by letting Charity in here."

"Thank you, Frank," Judy hollered from her bunk.

Charity was soon back with another armful of clothes and several heavily loaded shopping bags. "Audrey, I hope you don't mind. I called Phil and he said he had a key to your house, so I just let myself in and chose something."

"Phil has a key?" Hazel perked up.

Audrey turned away, blushing. "Sometimes he stops by to fix things around the house when I'm not there, that's all."

"Right," Judy said with a smirk. "That's why they call him 'the fix-it man.'"

"Judy, leave Audrey alone," Hazel warned.

Charity waved a pair of brown pumps in the air. "Who do these belong to? The tag fell off."

"They're mine," Judy said. "They go with this plain brown dress that makes me look like a preacher's wife...no offense, Berlene."

"None taken," Berlene assured her. "Charity, how did you decide which clothes to bring?"

I talked to Benny Wonderland, the Top Cats' attorney. He said to bring outfits that make you look like pillars of the community."

"As we are," said Judy.

"Except for Judy," Hazel said, poking the younger woman.

"I can't stay," Charity announced. "So I hope everything you guys need is here."

Judy emptied makeup out of one of the shopping bags. "If there's no mascara, I'm sending Reggie out to get some."

"This is cruel and unusual punishment," Hazel complained, collapsing back onto her bunk. She bent over and rubbed her legs. "My ankles are starting to swell from lack of exercise."

Frank Beemer, shifting in his uncomfortable desk chair, overhead Hazel's complaint and understood exactly where she was coming from. His own rear ached from sitting in one place so long. He could barely draw a proper breath in the stuffy office. Inhaling the stale odor of that morning's sausage gravy didn't help much. He stooped to retrieve the foam containers from his trash basket. At least he could be rid of those.

Frank got as far as opening the door to the clerk's office when he was waylaid by Irene Slump and Sylvia Crocker. The pair pushed past him and headed directly toward the holding cells. Both were clutching foil-covered containers.

The chief stepped in front of them. "Excuse me, ladies. May I help you?"

"We're here with hot dishes," Irene announced, as if that explained everything. She dodged left to get around Frank.

"Irene, I'm sorry but you can't go in there." Frank held out his arm, blocking her progress. "The only people allowed in are lawyers who need to confer with their clients."

"But I brought my famous tuna noodle casserole. Hazel's been asking for the recipe for years. I know she'll want to eat some right now. It will make her feel better."

Frank felt his stomach rumble. He craned his neck and sniffed at the plastic bowl Sylvia was carrying. "What have you got there?"

"My special lime Jell-O salad. It's made with coconut, miniature marshmallows and cream whip."

"Put all the dishes on my desk," Frank suggested smoothly. "I'll be sure the prisoners get them,"

Irene gripped her hot dish closer, not giving an inch. She feigned a step left, then ducked right. "That's impossible. We must speak to our dear friends; let them know they have our support."

"Support?" Frank frowned skeptically. "You're the ones who called the liquor control board. What kind of support is that?"

"Who gave you the idea I called anybody?" Irene puffed with indignation.

Frank stared at her a long minute. "The head of the liquor control agency. He told me he talked to you personally."

"Well, the man's a liar," denied Irene hotly.

"Be that as it may, you can't talk to the prisoners." The police chief took up position with his feet spread and his hand close to his weapon, just to let the pair know he meant business. "I'm going to have to ask you to leave immediately."

"But we brought food," Sylvia objected. "The prisoners need to eat. It's time for lunch." She inched over, hoping to get a peek past Frank into the holding cells. "Why don't you ask them what they want to do? I'm sure they'd love some of Irene's tuna casserole."

"Go now!" the chief roared, losing patience.

"You don't have to be rude, Frank. Just remember your salary comes from my taxes."

"I'm well aware of who pays my salary," Beemer said through clenched teeth.

Haughty as a goose, Irene swept off. "I hope those women get what they deserve!" she said, voice full of spite.

"Ten years isn't enough," Sylvia concurred. "They've ruined the good name of women everywhere, not to mention setting a poor example for the town."

"This can't be real," Frank moaned as he watched the two exit in a huff. He felt as if he'd been accidentally transported into the middle of a made-for-TV movie.

22

"Let me see if I've got this right," a weary Judge Potter said as he sorted through the stack of legal documents in front of him. "These women...and gentleman...were arrested at a fundraiser called Ladies Night Out. The fundraiser in question featured a group of men who performed in a male exotic dance review. In other words, they were doing a strip act. Except for the defendant, who was the emcee and did not dance.

"Representatives of the liquor control board entered the premises because they'd been notified of under-age drinking. An altercation ensued, and somebody hit the deputy. The defendants were then arrested for public drunkenness, resisting arrest, and assault of a police officer...is that correct?"

"Yes, your honor, except that it wasn't 'somebody' who hit the deputy, it was Jeffrey Constantine. My client, Audrey Miller, had no part in it. And the other women didn't either."

The young lawyer representing Audrey stepped forward. His name was Dean Falls Junior. Phil Miller first tried to enlist Dean Falls Senior, a frequent golfing partner, to represent Audrey, but Senior was tied up with another case.

The elder Falls recommended his son. "Junior's fresh out of law school and is an eager beaver. He'll work hard for you. Besides he needs the experience."

"Ummmm," the judge murmured. He was ready for a couple of days off. The case he'd just completed had been long and complicated, requiring his full attention for over a week. He slowly rubbed his cheeks, hoping the mini-massage would bring more blood to his head and keep him alert.

He gazed out over the crowded courtroom. Every seat was taken; the only open space was a small divide between supporters of the defendants and members of the decency committee. Irene, Sylvia and Pansy sat together in the front row behind the prosecutor, with Boyd-The-Barber and the church deacons in the row directly behind them. Phil, Reverend Goss, Clint Small and Harry Bell formed a solid wall of support in the first row behind the defendants. Rita Lee and the rest of the Beauty Mark regulars were seated midway back on the left. Walt sat in a seat close to the exit.

"Your honor." Dean Falls Junior cleared his throat nervously. "I have a number of witnesses on hand who are prepared to testify that my client was nowhere near the deputy when the assault occurred." He turned and pointed in the direction of a group of at least twenty women whispering among themselves in the spectator section.

Judge Potter frowned and tapped his gavel lightly to stop the buzzing, which reminded him of a hive of bees.

His eyes traveled to the prosecutor. "Are the liquor control board agents in the courtroom?"

"No, your honor. They...they had to be at a meeting."

"A meeting that took precedence over this hearing?"

"I guess so, sir." Winston Buscrut shuffled a few papers on his desk. "Maybe they didn't understand the importance of the case."

"Perhaps not," the judge observed dryly. "Well, let's get on with it. I suppose you want to call the chief of police."

"Yes, your honor," Win Buscrut replied, examining his notes again. He surreptitiously glanced down to be sure his suit jacket still covered the spot of thousand island dressing which landed on his shirt during lunch. Then his eyes narrowed and he stood a little taller. It was time to go to work. Winston Buscrut was a man with a dream, a destiny. He was determined to be elected state attorney general. Serving as Fox County prosecutor was only the first play in a personal game plan devised to lead straight to the state's top legal post. When his current term was over, Buscrut intended to move up the ladder to a prominent position in a county with a larger population. Meanwhile, he was doing his best to build a record as a tough-as-nails prosecutor.

Once Frank Beemer was sworn in, the prosecutor questioned him closely, asking the chief of police to describe in detail events on night of the fundraiser. When the chief got to the part about the audience tossing plastic cups at law enforcement officers, Win Buscrut stopped him. "Did you see any of the defendants throwing cups?"

"No, but I couldn't watch everywhere at once. I was mostly looking at Alice's chest."

The spectators snickered, provoking a stern rap of

the judge's gavel.

"What I meant to say," Frank quickly explained, "is that Alice had wine all over her blouse, and that drew my attention away from the defendants. Also I was worried about my officers getting hit with flying cups, and I wasn't observing what was going on with the defendants exactly."

The prosecutor moved on. "Then were you watching the defendants when the physical assault occurred?"

"Of course," Frank replied, insulted. "I was standing right next to them."

At the prosecutor's request, the police chief described the events leading up to the arrests.

On cross examination, Benny Wonderland inquired how long it had been since the chief had his vision checked.

Dean Fall Junior took copious notes, but asked no questions.

When Frank Beemer finished testifying, Win Buscrut called Reggie to the stand.

He asked Reggie to tell what happened on the night in question, and the deputy was happy to back up the chief's story--right up until the moment Jeff Constantine took the swing at him. "That's when I fainted," he explained to the judge.

"Fainted?" the judge asked, mystified.

"I guess it was the bloody nose," Reggie clarified. "Ever since I was a little kid, if I get too excited, I get a nose bleed."

"Are you saying no one hit you?"

"What about that bruise on your face?" Frank Beemer squeaked from his second row seat behind the prosecutor's table.

"I think I got that when I fell," Reggie called out to his boss.

Judge Potter rapped his gavel again. "Please confine yourself to answering questions from the prosecutor and defense attorneys."

"Yes, your honor," Reggie promised cheerfully."

"Mr. Buscrut, please continue."

"Thank you." The prosecutor faced the deputy once more. "Did any of the defendants appear to be intoxicated?"

Reggie tried to remember. "No, no sir. In fact, I think the pastor's wife may have been drinking water."

"Hmm," the judge muttered. "Deputy, you may step down for the time being." He directed his attention to the attorneys. "Gentlemen, please approach the bench."

Judge Potter glanced down at the documents in front of him and then over the top of his half-glasses at the lawyers.

"It appears to me there's some confusion here. No one was assaulted; there's no proof of intoxication since the chief of police was looking the other direction and the liquor agents didn't show up to testify. And it sounds like the rest of the audience caused quite a bit more ruckus than the defendants. I fail to see a good reason to hold the defendants any longer."

An excited clamor erupted among the spectators, which Judge Potter quickly silenced.

When order was restored, Benny Wonderland stepped forward. "Your Honor, as long as all charges are being dropped, my client withdraws his intended complaint against the chief of police for sexual harassment of a member of the opposite sex."

"How's that?" Judge Potter wasn't sure he'd heard right. "The chief is a male and your client is a male, so who's the opposite sex?"

"At the time of the harassment, the chief believed my client was a woman. I'm prepared to bring into court audio tapes of the voice of Joan Rivers and of my client. The jury will see that you can't tell the difference between the two voices. Also I will call to the stand a group of witnesses," Wonderland pointed to the buzzing women, "who will testify they were convinced at the time of the show that my client was a woman. In addition, I will..."

"That's enough. I get your point. Since you don't intend to file the complaint, I think we can let it go at that." A yawn Potter had been forcing back since the start of the hearing finally escaped, and the exhausted judge opened his mouth wide and exhaled a mighty breath. He then picked up his gavel. "This case is dismissed for lack of evidence."

Applause and cheers followed the finding. The defendants were immediately surrounded by family and friends, with hugs exchanged all around.

"Just because the judge has gone soft on crime doesn't mean it's right," grumped Sylvia Crocker to Pansy as they made their way toward the exit.

"The judge let them go on a technicality," Irene stated without equivocation.

In the hall outside the courtroom, small groups tarried, discussing the hearing.

"All's well that ends well," Arvid Smiley assured Rita Lee. "It was a struggle at times, but the fire department will make good use of the money. Can we talk you into doing this again next year?"

Rita Lee was speechless.

A few feet away, Berlene Goss stood repentant before her husband. "Can you ever forgive me?" she asked, close to tears.

"What's there to forgive? The judge dismissed the case for lack of evidence."

"But I..."

"It doesn't matter," the reverend interrupted. "You're perfect in the eyes of the Lord, and who am I to judge you to be any less?" He gave her quick kiss on the cheek. "Let's find Charity and go home."

Phil and Audrey, holding hands, followed the Gosses out of the courthouse. They were accompanied by Dean Falls Junior, who had a smile that lit his face.

"Thank you so much," he kept repeating. At the curb Junior vigorously shook hands with both of them. "My dad is going to be so proud of me, winning my first case and all. I just passed the bar exam two weeks ago."

"Imagine that!" Audrey said, weakly. "I guess every lawyer has to have a first case."

"Your father said you were recently out of law school. He neglected to mention this was your first time in court," Phil gruffly informed the eager young attorney. He stood for a moment, trying to decide whether he should be angry with his old golfing buddy for foisting a green kid on him. But Junior's pleasure at winning the case was so infectious Phil couldn't find it in himself to be upset. He grinned instead. "I suppose it's something to tell the grandchildren--your first client was a senior citizen arrested at a male strip show."

"Oh, wow!" Junior exclaimed. "The legend begins."

"Congratulations, counselor," said Benny Wonderland, walking up to Junior with his hand extended. "Excellent job in the courtroom. Couldn't have done better myself." He slapped Junior on the shoulder. "Do you have time for a cup of coffee? I'd like to tell you about my mistaken identity defense. It might come in handy some time."

Dean Falls Junior happily accepted the invitation. He gave one more round of ardent thanks to Phil and Audrey, and then headed down the street with Benny to the Pub & Grub.

Rita Lee didn't quite know how to respond to those who came up to congratulate her on the victory. She didn't feel she'd done anything to earn their gratitude, but it was nice to know she appeared to be back in the good graces of the town.

She steeled herself when Clint Small approached with a scowl on his face. Rita Lee fully expected a well-deserved rebuke from the mayor.

"Don't worry, Ree, I'm right here with you," Teenie murmured.

Without preamble, Clint began. "Tell you what. If you'll agree to put on a Valentine's dance next year, I promise to come without a single protest. The Top Cats show was okay once, but I don't know if I can handle Judy getting arrested a second time."

"Next year we're thinking of selling tickets to not put on the show," Teenie told him, grinning.

"I'll buy those tickets and tickets to the dance both," he vowed. "When I married Judy, I didn't know how hard it was going to be to keep her out of trouble. She was a firecracker then, and she's a firecracker now." Clint gazed affectionately at his wife, who was standing across the way conversing with Harry and Hazel. Without warning, all three burst into loud laughter.

"Telling Harry some story about their night in the lockup," Clint guessed. "I betcha Frank Beemer's glad to have that crowd gone from his jailhouse. He looked pretty worn out when I left last night."

"Serves him right. That idiot wrecked our show," Teenie exclaimed angrily.

"It's going to be a while before anyone lets him forget this one, especially the women who were there. Most of them are mad as wet cats...when they're not laughing their heads off."

As he talked, Rita Lee's eyes roamed around the

crowed courthouse hall, hoping to catch a glimpse of Walt. Finally she found him, standing near the wall, deep in conversation with Boyd-The-Barber-No-Waiting. Her breath snagged as she struggled to conquer her rampaging emotions. Though she and Walt were only feet apart, the distance seemed immense. She took a few steps in his direction, then stopped.

Walt's voice carried to her and Rita Lees strained to hear what he was saying. Even though she was embarrassed to be eavesdropping, she wanted to hear Walt's voice.

"Does this mean you're considering a run for mayor?" Walt was asking the barber.

"I'm currently evaluating several options," Boyd told the editor, making noises like a candidate running for office. "There's a growing groundswell of support for my candidacy, and Hobart Junction certainly needs a fresh face in town hall. Many voters seem to believe I can provide the leadership that's sorely lacking in the present administration." He shrugged his shoulders and smiled modestly. "The filing period is still several months away. We'll wait and see what the people decree."

Rita Lee listened to Boyd-The-Barber's declaration with fascination. There was something about his voice that reminded her of someone. She'd heard the voice before, but it didn't sound precisely the same. It was like this voice, only lower and muffled. She closed her eyes, letting her brain sort through its card file. Stored somewhere in her unconscious was the memory of a voice that matched the one she was hearing now.

Walt glanced away from Boyd-The-Barber and noticed Rita Lee, about eight feet down the hall, standing frozen, with her eyes closed. Was something the matter?

"And if I'm elected," Boyd-The-Barber continued, "I

guarantee there'll be no more strip shows in this town. The women who organized that disgusting performance should be run out of town."

Rita Lee suddenly felt dizzy. She recognized the voice! It was his venomous tone when Boyd said "disgusting," that finally triggered her brain to find the match. Rita Lee slowly backed away, turned, and grabbed Teenie by the arm. "It's him," she said hoarsely. "That awful voice on my answering machine, the one who's been threatening me. It's Boyd-The-Barber."

"Oh my gosh, Ree! What are you going to do?"

"Right now I'm getting out of here."

Rita Lee dashed toward the door, brushing past several people who waited to congratulate her. "Rita Lee isn't feeling well," her friend hastily explained. "She feels like she's going to be sick."

Which was true.

23

Walt watched Rita Lee and Teenie rush from the courthouse and wondered what was up. It took a moment to extricate himself from Boyd-The-Barber, and by the time he arrived outside the woman were nowhere in sight.

He was still standing forlornly on the curb when the Top Cat's elderly silver tour bus came around the corner.

As soon as the bus rolled to a stop. Max and Jeff, poised for flight behind a shrub at a corner of the courthouse lawn, hustled forward and climbed aboard. The door closed behind them.

Max did a quick body count. "Where's Shotgun?"

"He's with the preacher's daughter," the driver reported. "We're supposed to pick them up at the parsonage."

"Well, what are we waiting for?"

"We're out of here," the substitute driver said, and

slid the bus into gear. He tooted the horn once and headed out of the courthouse parking lot.

Gilford Goss was grateful to be back in the quiet comfort of his study. Late afternoon sun streamed in on an ancient oriental rug which had once decorated the floor of his parent's living room. Even the dust that floated in the sunlight above the carpet was familiar. Gilford idly watched the dust dance and wondered if the particles were the same he'd seen as a kid. Maybe the dust just rose and fell each day, evading every resolute effort by his wife, and his mother before her, to vacuum them away.

He heard Berlene rattling around in the kitchen and knew by the sound that a soothing cup of tea would soon appear. It felt good to be back at his desk, back in his usual Thursday routine of composing a sermon.

It didn't bother the pastor that he was getting a late start, that the white lined pad before him was blank. He was perfectly content to sit comfortably and wait for inspiration to arrive.

"Daddy, are you asleep?" he heard a whispered voice ask.

"No, just resting my eyes. Come on in."

"We've got something special to tell you," Charity announced, elated. Behind her stood Shotgun, dressed in clean jeans, a white shirt and a black leather vest. His long hair was tied back in a pony tail.

"I know this happened pretty fast, sir," Shotgun said earnestly, "but we didn't want to leave town without your blessing."

"My blessing?" the reverend asked, fearing the worst.

"I'll treat her right, sir. You can count on that."

Gilford Goss gripped the arms of the desk chair, trying desperately to keep hold of a life flying out of control. He couldn't make sense out of any of it. Last night his wife was arrested at a male strip show, and now a hippie with a pony tail was walking off with his daughter.

"I've got a job with the Top Cats," Charity bubbled. "Max hired me as his administrative assistant."

Before Gilford could tell his daughter exactly what he thought of her traipsing off with a busload of sleazy show business sex fiends, Berlene entered balancing a silver tray. She was still wearing the dress from court but had changed from pumps to bedroom slippers. The scuffs slapped softly on the oriental carpet as she moved around the study serving tea and sugar cookies.

"Don't be too hard on Charity," she begged her husband. "This is all my fault. If I hadn't gone to the Top Cats show, none of this would be happening."

"Mom, you had nothing to do with it," Charity objected. "I met Shotgun before you even went to the show." She poured tea into her cup and added a squeeze of lemon. "We're not thinking of getting married right now, or anything like that. But we've got so much in common, we want to give the relationship a chance."

Gilford looked at the couple and wondered exactly what it was they thought they had in common. Other than looking a little bit alike, with the earrings, tattoos and similar clothes, he didn't see anything that predicted a rosy future.

"Do you have parents?" the pastor asked in a voice suggesting the young man was from some strange, outer planet where parents might be unknown.

"Yes, sir, I sure do. Their names are Dora and John Phillips. I grew up in Miami, but they live in Peoria now. My dad's an electrician and my mother's a checker at Food Giant. I have one brother, Billy, and a sister, Mary

Lou. Billy works at a transmission shop. Mary Lou's a nurse. She's married and has two little kids--cutest things you ever saw."

"And which church does your family attend?" Berlene inquired, feeling somewhat better. The young man obviously loved his family, always a good sign in a potential husband.

"Ah well, we're not exactly a church-going family," Shotgun admitted. "I think my mom was raised Catholic. I don't know about my dad."

Gilford frowned. This was not good.

"Here's the plan," Charity quickly inserted, hoping to steer the conversation away from religion. "I'll stay on tour till we get to Denver, then fly to Chicago to find an apartment for Shotgun and me. There's a two-month break, and then the tour starts up again." She clapped her hands in delight. "Finally, I'm going to get to see Alaska."

"I've always dreamed of visiting Alaska," Berlene murmured.

"Why don't you fly up and join us for a week or two?" Shotgun suggested. "Charity would love to see you, and the boys would love to have a mother along for a little while, especially if you promise to make cookies like these." He helped himself to two more.

"Berlene, I don't think going to Alaska is a good idea." Reverend Goss said, expecting that to be the end of the matter.

"How much do you think a plane ticket will cost?" Berlene asked Shotgun, as if her husband hadn't spoken.

"You've never traveled by yourself." Reverend Goss objected. "You'll get lost and your luggage will be stolen."

"Gilford dear," said Berlene patiently. "I really think I can do this. I've been arrested, been put in jail, and been to court. After all that, I probably can make my way through an airport."

The pastor sagged. It was obvious his wife and daughter intended to do whatever they pleased. His sound advice was wasted on both of them. He might as well give the kids his blessing and get it over with. He didn't know what to do about his wife. He fervently hoped she'd go back to being her old self once Charity was out of town.

It's that haircut, he told himself darkly. I should never have let her go down to the Beauty Mark. She hasn't been the same since.

Late in the afternoon Phil and Audrey strolled through her rose garden. They were trying to decide the best location for a new decorative trellis. There was also a discussion going on about which variety of climbing rose to plant next to it. Audrey thought yellow, Phil leaned toward white. A gentle gurgle of water fell from the stars clutched by the fountain's mermaid. Audrey was delighted to be home.

"It was quite something," she told Phil, describing the Top Cats show. "But to tell the truth, I got bored. I was just getting up to leave when the police came."

"From the chief's description, it sounds like things got pretty wild."

"They sure did," Audrey laughed. "I couldn't believe it, the way some of those women were carrying on, hooting and hollering and throwing cups. It's a good thing you weren't there. You would have been quite shocked to see women you know acting so silly."

Audrey became serious. "I have no idea how I'm ever going to find a way to thank you for hiring the lawyer to defend me."

"I can think of one way," Phil said with a merry

twinkle. "You can agree to become my wife."

Stunned, Audrey turned and searched his eyes. "Are you proposing?" she asked weakly.

"Yes, I am" Phil said resolutely, taking her hand and giving it a kiss. "I know you'll always treasure the memory of your first husband and I don't expect to replace him, but I think we could make a happy life together in the years we have remaining."

Audrey loosened his grasp and knelt to pull a weed. She needed time to think, to get used to the idea that Phil was asking her to marry.

"If money is a concern, you needn't worry," Phil quickly assured his sweetheart. "I don't blame you one bit for wanting to be practical about this." He knelt beside her. "I've got a good-sized pension check coming in every month, along with social security. And there's stocks and a few pieces of real estate. I can provide well for you. We'll be able to travel, and buy new furniture if that's what you want."

"It's not about money," Audrey said, sitting back on the grassy path between the rose bushes. "This is just so unexpected. I never imagined I'd marry again. I've always thought I'd live my life out as a widow."

Phil sat down stiffly on the path beside her. "Would you prefer to remain single? If you do, I understand. I'm probably too set in my ways for you anyway."

"No, you're not," exclaimed Audrey. She reached out to move aside a thorny rose that was just about to snag his hair. "Can we live at my house? I don't think I can bear to leave my flower garden and fountain behind."

Phil shifted uneasily. "This ground is just too hard. I've got to stand up."

When he was on his feet again, Phil reached down to give Audrey a hand. He brushed off the dry leaves clinging to her sweater and then led her to the edge of the fountain. "There's something I've got to tell you. It might influence your decision. You may not want to marry me after I tell you."

Audrey stared, mystified, as the apprehensive Phil shifted from one foot to the other. He seemed to be having trouble forcing the words out of his mouth

"It's about the fountain. I was so ashamed when you were arrested. It should have been me in jail, not you. I'm the criminal, not you. That's part of the reason I hired Dean Fall Junior. It was the least I could do."

"I don't understand. You hired Junior because of the fountain?"

"I'm a thief," Phil blurted. "I'm the one who stole the town park fountain."

"Well, I'm sure you had a good reason, dear" she said after a moment's thought. "Why don't you come in the house and tell me about it. I'll make a pot of tea."

Between sips of orange spice, Phil made a full confession.

It took ten minutes to recount the tale from beginning to end. By the time he finished, Audrey was smiling. "You mean that was my fountain Don Johnson threw the tarp over? How hilarious. I thought he was worried about rain."

Phil nodded mutely, eyes downcast.

Audrey sat quietly for moment, stirring her tea and considering all she'd been told. "I can't believe you went through all that just for a birthday present."

"I wanted it to be a special gift. Because you're a special person."

Audrey continued to absently stir her tea. Phil listened to the steady ticking of the heirloom clock in the living room, barely breathing.

"I'll make you a deal" Audrey proposed at last. "I'll

marry you. But you have to agree to forget I was arrested at a male strip show. In exchange, I'll agree to forget you stole the fountain."

Phil slowly let out a long sigh of relief. Then his face went blank. "What male strip show?" he asked.

"What park fountain?" Audrey responded, and then gave him a mischievous wink.

In the waning sunlight of a warm afternoon, they reached across the table until their fingers touched and entwined, their happiness complete.

"Can we get married in the rose garden?" Audrey asked, her eyes sparkling.

"At our age, we can do whatever we want. And right now I want to give you a hug and a kiss."

Sylvia Crocker, driving by in her ancient Pinto, craned her neck when she spied Phil and Audrey, standing right in front of the big picture window, wrapped in a passionate embrace. Recognizing a juicy bit of gossip when she saw one, Sylvia put pedal to the metal. In a few minutes she was home and on the telephone.

"Are you sure you're okay?" Teenie asked with concern. "You've hardly said a word the whole way back from the courthouse. Is it Boyd-The-Barber? Do you think we should call the police"

"No. I was sort of shocked when I heard his voice and figured out he's the one who's been calling me. But I've known Boyd for years, and he's harmless. He's an idiot, true, but he wouldn't actually hurt anybody."

They were sitting in Teenie's cluttered van in front of the Beauty Mark. The sun was low on the horizon and scattered clouds to the west would soon turn a pale pink. Two boys rode past on bicycles and waved.

"Joey Spilling's sure getting big, isn't he? I barely recognized him."

"Hmmm." Rita's head bobbed like it was on a spring.

"For someone who's supposed to be so okay, you're sure acting funny," Teenie said sharply.

"I'm fine," Rita Lee insisted, gathering up her handbag and sweater. "You go get the kids from soccer practice. Edna Olson's coming at 4:30. When I'm through with her, I'm going home."

"Can't you get Wendy to take care of Edna?"

"I've been doing Edna's hair every Thursday for years. Friday is dance day at the senior center and she likes to look good."

"I'll be back," Teenie promised, as Rita Lee got out of the van.

For a fleeting instant, Rita Lee reconsidered handing Edna over to Wendy. But the prospect of sitting home alone trying not to think about Walt wasn't very appealing. Not that she planned to mope. In order to mope, you had to care. And Rita Lee didn't care.

Her life was grand just as it was. Edna was one of her favorite clients--always cheery and ready with a funny remark. For sure, she was way better off standing behind her chair laughing with Edna than hanging out at home not moping.

On Friday morning it was business as usual at the Hobart Junction post office. Postmaster Freddie Dunfield sold stamps and passed out packages to a steady stream of customers. The talk in line was mostly about whether it was safe to put out tomatoes. The risk takers bragged that they'd had their plants in for a month. "We haven't had a frost in May in years," they scoffed.

"Yeah, but how tall are they right now? In two weeks my tomatoes will catch up with yours."

The debate went on every spring.

Outside on the sidewalk people exchanged gossip

about the show and court hearing, but since almost everybody had already heard several versions of the affair, or been at one or both events, it was mostly a rehash. But that didn't stop folks from telling each other what they knew and thought about the whole deal.

Several patrons stopped on their way out to read hand-made announcements pinned on the bulletin board in the lobby. A family dog was missing; Doyle Baxter was selling his farm truck; the Christian Women were holding a rummage sale on Saturday.

Sylvia Crocker was in her regular spot just to the right of the post office boxes, looking over shoulders and handing out free advice.

"Good morning, Sylvia," said Twila Switzer brightly as she inserted a small gold key into the lock of her post office box. "Too bad you didn't go to the show the other night. You missed quite a spectacle. It would have given you something to blab about for months. And your friend Irene could have taken down lots of names."

Twila reached deep inside the box to pull out one last piece of mail stuck in the back. "Did you hear? They're already selling tickets for next year's Top Cats show."

"Ciao," she called over her shoulder.

That should give the infernal pest something to think about, a satisfied Twila chuckled to herself as she headed back to the bookstore.

"Better close your mouth or flies will get in," Pansy advised the slack-jawed Sylvia a moment later.

"You'll never believe what I just heard from Twila," Sylvia hissed. "They're going to have another one of those strip shows next year."

"Maybe not," Pansy said with a sly smile. She lowered her voice to just above a whisper. "Don't breathe a word of this to anyone because he wants to wait to make an official announcement until the time's right. But I've been talking to Boyd-The-Barber. He's decided to run for mayor. He promised one of the first things he's going to do when he gets elected is pass an anti-smut ordinance."

"Well, Boyd can count on my vote." Sylvia declared.

Pansy marched over and snatched the poster with the photo of the bare-chested Top Cats off the bulletin board. "At least we can get rid of this filth."

"Collecting a souvenir?" Ruth Smiley asked when she entered the lobby and saw Pansy pulling down the poster.

"Not on your life. I'm removing disgusting smut." Pansy angrily crumpled the poster and threw it into the trash basket beneath the bulletin board. "I'm warning you right here and now that the fire department isn't going to get away with it next year."

"Get away with what?" Ruth asked, perplexed

"Putting on another one of those nasty strip shows."

"At this point there's no plans for another show that I know of. Where did you hear something like..."

"Twila told me..." Sylvia broke in.

"I think she was pulling your leg, Sylvia."

"They wouldn't dare put on another show."

"I don't know about that," Ruth said. "But right now the department considers this a one-time fundraiser. They raised the money they needed and that's it. But since Charity Goss is now part of the Top Cats production company, you never can tell what might happen in the future."

"What's that about Charity?" Sylvia went on high alert.

"You'll have to ask her." Ruth said, ice in her voice. Then she quickly moved away.

The Top Cats show and the ensuing arrests were the talk of the town for about a week. Charity's sudden departure caused a huge sensation, especially among members of her father's church. Some women said she eloped with that cute blond dancer with the mole on his left buttock; others claimed she was seduced by the manager, though they couldn't imagine why she would even look at a man that dumpy.

For several days a rumor circulated that the chamber of commerce was going to take the Citizen of the Year award away from Hazel Bell. But that died a quick death.

By the time Stitch and Bitch rolled around on Tuesday, there wasn't too much left to talk about. Everybody had heard it all.

At the chamber of commerce breakfast meeting on Wednesday, a whole new commotion erupted. One of the newcomers, recently hired as a checker at Smitty's Food City, was caught with her finger in the till. Now all newcomers were under suspicion. The newcomers reacted as you might expect, accusing the old-timers of being narrow-minded and provincial. Letters poured in to the editor on both sides of the issue.

Then Jerry Beemer announced he was going to chef's school in Paris, one of the cheerleaders got pregnant, and Ladies Night Out turned stone cold as a hot topic.

Everybody forgot about it. Except Rita Lee. In a surprising turn of events, she started getting occasional calls to go out. She wasn't sure if it was notoriety, or if her name and number in the advertisements jogged a few memories. Whatever the reason, she was having more fun than she'd had in years. Not that the men themselves were all that interesting, but it felt good to be in circulation.

The yard was another surprise. Her bedding plants were spreading and the early bloomers gave the garden a showiness that indicated Rita Lee's brown thumb might be turning a pale shade of green. She was as astonished as her neighbors.

Memorial Day was coming up and with it the American Legion fried chicken dinner. The dinner was an annual event to honor veterans--they got in free. Everybody else paid six dollars, except kids under twelve, who were charged three dollars.

Rita Lee was between appointments one morning when Carl stopped by with a complimentary chicken dinner ticket and a special invitation.

"The new pool table is coming Thursday. The Legion is having a small get-together to inaugurate it. Since you're the person who made it all happen, we'd like you to come and be one of the first to try it out."

Rita Lee was both pleased and flattered to be included. For one thing, it meant the members held no grudge about the police raid at the Legion Post. "I'll bring my own cue," she told Carl.

"Oh no, a hustler. I better warn the boys to practice up."

"No need for that. I used to play a lot when I was a kid, but it's been years...except for one night down at the Pub a couple of months ago."

Rita Lee's emotions remained in neutral, which surprised her. She could actually think about Walt and their romantic evening without one ounce of feeling. There was no ripple of regret, no fluttering of the heart. She was back to normal.

So why did normal not feel right any more?

24

The gravel crunched under Rita Lee's sandals as she crossed the parking lot in front of the Legion hall. Lilac bushes along the street bathed the air with fragrance. Summer was on its way, and some in Hobart Junction claimed they could actually hear their gardens growing. The plant-early contingent predicted they'd be eating tomatoes by the middle of July.

A dog barked nearby and a cat in full huff streaked out from under a lilac bush, tail fur as stiff as a bottle brush.

Rita Lee stopped up short to let the enraged feline pass, and the long narrow leather case she was carrying banged against the side of her leg. She debated whether to bring the pool cue. Considering her current skill level, it might look like she was showing off. But the cue was a gift from her father on her fifteenth birthday, and she knew he'd be pleased to know she was still using it.

Maybe not well, but still using it.

The front door to the Legion hall was off its hinges and propped up against the wall. A plastic toolbox stood open next to it.

Rita Lee entered the hall and heard voices coming up the stairs from the basement pool room. She followed the laughter down the stairs to find the post commander and the rest of the officers, Harry and Hazel, Arvid and several firemen admiring the new table.

"Just feel this felt," Carl was saying as he reverently ran his fingers over the green top. "Not a lump, not a dimple."

"Top of the line," The Commander boasted. "Best they make. It should outlast us all."

The Commander was known to one and all by his title, which referred both to his position as long-time head of the Legion Post and to his former Navy rank.

"Certainly is a fine piece of furniture," Carl agreed.

"I don't know if I can play at a table without dents and cigarette burns. It could screw up my game."

"What game?" The Commander joked. "Even Rita Lee here can give you a mighty shellacking."

"Be careful what you say about Rita Lee. Did you notice she brought her own cue?"

All eyes turned to Rita. "It was a gift from my dad," she quickly explained.

She took the cue, broken down into two parts, out of its case and screwed them together, then wiped the cue down with a hand towel she pulled out of the case. "I'm not that good."

"As soon as Walt gets here to take the pictures, we'll find out," Carl told her.

"I'm here," the editor announced as he started down the stairs.

Rita took a deep breath. She gave Walt a noncommittal smile, and his greeting in turn was equally detached.

It took a few minutes to get the shot posed. There was some discussion about who should break the balls. Eventually it was decided that since it was a photo for the newspaper, not a real game, Arvid, Rita Lee and The Commander would all have cues and bend down over the table, aiming at the triangle of balls in the center of the table. The Legion officers and fire captains would crowd around behind them, pool cues gripped upright like lances.

Better than the usual "grip and grin" handshake that usually accompanied the hand-over of a fundraising check, Walt reflected as he snapped the happy group around the new table.

"Too bad you weren't here a little earlier to get pictures of us trying to get the monster through the front door and down the stairs," Arvid told him. "The darn thing weighs a ton."

"Carl, move your cue," Walt ordered. "You've got it right in front of Harry's face."

"Oops, sorry."

"That should do it," Walt said, snapping the lens cover back on his camera. "It's time somebody tried out this new table."

More discussion ensued over who was going to initiate the table. Finally, the honor went to The Commander and Harry Bell playing Rita Lee and Arvid Smiley.

Harry racked the balls, The Commander hit a breaking shot, and the inaugural game of 8-ball was underway.

Walt decided to stick around for awhile and watch. The legionnaires, both Korean War vets, obviously knew their way around a pool table. He'd played with Rita Lee and felt sure Arvid was going to have to hold up their team. Walt figured the legionnaires would win the first game handily. Perhaps after a round or two, Rita Lee would see how outclassed she was and drop out. Then maybe he could play.

Rita Lee truly didn't care one way or the other about winning. She was relaxed and having fun. When her turn came, she had an easy shot and without effort hit the red ball into the side pocket. The next time her turn came, she sank the blue ball. And so it went each time she picked up her cue. Before long she and Arvid were declared the winners. Arvid gave a whoop and pounded Rita Lee on the back.

Then they changed partners.

Walt watched Rita Lee miss a shot or two during the next game, but everybody else goofed up more. Once more, her team won.

The Commander was the first to announce he was dropping out and asked for a volunteer to take his place.

Nobody else jumped at the chance, content to kibitz and make quarter bets on the side, so Walt took a pool cue from the tall wooden rack on the wall, sighted down its length to be sure it was straight, and stepped in.

Walt and Harry had a little better showing against Rita Lee and Arvid, but not much. Friendly, smiling, bantering as she went, Rita Lee pulled off one tough shot after another.

After a couple of games, Arvid and Harry declared it was time for a break, and left Walt and Rita to play for the championship.

Rita Lee was as surprised as anyone that she was doing so well. Dumb luck was the only explanation she had...unless maybe it was the pool cue. She'd hit thousands of balls with it while she was growing up, and it just felt right in her hand.

"Looks like you've put some miles on that cue," Arvid commented, pointing to the well-worn linen grip.

"Many miles. My dad gave it to me for my thirteenth birthday. We played a lot when I was in high school."

"He taught you well," Arvid noted with admiration.

A shadow of annoyance passed over Walt. She wasn't all that good.

"So what's the game?" the editor asked sharply.

Startled by the challenge in his voice, Rita Lee hesitated for a moment thinking it over.

"Straight pool is fine with me. Play to 50?"

"Sounds good. You break."

Walt gathered up the balls and positioned them in the triangular wooden rack so all were touching. He checked to be sure the rack was placed in the right spot and stepped back. "It's all yours."

Rita Lee applied a little chalk to the tip of her cue, took her stance, then aimed. She hit the cue ball with a soft stroke that sent the ball off with a right spin. The cue ball clipped the back corner of the racked balls, which set one ball rolling straight out to the side cushion on the left side of the table. It bounced off and rolled back almost to where it started. The cue ball was frozen against the top cushion a full table length away.

Without a word, Walt walked up to the other end of the table and scrutinized his options, none of which was really acceptable. After half a minute, he chalked his cue, bent into position, and made a safe shot he hoped would create a tough follow-up for Rita.

He did as intended. "You didn't give me a lot to work with, you know," Rita Lee said with good humor and set out to find her own next shot.

After another turn apiece, Walt made a mistake that left Rita Lee with the cue ball in a favorable position on the table. She ran seven balls into the pocket before she overdid it trying a tricky bank shot.

"That's what I get for showing off," she told the group watching the game.

Walt stared at her a moment and then broke out laughing, his dark mood vanquished by her high spirits.

When all the balls had been eliminated from the table, there was a pause while Rita Lee racked them up again.

Hazel, standing close to Walt, gave him a nudge. "Isn't it about time you went in to see Rita Lee at the shop?"

Walt was at a loss for words. He couldn't imagine what the outspoken woman had in mind. Was she trying to get them back together? Did she think they should start seeing each other again?

"It's your hair, Walt. You look like an overgrown porcupine."

Oh that.

"Nothing wrong with a good military cut," The Commander stated with authority. "Wore one myself for years, all during my Navy career."

"I'm letting it grow out, actually." Walt ran fingers through his hair. It had been some time since he'd stood in front of a mirror and taken a good look at himself.

"Well, just don't let it grow too long before you make an appointment," Hazel advised. "I'm sure Rita Lee will give you a free trim, since she's the one who butchered you in the first place."

"Don't even remind me," Rita groaned as she gave the rack of balls a final little push into position on the foot spot. She was on the verge of telling Walt to call for an appointment, but a warning voice inside told her it wasn't a good idea. He might tell her no, and that would hurt. No point in setting herself up for that, especially in front of all these people.

"Your break," Rita Lee said.

The game continued for a while longer, but its outcome was never in question. Rita Lee won fifty to twenty-seven.

"That was fun," The Commander said, hanging up his cue. "Rita Lee, I had no idea you were such a good pool player."

"Neither did I. To be honest, I played better today than I have in my whole life." Rita Lee twisted her cue apart and carefully put the two sections back in their case. "Walt's actually a lot better than I am. Last time we played, he made me look like a beginner."

"Well, you sure showed your stuff this time." Walt said. Amusement flickered in his eyes.

"I'd say we've given the table a proper initiation," The Commander announced. "When Frank and the boys showed up at the strip show, I wasn't sure what we'd gotten ourselves into, but all's well that ends and all that, as Shakespeare says."

Arvid and Rita Lee thanked The Commander again for letting them use the Legion hall for the Top Cats show, and The Commander thanked them again for splitting the liquor profits. Arvid and Carl reverently draped a blue plastic cover over the new pool table, and everybody gathered up their things to leave.

In the parking lot, Walt hesitantly approached Rita Lee. "Any chance you'd have time this afternoon to trim my hair?" There was a spark of emotion in his eyes she couldn't read.

"I can do it right now, if you want to come down to the Beauty Mark." She was clearly surprised he'd asked.

"See you there in a few minutes," Walt confirmed, and headed for his car with an unexpected feeling of elation. He grinned and straightened his shoulders. The gravel beneath his feet crunched in an upbeat groove.

Rita Lee came in the back door of the salon, and stopped at the first mirror to check her appearance. She gave her short hair a few quick swipes with a brush and frowned. She wished she'd been a little more careful in the morning about selecting an outfit. Too late to make a change now, though. Maybe a little lipstick would help.

Wendy was just finished with Gloria Spilling's haircut. Gloria spun around in the chair, mirror in hand, to check out the back of her head. "You always do such a good job," she said with satisfaction.

Gloria slipped a dollar bill into Wendy's hand. Tipping your hair stylist wasn't always done in Hobart Junction, but Gloria Spilling, born Gloria Hobart, saw herself as a cut above most of the women in town.

Wendy noticed Rita Lee's buoyant smile and inquired, "Does this mean you didn't embarrass yourself playing pool at the Legion hall?"

"I played great" Rita said, still in awe of her performance. "Walt is on his way over to get his hair trimmed. I beat him fifty to twenty-seven."

"He lost so he has to get another haircut from you. Is that it?"

Gloria passed Walt coming in the salon. "Hear you got beat playing pool," she teased.

"All too true," Walt said with chagrin. "Word travels fast." His eyes traveled past Gloria searching out Rita Lee.

He found her standing beside her chair, indicating for him to come on back and sit down.

Walt settled into the chair, and thoughtfully examined his hair. Hazel was right, he did look like a porcupine with one paw in an electric socket. But, despite his obvious tonsorial needs, Walt was feeling a much deeper necessity. He could no longer ignore that the primary reason he was sitting in the Beauty Mark on this beautiful Thursday afternoon was to share time with Rita Lee. The harder he tried to ignore the woman, the more she became a part of his life. The luster was gone from his protected life as a hardboiled bachelor. He wanted more, and he wanted it with Rita Lee.

"Shampoo first," Rita Lee reminded Walt, leading him toward the sink.

Walt sank back to enjoy what he now considered to be the best part of a visit to the Beauty Mark. "Can't believe anybody goes to Boyd-the-Barber-No-Waiting," he said as Rita Lee gently massaged his scalp. "Those guys sitting around reading Field and Stream and listening to Boyd's lame knock knock jokes have no idea what they're missing."

Back before the mirror, Rita Lee somberly contemplated the hair in front of her. "No probleemo," she declared after a few seconds.

"Are you sure?" Walt was doubtful, especially now that his hair was wet and sticking out even worse.

"I could do it blindfolded."

"I dare you," Walt challenged.

"Wendy, where's something I can use as a blindfold?" asked Rita Lee, recklessly accepting the dare.

"You can't be serious." Wendy couldn't believe what she was hearing. Now she was really convinced Rita Lee had gone over the edge.

"Just tie the blindfold over my eyes," Rita Lee instructed.

"Are you sure?" Wendy asked Walt, who gave a firm affirmative nod, a gleam in his eyes.

"This is totally insane," Wendy flatly stated. But she tied a scarf in place around Rita Lee's head and stepped back to await disaster.

"Hand me the silver barber scissors sitting on the

left side of the shelf," Rita Lee told Wendy.

Rita Lee accepted the scissors and carefully touched the hair beneath her fingers. She'd been cutting hair at least five days a week for over ten years. She was confident that muscle memory would take over now that sight was eliminated. All she had to do was stay focused on feel.

"Try your best not to move," she ordered Walt. Then she took a deep breath and made the first snip.

Walt didn't have to be told twice to stay still. He watched the mirror in frozen fascination as Rita Lee made snip after snip, each careful clip bringing his unruly hair closer to being acceptable.

"You're doing fine so far," he reported.

"Don't talk. You move your head and I might cut off your ear."

Rita Lee was only joking. In truth, she could tell her physical abilities were operating at a much higher level than normal--just look at her amazing run at pool. She felt like Wonder Woman! She also knew without seeing that Walt's haircut was going to be one of her best ever.

Blindfolded, Rita Lee had a whole new awareness of the man sitting in front of her. She could smell the faint lingering aroma of conditioner and feel his warmth beneath her hands. She was flooded with wonder that he trusted her enough to allow her to cut his hair blindfolded. It might be a silly dare, but it also said something about the confidence he had in her.

Confidence and trust...the two words kept repeating themselves in the protected part of her heart as she slowly made her final snips.

The crazy events of the past few months surely had given her more confidence in herself.

Now it was up to her to place her trust in Walt.

He was squarely in her life and it felt good. She was

tired of fighting with the fearful voice within. In fact, she didn't have time for the pain any more...or room in her heart.

Rita Lee ran her fingers around his head one last time, searching for a hair out of place. Finding none, she stepped back, exhaled deeply and announced, "That's it. I'm done."

"Un-believable." Wendy said, awestruck.

Rita Lee untied the knot at the back of the scarf, then critically examined her work. "Okay in the front, iffy in the back."

Walt snatched the hand mirror off the shelf and spun around in the chair to see how bad it really was.

No matter which way he turned the mirror, every hair appeared to lie flat and he couldn't even tell where the original gouge had been. "Not bad, not bad at all," he praised Rita Lee. "I have to take back of half of what I said about you."

"Thanks for that at least." She tried not to smile.

"You two are crazy," Wendy declared. "And the strangest part is that you're both crazy in the same way."

Walt and Rita Lee's eyes met and held, just as they had months before in Walt's kitchen.

"We know," Walt said softly, speaking for both of them.

Can lightening strike twice? It sure felt like it.

Walt rose from the salon chair. "What about that canoe trip we talked about when the show was over? You still want to do it?"

"Yes," Rita Lee told him clearly. She gave Walt a huge hug.

"Have you ever eaten sushi? I'll make a Japanese picnic."

Acknowledgements

Thanks to Sue Roberts, Kristina Christmas, Sally Portman, Rayma Hayes and Gloria Spiwak, who read an early version of the manuscript and provided invaluable comments.

Kudos to Mary Sharman for her great cover design.

Special thanks to my brother Bob Van Valkenburgh and his wife Jayne for their continuous support. Bob saved the book one day when I was ready to kick my computer down the stairs.

My gratitude always to my sons Aaron and Ian Rea for their expertise and encouragement.

Made in the USA
Charleston, SC
14 January 2011